COFFIN'S GAME

COFFIN'S GAME

A JOHN COFFIN MYSTERY

GWENDOLINE BUTLER

ST. MARTIN'S PRESS
NEW YORK

THOMAS DUNNE BOOKS.
An imprint of St. Martin's Press.

COFFIN'S GAME. Copyright © 1997 by Gwendoline Butler. All rights reserved. Printed in the United States of America. No part of this book may be used or reproduced in any manner whatsoever without written permission except in the case of brief quotations embodied in critical articles or reviews. For information, address St. Martin's Press, 175 Fifth Avenue, New York, N.Y. 10010.

ISBN 0-312-20512-0

First published in Great Britain by Collins Crime, an imprint of HarperCollins*Publishers*

First U.S. Edition: July 1999

10 9 8 7 6 5 4 3 2 1

My thanks to Professor Geoffrey Lee Williams for help about terrorism and terrorists, and to Inspector Euan Forbes and John Kennedy Melling for details of technical procedures.

AUTHOR'S NOTE

One evening in April 1988, I sat in Toynbee Hall in the East End of London, near to Docklands, listening to Doctor David Owen (now Lord Owen) give that year's Barnett Memorial Lecture. In it, he suggested the creation of a Second City of London, to be spun off from the first, to aid the economic and social regeneration of the Docklands.

The idea fascinated me and I have made use of it to create a world for detective John Coffin, to whom I gave the tricky task of keeping there the Queen's Peace.

A brief Calendar of the life and career of John Coffin, Chief Commander of the Second City of London Police.

John Coffin is a Londoner by birth, his father is unknown and his mother was a difficult lady of many careers and different lives who abandoned him in infancy to be looked after by a woman who may have been a relative of his father and who seems to have acted as his mother's dresser when she was on the stage. He kept in touch with this lady, whom he called Mother, lodged with her in his early career and looked after her until she died.

After serving briefly in the army, he joined the Metropolitan Police, soon transferring to the plain-clothes branch as a detective.

He became a sergeant and was very quickly promoted to inspector a year later. Ten years later, he was a superintendent and then chief superintendent.

There was a bad patch in his career about which he is reluctant to talk. His difficult family background has complicated his life and possibly accounts for an unhappy period when, as he admits, his career went down a black hole. His first marriage split apart at this time and his only child died

From this dark period he was resurrected by a spell in a secret, dangerous undercover operation about which even now not much is known. But the esteem he won then was recognized when the Second City of London was being formed and he became Chief Commander of its Police Force. He has married again, an old love, Stella Pinero, who is herself a very successful actress. He has also discovered two siblings, a much younger sister and brother.

For the urban terrorist, logistics are expressed by the formula MDAME.

M   mechanisation
D   money (*dinheiro*)
A   arms
M   ammunition (*municos*)
E   explosives

Minimanual of the Urban Guerrilla
Carlos Marighella

Despite the popular image there is no reliable archetype of terrorist personality. While they are undeniably cruel, virtually none has been found to be clinically mad. But there are always exceptions.

A recurring syndrome is what psychiatrists call externalisation, coping with failure by blaming an outside source.

Terrorism
Professor Geoffrey Lee Williams
Alan Lee Williams
Institute for European Defence and Strategic Studies

PRELUDE

'The Chemin des Dames, that's the name,' said Charles. 'Do you know that in 1917 the whole French Army was in revolt because of the terrible deaths on the Chemin des Dames. That wonderful army that Napoleon built, reduced to chaos and despair . . . that's the mood I want to create with our bombs. Then we can rebuild society.'

Not me, thought Jerry. I'm a soldier, I get instructions from above, I do the job, and walk away. Also, I get paid.

There were three of them in the rented room above an empty shop in Mordecai Street; the neighbours, such as took any interest, thought they were charity workers helping Africa or Tibet.

Present were Jerry, the supreme professional, the leader and the technician on the bomb, Andrew, an old colleague on the bomb run, and Charles, the college graduate, the sort to go out on a crusade. Jerry found him useful, but did not trust him.

Nor did he trust the fourth member of the team, known as the Secret Card, brought in by Pip for local knowledge and inside information on the Second City Police.

None of them used their own names, not even Jerry and Andrew. Only Jerry knew and had contact with the man next in the chain of command, and he knew him only as Pip. Jerry knew that they were only the second team, not entrusted with the bigger bomb, but they were operators.

The local knowledge of the Card had told them which street was strategically placed for a bomb, near a big supermarket for maximum damage, yet neutral; a thoroughfare where people took not much notice of each other and where cars and vans could park unnoticed. Arch Road, with Percy Street, in which many houses were empty, just round the corner. Arch Road – put the bomb there.

'Cameras, videos?' Jerry had queried, having observed the police cameras going up on street corners in the Second City.

'None in Arch Road, nor Percy Street yet. The city has to persuade local businesses to come up with the cash.'

That was where the Card's knowledge of the police had come in useful.

The Card was not present at this last meeting before the bomb. Might be due for a quick exit. Jerry would decide.

In any case, the group (and there were others of whom this little coterie knew nothing) would soon split up and disappear.

Job done.

But Jerry had not quite taken in the tricky character Pip had enlisted in the Card.

Pip could have enlightened him, but saw no reason to do so.

1

There were two great explosions on the same day in the Second City that autumn. One bomb went off, near the entrance to the new tunnel under the Thames which the Queen had opened but two years before. The tunnel was not damaged. The other bomb went off later in a shopping street. Most of the damage was in the ancient riverside borough of Spinnergate, but it had been heard as far away as East Hythe, and even Swinehouse, further east, had felt the blast. The new rich areas of Evelyn Fields and Tower Hill with their loft conversions in old warehouses and their smart flats in former factories had been spared – to the fury of Spinnergate, which was not smart or converted in any way. There had been deaths and more injuries in the second bomb, houses and offices nearby were blasted, but the tunnel itself was already open, with traffic running through it. Still, the Second City was used to surviving onslaughts, having come through the ravages of Romans, Vikings, and Normans, not to mention later enemies, amongst whom they numbered all governments, whether home-based or across the Channel. The habit of the population was to pick itself up and get on with living while cursing its rulers.

They did regret that the complex system of video cameras placed high on many buildings around the Second City had yet to be extended to lesser streets, where it might have provided better clues. Instead they had to wait for the bombers to claim their work. Which they did, only when they thought they were safely away.

It was war, after all.

The other explosion, more personally aimed, was about to happen.

Six days after the explosions, a row of houses which had been damaged in the blast was being tidied up. There was no major structural damage and the repairs, which were in the hands of a local firm, were expected to be finished quickly. The firm, William Archer Ltd, a small outfit which knew Percy Street well, glad of the work, was not going to rush, tacitly admitting that if the bomb brought work it was not altogether a bad bomb.

Bill Archer, the boss and owner of the firm which his father had started, was in a bad mood, irritable because of the absence of his office manager who had taken some days off. Peter Corner had gone sick, sending a brief message that he had migraine.

'Didn't think men got migraine,' grumbled his employer, 'that's for women. Why can't he just take an aspirin and come in?'

'You can be quite ill with migraine,' said his wife, who had taken the message on the telephone. She was in the office doing the work herself so that if anyone had a grievance it was her. 'You pay him women's wages anyway.'

'I pay him what he deserves, and I won't pay that if he doesn't turn up. Nancy boy. I bet it was a man on the phone to you.' Mrs Archer admitted silently that it was. 'Gone off together somewhere, I bet.' Bill was sharp. He often had labour problems. He employed casual labour, taking them on for a job and then sacking them. It was the way of his work, he would say; there had always been casual workers in the building trade. There were always men to be had. For instance, at this moment, he had a former bank clerk, a university graduate doing a thesis on economic history, and a seaman without a ship. His son and a nephew – his sister's son – he employed all the time.

'I'll be round the corner in Percy Street.' He picked up his jacket as he departed.

Bill Archer's son, George (they went in for royal names),

was in charge and his cousin, Phil, was doing most of the work.

Number five Percy Street was the third house in the row and had been empty and up for sale for six months or so. This was known by both George and Phil who had been given the key by the house agent and told to get on with the roof and the windows and ceiling in the top floor front room.

Phil ran up the stairs cheerfully, his first job of the day and a light one. It was very early in the morning; he liked to get a good start. He was a thin and eager man. Behind him came Tom McAndrew, taller, heavier and older, he it was who was working on a thesis and looking for a university job. Any job. But he was a good brickie and could turn his hand to anything electrical. Woodwork and plumbing, no.

Phil pushed open the door. The wind blew through the shattered windows and shivered up to the rafters through the torn ceiling. If it had not been for the wind, he reckoned, there would have been more of a smell.

On the floor, face in profile, was a body.

'Don't touch,' said Tom, putting out a restraining hand, 'better not.'

Bill, who had been talking to his son in the street outside the house, could be heard coming up the stairs. He was not going to be pleased.

A call from George Archer in his capacity as works foreman on the job brought a police patrol car to inspect 5 Percy Street and then two more senior officers to take another look.

Sergeant Mitchell and Detective Ellis Rice arrived before the police surgeon and before the Scene of Crime team. They stared down at the body lying on the floor of a room where the ceiling was half down and the windows out. They made a quiet, delicate, gloved inspection of the corpse and her possessions. She had a short fall of fair hair, she wore jeans, a white shirt, tucked in and belted, and on the hands were bloodstained white cotton gloves. There was a handbag on the floor. Mitchell carefully put on plastic gloves, then opened the bag and looked inside. He raised an eyebrow. Silently, he let Rice see what he had been seeing.

'That bag hers?' asked Archer, who had come up the stairs with them. They had told him to stay behind, but he had ignored this advice.

'Could be.'

'It's a good bag.'

It was; soft leather with an initial in gold.

'That is no bomb injury,' said George Archer, staring at the corpse. 'Not the face.' He said this sadly; he was a former soldier who had served in the Falklands, he knew what wounds were and how they were made. Hands had done this work. Brutal, determined hands.

'No,' said Mitchell. 'Not disputing that.' He crouched down to replace the woman's handbag on the floor beside her. He turned in query to his colleague. A meaning look passed between them: a question wanting an answer.

'It can't be,' said the other. 'Can't be her.'

'There's the handbag,' said Mitchell. 'That means something. Could have been stolen, I suppose.' He walked away. 'This is too much for us.'

'SOCO will be here soon.'

Mitchell had made up his mind. 'That's not enough,' he called over his shoulder. 'I am going to telephone.'

Within the hour, two very senior detectives had arrived. The first to march up the stairs, quickly and lightly, was Chief Superintendent Archie Young. Behind him, climbing with that soft creeping movement that had won him the nickname of the Todger, was Inspector Thomas Lodge, a man of specialized knowledge and many tongues. He was an outsider who ran his own game.

The two men walked into the room together, one tall and burly although quick moving, and the other several inches shorter, while the recently arrived SOCO team stood back.

Archie Young surveyed the body, then knelt down for a

18

closer look. 'I can't say; I ought to be able . . . I knew her –
know her,' he amended. 'I simply can't say, the face has
gone.' He looked at Inspector Lodge. 'Any views?'

'That can probably be reconstructed. To some extent. In
the long run it will be of use. Fingerprints also.'

'You are looking at this from your point of view,' said
Archie Young with some irritation. As you usually do, he
muttered to himself. 'I can't go round collecting fingerprints
to check if this is the body of the woman we think it is. Not
this woman.'

'The circumstances are unusual,' said Inspector Lodge
calmly.

'They bloody are.'

Lodge drew his lips together. He rarely swore, but when
he did he had a wide-ranging vocabulary in which to do it,
from Russian to a couple of Chinese dialects, picked up in
Soho.

'There's nothing for it: we have to get the Chief Commander himself.'

'He's away, isn't he?'

'Back today, here now.' Archie Young looked at his watch.
Still early, but he reckoned the Chief Commander would be
in his office.

'In situ?'

'Yes, here and now.'

Lodge nodded gravely, watching as Archie Young drew his
mobile phone from his pocket. 'I hope that phone is protected,' he said.

'It is, as you know very well. All mobiles are in this Force,
no one can eavesdrop.' And to himself, Archie Young said:
No wonder they call you the Todger. I wouldn't have you
with me now if I didn't have to; you are the king of this
particular territory. 'Sir,' he began, when John Coffin, Chief
Commander of the Second City Police, answered on his private reserved line, and found himself stumbling, wondering
how to go on.

*   *   *

Four days after the explosions, Stella Pinero had gone away.

Before her going, there had been a moment of confusion and despair. And in the theatre, too.

Stella Pinero was lost. She had stood centre stage and realized she had lost her words, lost where she was in Act One (that bit she could remember), and very nearly forgotten what play it was.

Tension, that was the cause. Fear, yes, she could say that too.

A voice prompted her: 'What letter?'

Stella came to herself. 'You thought the letter had been destroyed. How foolish of you. It is in my possession, it was a swindle, Sir Robert.'

An Ideal Husband, she said to herself, that's the play. Why on earth did I choose to produce that play here in my own theatre, when I had a free choice? Because it is popular with my audience, and I serve that audience.

And because I have husbands on my mind; I am terribly, terribly worried about my own husband.

At last a voice got through to her: 'Your carriage is here, Mrs Cheveley.'

Stella once more came to and obliged with the speech: 'Thanks. Good evening, Lady Chiltern.'

Then she realized what she had said and what it meant. It was a painful moment. Oh God, I must have gone through almost an act on autopilot. This could happen, all actors knew the phenomenon, but it would not do. She gathered herself together and carried on.

Stella Pinero as Mrs Cheveley – she had naturally given herself the female lead – went backstage and sought comfort. Alice Yeoman was standing in the wings, watching.

Stella had been persuaded to employ Alice by her husband, John Coffin. 'She's the child of a chap I served with,' he explained. 'We did a job together, he saved my life, got hurt himself. When he died last year, he asked me to look after the girl . . . he'd been too old a father and her mother was gone. I don't see myself as a father-figure, but I promised I would see the girl through.' There had been a bit more to

20

it, but this was not something to talk about. Alice was like Bill Yeoman and yet different.

'That was the time I was out of touch with you,' said Stella.

'I wasn't in touch with anyone much, I was fighting my way back.' After a bad time in his life and career, but he did not say this aloud. 'I owe her, give her a chance.'

'Sure. She will have to be a good worker.' But Alice was quiet, alert and industrious. There was a private side to her: the easy, all-knowing, uncensorious commonwealth of the theatre observed that Alice trawled the town a bit. Stella wondered whether Coffin knew – but did it matter?

Alice was a tall, well-built young woman, not a very good actress but not one to be underrated. Stella grabbed her, physically took her by the arm and stared in her face. Alice opened her eyes wide with surprise. 'Tell me, quickly, was I terrible?'

'No, just the same as usual. Good, I mean. Stella, you're always good,' said Alice quickly. Alice was a minor member of the company with a few lines that prevented her being a mere walking understudy, but she was also deputy stage manager and helped with props; in short, a humble member of the theatre, while Stella Pinero was a famous actress with a long career behind her and this very theatre named after her. But this was a democratic company in which leading lady and minor actress could talk to each other on friendly terms. Alice admired Stella and also feared her. Not only was Stella famous and practically the owner of the Pinero Theatre in the old church, together with the Theatre Workshop and the small Experimental Theatre – all great things in themselves – but her husband was Commander John Coffin, Head of the Police Force of the Second City.

Stella went into her dressing room, sat down in front of her looking glass where she stared at her reflection. She was still a beauty, would be till she died; she had grown into beauty, a rare benefaction of nature but one given to her.

Her make-up needed touching up, and mechanically she redid her lips and puffed on some powder. Her mind was not on it, but her hand was so used to the job that it smoothed

21

her eyebrows and checked the line of her lips with its usual skill.

She was not on for some time in the next act so she could sit back, breathe deeply and give herself good advice. Such as:

Stop going into a panic.

Pretend it's all a joke.

Tell your husband.

Oh, no, not John, not yet.

Her call came, the first call, to remind her she should soon be in the wings awaiting her cue. Stella remembered the days when a boy came round to bang on your door with the news: you're on, Miss Pinero. Now, the word came over the intercom.

She moved towards the wings, not waiting to be prompted.

She could hear the dialogue. Here was Lady Chiltern (acted by Jane Gillam, a beautiful girl, very nearly straight out of RADA where she had won an important prize). Lady Chiltern was a difficult part because she was so humourless and stupid, but Jane was doing what she could with it.

'Mrs Cheveley! Coming to see me? Impossible!'

And here was Fanny Burt as Mabel Chiltern – she had better lines and even a few jokes, but Wilde reserved the best dialogue for the men: 'She is coming up the stairs, as large as life and not nearly so natural.'

Not brilliant dialogue, Stella thought as she moved forward, but it got you on stage.

Here she went: 'Isn't that Miss Chiltern? I should so much like to know her.'

Stella stayed alert through the rest of the play. She had come to a decision. Speed seemed necessary, so she was off the stage as soon as the applause finished – to her pleasure there was a good show of enthusiasm – and slipped away to her dressing room without a word to the rest of the performers.

There were thirteen members of the cast; in the original production there had been fifteen, but money was easier then, and Stella had been obliged to cut out the two footmen.

22

Of the remainder, ten were what she thought of as her 'repertory company' inasmuch as they performed for her whenever she produced a play herself and did not buy one in. Most of these actors were young, and local, from the drama department in one of the nearby universities. Stella had early realized the importance of cultivating your neighbourhood to win affection and bring in the audiences. She had a lot of support always from the friends and families of her young performers.

But you also needed an outsider to provide some extra excitement and here Jane Gillam, a star in the making, and Fanny Burt came in. The two men, Michael Guardian and Tom Jenks were attractive performers. Stella Pinero herself provided glitter.

In her dressing room, Stella let her dresser remove her hat and garments as Mrs Cheveley. She did not appear in the last act, but had duly turned up for the last curtain. 'You pop off, Maisie,' she said to her elderly dresser. 'I know you want to get home. I will finish myself off.'

'I'll be dressing Miss Bow next week?'

'That's right.' Stella was creaming her face, removing the last of her make-up – she never used much, the days of heavy slap were over.

Stella had introduced a fortnightly change of programme to entertain her limited audience in the Second City, which made a frequent change of programme an economic necessity.

'A bit of an unknown quantity,' said Maisie, hanging up a green silk mantle. As an old hand, she was allowed a certain freedom of speech. 'But she's done well; starring roles straight from college.'

'Yes.'

Irene Bow was a graduate of the University drama department; she had been lucky with parts and had performed well in the Theatre Workshop production of *Barefoot in the Park*, and her crisp, rapid style of delivery would go down well in Michael Frayn's *Noises Off*. Stella now had two weeks to herself.

'You have a nice rest then, Miss Pinero,' said Maisie. 'You've earned it.'

If only, thought Stella.

Maisie turned round at the door. 'Are you all right, Miss Pinero?'

'I'm fine.'

'You look a bit white.'

'Don't you worry, Maisie.' Stella was rapidly doing her face, repairing what ravages she could and concealing any paleness with a thin foundation cream from Guerlain. 'You get off.' What she meant in her silent heart was: Please go away and leave me to think.

Stella went to a locked drawer on the make-up table and withdrew a thickish envelope. She looked at it for a moment before opening it.

Three old letters, two very recent ones, and a photograph. How wrong she had been to let that photograph be taken.

Not drunk, not mad, just silly, she told herself. I cannot even claim that I was so young, she added. He was, I wasn't. Stupid, I was, carried away by emotion. Even now, when she knew what he was, what he had become, she remembered his physical beauty.

She looked away from the letters, and inside herself let the dialogue go on: I did not know then that I would meet John Coffin again, that I would marry him and become the wife of a top policeman. When I married John, I tried to tell him of a few past affairs, but he laughed and said he did not want a General Confession, and he had not been without lovers himself.

It was, she admitted to herself, one of her treasured moments, because it showed what a nice man John Coffin was, with a knack for good behaviour. He was also tough-minded, resolute and quick-tempered. Oh dear, she could hardly bear to think of all that being turned against her.

He was fair, she told herself, very fair.

For some reason, she found this no comfort as she stared at her face in the looking glass, for fairness could be a very sharp weapon. She touched her cheek with a careful finger.

'I must look after my skin, stress is bad for it. Maisie was right, I am a wreck.'

She leaned, resting her chin on her right hand, and, ever the actress, mimed tragic despair.

Possibly not a wreck, she allowed herself, withdrawing her hand, she had been a beauty and still was. Like many actresses she could make herself beautiful. She turned away from the looking glass to get dressed.

Her hasty movement knocked the letters and the photograph to the ground. Three old letters from her, and two new ones from him. Unwelcome, unwanted letters, threatening letters, demanding letters.

Pip Eton, student, actor, stared up at her from the photograph on the floor. How he had changed from what he had once been, to a treacherous beast. Once her lover, now . . . What could she call him but a blackmailer, a criminal, a traitor?

No, be fair, she told herself bitterly, it is you, Stella Pinero, whom he invites to be the traitor. And to betray whom? Your own husband, not sexually as a lover, but professionally as a policeman.

A reviewer had once called Stella the 'modern comic muse'. Stella had valued that comment, she knew that she was a very good, possibly great comic actress, but now she felt a sting. Life had offered her a comedy, she reflected bitterly, and now she was being asked to play it as tragedy.

She put the letters and the photograph into her big black crocodile handbag which she had bought when she had won the Golden Apple Award on Broadway, and forced herself to calm down.

She could always kill someone. Preferably, Pip; if not, then very likely herself.

Her husband was away from home tonight, she would have the place to herself. There were times when it was better to be on your own.

Dressed in her street clothes, Stella sped through the back corridors of the Pinero Theatre, ignoring a wave from Jane

Gillam and a cheerful shout from Adam Fisk, who had played Lord Chiltern, to join them for a drink – they were going on to Max's for a meal afterwards. 'Can't manage tonight,' she called over her shoulder. 'Have a lovely time.'

'What's the matter with her?' said Adam to Fanny and Jane. 'She always comes at the end of the run. Tradition.'

'Her husband, I expect,' said Jane.

'Why do you say that?'

Jane shrugged. 'Just think so.'

Stella stepped out into the open air, took three deep and calming breaths, then walked briskly to where she lived with the Chief Commander in the tower of the old church now converted into the theatre. There was one good thing about living on the job: you did not have far to walk home.

She let herself in, switched on the light that illuminated the winding stair and listened, in case Coffin had come back, then walked up the stairs into silence.

There was no cat or dog to greet her, both animals of the earlier generation had died within a few months of each other, as if, rivals and enemies as they were, they could not endure life without each other. And although Stella had often cursed the old cat, a battered old street cat, for waking her in the morning with its paw on her face, and grumbled at the dog for demanding that late-night walk, she missed them, too. They had been replaced by a sturdy white peke called Augustus, but he had declared himself Coffin's dog who must go where the boss went, so he was off now with Coffin on his travels.

She made herself a pot of coffee, prepared a sandwich with cheese and, defiantly, a crisp spiced onion, something no performer would normally do, which she sat at the table in the kitchen eating. The strong hot drink together with food helped her to clear her mind.

'I don't see the way forward yet, but I know I need to think it over and I will do that best on my own.'

She could not talk it over with her husband because it was his career that could be ruined.

'I am not a fool,' she said aloud. 'I know it is not the

sexual element that would do him in – society is not so unsophisticated – nor the fact that I look as though . . . No, I won't utter what it looks as if I am doing. And it's not that, even, it's the security side that would destroy him.'

She drank some coffee. The darkness outside seemed to creep in behind her eyes so that she could not see. 'Emotional mist,' she said in a loud voice, shaking her head.

She went down the stairs to the large sitting room one floor below and poured herself a large glass of whisky which she then carried upstairs. She had seen tired detectives come back to life after a slug of it, so she guessed it would do the same for her.

As she sipped it, she heard a rustle at floor level. She turned slowly to see what was there. A small grey mouse sat staring back at her. In the old days the cat had brought them in as an unwanted present for her mistress. This one must have made its way there under its own steam, or be a survivor. She found that thought comforting.

'Hello, friend,' she said. 'Don't worry, you are safe with me tonight. I know how you feel: trapped in a hostile world.' She drank some more whisky. 'Fear not. Appearances to the contrary,' she added, 'I won't eat you.'

The mouse slid quietly away on his own business. He was a resident, knew the ways of the house, would not be seen again for some time.

Stella finished her whisky, then took herself upstairs to her bedroom. Off the bedroom was a small dressing room contrived out of a corner of the room.

She looked at her clothes hanging in a neat row behind a glass door. She changed into a comfortable trouser suit, packed a small bag.

One more task and the most painful: a lying letter. She hated deceiving her husband, partly because she was a naturally truthful person – which all actresses must be, since nothing shows up more on the stage than falseness – but also because the Chief Commander had a sharp eye for an untruth.

27

Dearest,

A late call from Silverline Films for the part of Annie Burnett, the prosecutor, in their new detective drama series. My agent says I simply must try for it . . . I am flying out to New York overnight.

Give me time. I will get in touch. I have to think.

Truth will out, she told herself, as she wrote the last words.

Then she scrawled: 'I really want this chance'. Again the truth; she did want such a chance, if offered. Her career had been on hold lately, and Coffin knew she fancied this part. Heaven knows, she had talked about it enough. He would believe her, accept the letter.

'All my love,' she ended.

Then she went across to the fax machine which lived on a shelf from which the messages popped out and slid to the ground. None there at the moment.

She wrote a note for her assistant in the theatre – Away for a few days – and the same to her co-producer, both of which she then faxed out to them.

Hardly had she moved a step away when the fax rang and a message spilled itself out in front of her. Slowly, feeling heavy with premonition, she bent down to pick it up.

IN THE NEXT MINUTE THE TELEPHONE WILL RING. ANSWER IT.

Stella picked up her bag and turned away. That was one bell she would not answer.

She was at the door when the telephone rang. It became hard to breathe. She hesitated, knowing that she wanted to ignore it, but she was like a rabbit before a stoat. Stuck, frozen.

But you never knew with telephone calls. Perhaps it really was a summons from her agent. She knew it would not be John Coffin. He was driving down the M40 – probably, she didn't really know where he was. He had a professional knack of disappearing. The thought went through her mind as she picked up the telephone; if he can disappear, so can I.

She held the receiver in her hand without speaking.

'I know you're there, Stella. I can hear you breathing.'

'How did you get this number?' Silly question, it was supposed to be secret, but it was this man's life's work to get at secrets.

A laugh came back as a reply. 'I want to meet you, Stella. I think you need to see me to take me seriously. This *is* serious.'

Stella did not answer.

'Come on, Stelly, I won't eat you.' He laughed, and Stella felt sick. 'Meet me at Waterloo, under the clock. Remember, that, Stelly? It was always the same place, wasn't it? Be there.'

Stella stood there, still clutching her bag. 'No, no, I can't, I can't.'

She picked up her bag, went down the staircase and out of the door.

Outside, in the night air, she looked around in case anyone was there.

Silence, quiet. Not a mouse stirring.

A whole day after Stella had gone away, John Coffin, Chief Commander of the Police Force of the Second City of London, let himself into his home. He was back some twenty-four hours before he was expected, and meant to have a quiet time working. He was accompanied by the white peke Augustus who had appointed himself dog-companion to Coffin and insisted on going everywhere he could with him. Coffin had gone away after the bombs had exploded; his departure had not been unconnected with that happening. His assistant, Paul Masters, kept him in touch.

Coffin was glad to be back; he had observed that the play running at the Pinero Theatre was no longer *An Ideal Husband* which meant, he hoped, that he would find Stella at home.

He put down his bags and ran up the stairs, calling out: 'Stella, I'm back.'

He was a big man, but spare of frame and light on his feet. His hair, which had been reddish in his youth, had darkened with the years and was now greying neatly about his temples. He was neat in everything he did. Thin as a young man he had never put on weight, although he took no exercise, other than running up and down the stairs of his home in the tower; he took part in no sports and never had. 'We didn't in my day in working-class London,' he said once, 'except a bit of street football and pavement boxing. Pugilism, more like,' he had added thoughtfully. But there was muscle beneath the suits, which, under Stella's control, were well and expensively tailored. Still done in the East End of London, but now he knew where to go. And how to pay.

'How come you have such muscles here and there?' Stella had said once.

'Inherited,' Coffin had answered. 'Runs in the family.' Though he had hardly had a family. Orphaned, he had only discovered in later life that he had a disappearing, much married mother, who had provided him with two siblings, one half-brother, a stiff Edinburgh lawyer, and the other, from another alliance, his darling half-sister. Mother herself remained an absentee, except for leaving some extraordinary memoirs.

Silence.

From behind a curtain on the window where the stair curved, he saw a tail, then a cautious beady gaze.

'Oh, hello, boy,' Coffin said. 'You still here? Better not let Stella see you. You and I are going to have to stop meeting like this.' Augustus bustled up the stairs behind him, ready to take part in the game, but the mouse was gone.

The quiet of the tower was telling its own story; it spoke of emptiness. Stella was not here.

The place did not feel like home without Stella in it. He knew why; marriage with Stella had given him the stable home life which a first disastrous marriage had failed to do.

Coffin had been in Edinburgh where, amongst other

things, he had visited his half-brother in the large, handsome, frigid house he inhabited. William matched the house; so much so that Coffin found it difficult to relate to him as a brother, even half a brother. Their meeting had been stiff and formal as they talked over the research Coffin was trying to do on the life of their eccentric parent. Sometimes, he thought his mother might still be alive and building up yet another family; though she would be near her century now, he did not put it past her. He wished he had known her, but disappearing was her game.

He was back home now and miserable. In Scotland he had been at a conference of top policemen held in a remote house. It had been one of those conferences which had appeared to be on one subject but which had had a covert purpose.

Coffin had learnt a few things at Melly House that would concern him and his district, and had been, tactfully, informed of certain others. He, in his turn, had passed on certain information.

Knowledge, he reflected, as he read Stella's note, is a painful thing. She will ring, probably from New York. I will know from the tone of her voice if I ought to raise what I learnt at Melly House.' He was desperately anxious but he kept calm; he knew he must.

The time passed quietly, with no call from Stella. He had ahead of him several busy days, a meeting in central London, two committees, one about finance. The bombs in his district, the need for increased security all round, had meant extra spending.

He knew that Stella usually stayed at the Algonquin, so he rang there first. Miss Pinero was not a guest, he was told politely. She was well known there and a welcome visitor, but, regretfully, she was not staying at the hotel just now.

If she could afford it, or if someone else, like the film company, was paying, Stella liked the St Regis.

But Stella was not there, either.

Finally, he did what he should have done at first, but disliked doing: he telephoned her London agent. He knew

31

that Doria Jones thought he was bad for Stella's career, that he kept her cooped up in the Second City when she ought to be adorning the London or New York stage. In short, she thought Coffin was a chauvinistic, oppressive spouse.

Doria's secretary answered his call, saying in her polite but chirpy voice that Doria was out of town and would not be back until the late evening.

In the evening, he worked on papers and prepared a speech he had to give at an official dinner. That done he had a meal, then a drink, and fell asleep. Then, late as it was, he telephoned Doria at home.

She replied in person, sounding surprised to hear him. She had a soft, sweet voice and always said that Stella was her favourite client – which may have been true.

'No, darling, I don't know where Stella is. I did not send her an urgent message. Definitely not.'

She was willing to go on talking about this, but Coffin was not. 'Thanks, Doria, I got it wrong. My fault. Sorry I bothered you.'

He put the telephone down. 'Stella, damn you, where are you?' Coffin's life had ruled out trusting people. Stella was an exception. He still loved and trusted her, but he wanted to know where she was.

Coffin did not sleep much that night. 'If I have lost Stella, either physically or emotionally, because she wasn't what I thought she was, I would not die. I would go on, because I have learnt how to survive, but I would be shrunken.'

In the dawn he went down to the kitchen and made some coffee, which he sat at the table drinking. The sky outside was pink with light. He couldn't see the mouse but he heard a rustle by the window.

'Could she be dead?' he asked himself. 'If what I heard in Melly House was true, then the company she is mixing with might easily kill her if they scented danger.' He felt a groan rising inside him. 'I am part of the danger, although God knows I don't want to be.'

It was not all his fault though, and he knew that, too. Stella had to bear her share.

'When she gets in touch, comes back, we will work this through somehow,' he told himself. He finished the coffee, made toast, put some cheese down for the mouse, then ate the toast standing by the window watching the sun slowly rise into view.

He felt better. At intervals he told himself that he would certainly know if anything had happened to Stella. He would sense it. Would he, though? Wasn't that precisely the sort of fallacy he would discourage in other people?

On the other hand, he would be told, someone would tell him, he was the person who was told things, he was in a position to know what was happening.

Anyway, Stella would telephone soon. Or walk in the door, then they could talk things over. 'I don't blame you for anything, Stella,' he would say, 'but I must know.'

Didn't that sound pompous, precisely the sort of comment that would make Stella stamp out of the room in a rage? Phrase it better, Coffin. You will when you see her, it will happen.

'You may never see her again,' a voice whispered in his ear.

The information appertaining to Stella – lovely professional phrase that, if a little pompous – was nothing much, merely her name on a list, but it had been fed to him so discreetly, almost anonymously and without comment. He had been observed, though; notice taken, as you might say.

He was surprised to find that during all this inner conversation he had driven himself to work and had arrived, safely, too, in his office.

He sped through the outer office where two uniformed officers manned the defences, then with a brisk good morning to them he entered the inner office where three people worked – his assistant Paul Masters, and the two secretaries: Gillian, and the new girl, Sheila, who had replaced the elegant Sylvia – before hurrying into his own room which was empty and quiet, and smelt of furniture polish with a touch of disinfectant. Pine, he thought.

'Got back early,' he announced, as he passed through to

his work-laden desk. The usual files to read and initial, a larger than customary folder of letters to sign (and there would be more when his secretary came in, but she was tactfully leaving him for a few minutes), and the notes of telephone calls received and to be returned.

A call from Archie Young, but no message. Coffin frowned. This was unlike Archie who was always businesslike and not mysterious. He rang his secretaries; Sheila answered.

'Do you know anything about these calls from Chief Superintendent Young?'

Sheila Heslop had been with him for six months now, more or less taking charge of the outer office and organizing Gillian, who was about to take study leave. In a quiet way, she organized the Chief Commander, too.

'He rang me first to see if you were in, sir,' she said carefully. 'I suggested that he speak to Inspector Masters, but he said he wanted you. I think he had something he wanted to talk to you about.'

'Oh, well, I expect I will be here.'

'I rather think he might be ringing again,' she said, with what might have been a touch of nervousness. This made Coffin answer her sharply.

'What makes you say that?'

'Just a feeling, sir.'

Coffin looked at his watch. Still early, still time for Stella to ring.

He took up the report on the bombings in the Second City, which came with photographs and a video of the bombers.

In two seconds the phone went. Coffin picked it up eagerly to hear Archie Young's hesitant voice. 'Something you ought to see, sir. A body . . . Percy Street.'

'I'll drive you round, sir,' Archie Young had said. 'Unless you would rather use your own driver?' He could see someone had better drive the Chief Commander. Coffin had a new driver – not a member of the Force; police officers cost too much to train to be used as chauffeurs.

'He's away,' said Coffin. 'Thank you, Archie, you drive.'

So tense he felt sick, Coffin let Archie Young lead him into the house in Percy Street. There was a ring of fellow officers there, the SOCO team, the police surgeon, and Inspector Lodge.

With automatic good manners he nodded towards them all, but did not speak. He looked at the body lying on the floor, the terribly damaged face staring upwards. He saw the handbag lying on the floor.

He walked forward, forcing himself to study well what he saw. He stared for some minutes before turning away. 'No, that is not my wife. Yes, she wore jeans like that; yes, she had such a handbag, but the body is not hers.'

Inspector Lodge met Coffin's eyes with a meaningful stare: I hope you know what you are doing.

Archie Young muttered something about the material in the handbag.

'I don't care what is inside the handbag. That is not my wife,' said Coffin in a quiet voice. 'It is not Stella.'

2

Archie Young and Coffin were back in the Chief Commander's office. Coffin had watched with an expressionless face as the body, which he refused to own, was packed into a black bag to be transported to the mortuary. The police used the one in the University Hospital where a special room had been allocated to them.

Archie picked up the blue leather handbag, now packaged in a piece of plastic. 'I think you should look at what was found in this bag.'

Coffin gave it a bleak look. He was not sure, but he thought he was angry with Archie. For certain, anger from somewhere, caused by someone, was welling up inside him. Perhaps it was from the pain, for there was pain all right. He said nothing but continued to stare at the bag.

'You thought you recognized the bag.'

The bag was dark leather, very soft and quilted with a gold chain and gold emblem on the front. Even Archie Young had seen similar ones around, swinging from the shoulders of the fashionable. Some were genuine, others imitation. This one looked the real thing.

'Stella has one like it. I gave it to her. Chanel, she chose it herself. But there must be many others, they are so fashionable.' Which was why he had given one to Stella, who had a taste for what was fashionable and expensive.

He studied the soft blue leather object, reluctant to open it, even to touch it.

'Better open it, sir. Or shall I do it for you?' A thin pair of transparent plastic gloves was held out, ready. Still reluctant,

Coffin smoothed on the gloves; he knew the rules.

'No.' Coffin stretched out his hand, now masked, and lifted the tiny gold fastening. The bag yawned open in front of him. 'It's been damaged, the bag should open more slowly.'

'Yes, I reckon it's been wrenched apart. Not malice, I don't think. Whoever did it wanted to be sure that it fell wide apart. So you could see what was inside. At a glance.'

Coffin looked at Archie Young sharply. 'You meant something by that.'

'Take a look, sir.'

Coffin frowned as he drew out a photograph. He laid it on the desktop in front of him. Archie, watching the Chief Commander closely, saw the colour melt from his face to be replaced by a pallor and then a flush that spread to his throat and touched his temple. Coffin put out his hand and covered the picture. He looked up at Archie Young: 'That photo is a fake. Stella is not mad, bad and dangerous.'

'No,' said Archie. 'Of course not.' But he said it awkwardly, half defensively.

'Stella does not eat human flesh. God, no. That woman –' he tapped the picture – 'is eating an arm, I can see the wrist. A bleeding human arm.'

'Bit of,' said Archie even more awkwardly. And it wasn't actually dripping with blood. The blood, if that was what it was, looked dry.

The picture, of course, was a fake, but why? And the face, and the body, what you could see of it, was certainly Stella Pinero's.

Archie felt miserable: it was a bloody awful thing to have happened. No, he mustn't keep using that word, there was too much blood around as it was. He looked with sympathy at the Chief Commander, who seemed suddenly older.

'The dead woman is not Stella,' said Coffin. 'And this photograph is not of Stella.'

He's a good man, Archie said to himself, whatever she's done to him, he doesn't deserve this.

The devil got a hold of his tongue because he heard himself

say: 'Some anthropologists think that kissing developed from biting.'

'Thank you.'

There was a pause during which Archie Young tried to think of something sensible and wise to say, before he decided that silence might be best.

Coffin shook himself, like a dog coming in from the rain. 'Let's get down to this. We are policemen, investigators. Who is the dead woman, and how did she die?'

'We don't know the answers yet to the first question. As to the second, it looks as though she was strangled. The face was beaten after death.'

'And the next thing, after establishing identity . . .' Coffin started the sentence.

If we can, said Archie Young silently to himself. He had dread feelings about this dead woman.

'Is to find out how and why she was carrying my wife's handbag. If indeed it is Stella's and not a replica,' Coffin pushed on. 'And that in itself is a strange thing. Why?'

It's all strange, Archie thought, mighty strange. 'Of course we will find out who she is,' he said, with more confidence than he felt. He grappled with another problem: how to refer to the Chief Commander's wife in the embarrassing present circumstance.

He compromised. 'Miss Pinero might be able to throw some light on it when questioned.' Coffin looked at him gloomily, even apprehensively. Archie floundered on. 'The bag might have been lost or stolen.'

'With the photograph in it?'

Wonder if he'll have a breakdown, Archie thought. He looks as though he could. On the edge. But no, he's a strong fellow, mentally and physically. Except he loves that woman, that's always dangerous. 'It's a joke that photograph,' he said.

'The dead body is not a joke,' said Coffin savagely.

Archie Young was silenced. From the outer room, Coffin could hear Paul Masters chatting away cheerfully. Too cheerfully, he thought sourly, and there was a woman laughing.

For a moment, he thought it might be Stella, but it was one of the secretaries. He knew the voice, there was a brassy ring to it which today he found irritating. She laughed again, damn her. He wondered if he could institute a no laughing rule like a no smoking rule.

'I don't know where she is,' Coffin heard himself saying. 'I have not the least idea in the world where Stella has gone.'

That, thought Archie, is one of the comments you are better off not hearing. He liked and admired the Chief Commander, he liked and admired Stella Pinero, too, but he wanted to keep out of their relationship. Let them sort it out. She would turn up. You had to allow actresses their freedom. 'She'll get in touch,' he heard himself saying.

Coffin looked at his old friend and colleague and suddenly realized he was being offered sympathy. He laughed and pulled himself together.

'I am sure she will, Archie, and it had better be soon.' There was a note in his voice which suggested that Stella, when she returned, would have some questions to answer. He stood up. 'I'd better get back to work.'

The Chief Superintendent rose too. 'Anything new on the bombers?'

Coffin shook his head. What he had learnt on his trip north was confidential even from Archie Young. 'Nothing much,' he said in a noncommittal voice. 'Inspector Lodge was first in to inspect the body in Percy Street, I suppose?'

'Pretty smartish,' agreed Archie Young. 'Asked to come with me as soon as he heard about it. He was told, of course.' Anything to do with the bombed area was for him to know about, he was their expert, the local, middle-range one. All the foremost terrorist watchers had probably been in Edinburgh or wherever it was the Chief Commander had really gone. On this point, Archie had his reservations. Edinburgh first, and then on to – where?

'I suppose he hoped he'd got a dead terrorist.'

'I don't know what he hoped. He doesn't show his mind, that one.'

The two looked at each other. They would be glad to be rid of the Todger, but life was not so simple.

'He's very good at what he does,' Coffin allowed. Not a loveable man, but who would be in that job. He could not regard himself as a totally loveable person. He heard Stella's voice: 'No, darling, not a cuddly person. Many good qualities and I love you madly, but not cosy.'

Was that why she had gone away? Was she running away from him?

Did Stella love him? He had never felt totally sure. You had to remember that she was an actress.

And where was she, damn her.

'I'll take the bag with me,' said Archie Young, reaching out a hand for the bag in its plastic container. 'Forensics, and all that.'

Coffin nodded.

'If I could suggest, sir, you might have a look round at home to see if Miss Pinero's bag is there or not.'

'I will, I will.' He would get round to it when he felt less sore.

'Or she might say herself . . .' Archie left the rest of the sentence delicately unsaid.

'When we speak again, I will certainly be asking,' said Coffin. He watched the Chief Superintendent depart with careful, depressing tact, closing the door quietly and not smiling.

Feeling unloved and out of sorts, Coffin slumped back in his chair and went to work on the mound of papers in front of him. Word processors, far from reducing this load, added to it daily. A truism, of course, but he was not in the mood to be original.

He wondered where Stella was and why she had said nothing which was true; but he shrank from the painful thought that perhaps it was better he did not know more. A lie had to hide something, didn't it?

'I would not have this feeling if it were not for that terrible photograph. Which was not a joke. A fake, but not a joke.' And also because of the information gently passed over to

40

him in Scotland. At the time he had tried to reject it, shrug it off as a case of mistaken identity, or a computer error, or someone's genuine mistake, which did happen even with the men he was being briefed by. Now he did not know.

He unlocked the bottom drawer of his desk. From inside, he withdrew a bundle of letters. Underneath was yet another, smaller bundle, older and grubby, as if much opened and read. All the letters were from Stella, he had kept every letter she had written to him: the older packet dated from when they first met, before they quarrelled and parted. The more recent letters were since they met again, and were written by Stella when away filming or on tour. He had asked her to write as well as telephone and he had written back.

'My secret hoard,' he said aloud. He never asked if Stella kept his letters.

There were no photographs. 'I hate being photographed except in the way of publicity business,' Stella had said, adding with a giggle: 'Besides, photographs are dangerous.'

Yes, Stella, they certainly are.

He packed the letters in his briefcase to take home where he could study them to see if they could tell him who took that photograph of Stella and, more importantly, who doctored it.

Who did you know, Stella, who could treat you in that way? Who wanted to make you look half-woman, half-beast?

He picked up the telephone. Paul Masters answered promptly, as if he had been awaiting the call.

'You know what's been going on?'

'Just a bit, sir. If I may say so, sir, don't worry.'

He's sorry for me. Coffin accepted the gift with resignation. No doubt there was sorrow and pity all around him at Headquarters, seeping out into the whole police division which he commanded. Many a laugh and a joke too.

But the photograph was not to be laughed at. Some strange fish had swum into his pool and must be accounted for, and, if necessary, caught.

'Get me Chief Inspector Astley, Paul, please.'

'She's here actually, sir. Outside. Shall I send her in?'

'Yes, do.' So had it been Phoebe laughing?

She swung into the room a second later, her face grave. She had not been laughing. But she smiled when she saw him. 'I was on my way to you. I knew I had to see you to tell you what the latest was.'

'You know about the body in Percy Street? Of course you do.'

Phoebe advanced into the room with the confidence of an old friend and ally; she perched herself on the windowsill. She invariably dressed soberly for work; today she wore black trousers with a cream silk shirt, but there was always the impression with Phoebe that underneath was lace and silk, probably in red. It was a tribute to her impact on her colleagues because, as she confided to her friend Eden when she heard the rumour going around about her red knickers, in fact they were white cotton, 'from my favourite high street store, and made in Israel'.

'Mind if I smoke?'

'Yes. I thought you'd given that up.' In an early brush with what might have been but was not something malignant, Phoebe had given up all sins of the flesh from food to sex. Rumour had it that those days were over. Rampantly, cheerfully over.

'I've started again.' She lit up. 'When under stress.'

'And you are under stress?'

'I'm catching it from you.'

'Right,' said Coffin. For a moment he said no more. He trusted Phoebe, to whom he would probably speak more openly than to anyone else. Except Stella. The Stella he had lived with and loved, but it looked as though there was a Stella he had never known. I won't allow this thought to enter my mind, he told himself. I have to trust Stella, to believe in Stella.

'I was coming to see you because the Todger called me in.' She looked at him gravely.

'He would do,' said Coffin. Phoebe's area of responsibility

touched upon that of Inspector Lodge. They did not like each other, but there was respect.

'I went round to Percy Street, the body had gone by then. I was told why they had thought it was Stella and got you round there, although I am bound to say I would not have thought it was her for a minute.'

'There was another factor . . .' he could hardly bring himself to call it a reason.

'The handbag? I was told about it and what it contained.'

'That was why I was brought round at speed,' Coffin said gloomily. 'I understand it, the bag has gone for forensic testing, and I am supposed to be going through Stella's things to see if the one she owned, her bag, is still there. But I am not doing it because I am perfectly certain the blue Chanel bag is the one and original.'

'Could be,' said Phoebe, 'but I shouldn't let it worry you, it's just a dirty trick. We'll sort that one out, don't worry. Her bag was used to create the illusion, someone wanted to distress you.'

'Someone succeeded.'

'But it wasn't Stella, and I am surprised that the illusion held for as long as it did. Once the body was moved and taken round to Dennis Garden for examination.' Phoebe picked a loose piece of tobacco from her lips, and smiled slightly. Professor Garden, an academic from the local university, was a pleasure to cross swords with. 'Once Dennis got it on the table – even before, I should guess – he knew not only was it not Stella Pinero but that it was not a woman. Too flat, no breasts.' She went on talking, giving him time to start breathing again; he seemed to have stopped. How long can the brain go without oxygen? 'The pelvic structure, of course. Quite different, you can always tell.'

'I suppose that, unconsciously, I saw that too. I knew it wasn't Stella.' Coffin went to the window to stare out. He could see across the road to the big car park where his own car had its privileged place; looking beyond was a large modern school where he had once given away the prizes, and further away the roof of the University Hospital where

Dennis Garden taught and operated on the living and gazed upon interesting corpses with whom he was able to set up a relationship at once intimate yet impersonal. He fancied he could see one of those discreet, black-windowed ambulances turning in now to deliver another customer for Dennis's attentions. Coffin turned back to Phoebe. 'I suppose as Lodge called you in he thinks there is some terrorist connection.'

'His antennae are twitching,' said Phoebe.

Coffin came back to sit at his desk. 'That needs thinking about.' He tried to wave away Phoebe's cigarette smoke. 'I wish you'd put that out.'

'Fag finished.' Phoebe crushed the cigarette out on the sole of her shoe, then threw the stub away. The need for the counter irritant was over: Coffin was back on the job.

'Pity about the face,' said Professor Dennis Garden. He sounded genuinely moved. 'The hair was a hairpiece on a band. Very good quality,'

'It does make identification difficult,' agreed John Coffin.

'Not only that, but from what I can make of the bone structure, he had a graceful, pleasing face. Small-boned altogether, or he would never have got into the jeans,' Garden said in a regretful tone.

'Strange there wasn't blood,' observed Coffin. 'Not much on the hair or hairpiece. What do you make of that?'

'Not much at the moment.' Garden was giving nothing away. 'I have not examined the body properly yet.'

'There was not too much blood in the room where he was found, but he was probably killed there. Interesting in itself. I wonder why?'

Professor Garden smiled happily. 'Your problem, my dear, not mine. I deal with only this end of the affair. It's for you to fiddle out the rest. If you can.' He waved a hand to an attendant. 'Seen all you want? Right, let's put this poor fellow away to rest.' The attendant wheeled the trolley to the refrigerated cage. 'I shall have to be at work on him later, but I promise you I'll do it delicately.' His pale blue eyes glinted with amusement at Coffin. 'Bit below you, isn't it, to be taking an interest in a simple case like this?'

'I always knew it wasn't my wife,' said Coffin bleakly. He knows all about it, every last detail, probably seen a copy of the photograph, or a drawing, or heard it with every elaboration and joke that his colleagues' humour could devise . . .

'Of course, of course. Very nasty moment it must have been. But soon over, you knew at once it was not Stella.' He crossed himself carefully. Amid a myriad of other interests in Dennis Garden's life was a feeling for a god. He was not always sure which god but he knew it was one to keep on good terms with. Besides, he liked Stella (inasmuch as he could admire any woman, his tastes not going that way), and wished her well. He would not have enjoyed doing a postmortem on her. He had an idea already that he was not about to enjoy this one.

'What about the hands?' Coffin asked.

'Ah, you saw the significance of the gloves?'

'One of the ways I knew it was not my wife,' said Coffin. 'I knew that Stella would not wear white gloves with jeans. So, what about the hands?'

'You were right to be worried; the fingers were cut off at the knuckles.'

Coffin nodded. 'No fingerprints then? What about the thumb?'

'Even the thumb has gone . . . Whoever did it was taking precautions about identification . . . But don't worry too much, science is wonderful, something might emerge that helps.'

But he was glad it was not Stella's body they were discussing. He was skilled in morbid anatomy; he taught it, even enjoyed doing so, but one does not want to cut up one's friends. Although there is always pleasure in a job well done. Already he had it in mind that he would identify this body for the police. No one got the better of Dennis Garden. Anyway, damn it, the face – he knew how to reconstruct the face. He had a sense of knowing that face.

He saw the Chief Commander to the door. What was she

doing though, the beautiful and talented Stella, wandering away without warning to her husband when their marriage was supposed to be a notable success?

Not a man you could play around with, he considered, watching the Chief Commander's retreating back. There was something to the set of Coffin's shoulders that suggested he might not be easy.

Coffin summoned Inspector Lodge to see him. Lodge arrived with speed, suggesting to Coffin's anxious mind that he had been expecting a call.

'You went round to Percy Street very fast. Was there any special reason?'

The Todger took it quietly. 'I wondered if we might have a terrorist there.'

'Any other reason?'

The Inspector became even quieter. 'Always interested when something like this turns up . . . it's my job.'

Coffin waited.

'In confidence, we have had an insider working here, I thought it might be my plant.'

'And is it?'

Lodge shrugged. 'No identification yet.'

'Is your insider a man or a woman?'

'A man,' he said with reluctance. How he hated to part with information, Coffin thought.

'So it could be the dead man?'

'I am waiting to find out more, see who's missing, run checks, but yes, I think, yes.'

'And why was he dressed up like my wife? With a handbag containing a photograph of Stella? Any views?'

Lodge looked away, then back so that his eyes met Coffin's bleak gaze.

'Ah,' said Coffin, understanding what he saw. No need to make mysteries here, he told himself, least of all to yourself. This man has been told what was shown to me with relative delicacy . . . yes, I have to say they tried to be humane.

No more was said on that secret subject. Lodge departed

murmuring that he would keep the Chief Commander in touch, but it looked at the moment that this was a terrorist killing. How his man had been flushed out, he did not yet know, but it was vital to find out.

'He was a good man,' he said. 'I don't know who got on to him or how, but by God I am going to find out.'

'A traitor in our midst,' said Coffin sadly.

'I hope not, but we may have to face it.'

'Let's meet for a drink sometime soon,' said Coffin. There was a hole here that needed mending, patching up, and it was his job to do it.

After Lodge had gone, Paul Masters came in with a tray of coffee and file of papers.

'Hot and strong. And this is today's list: a CC and Accounts meeting at midday. A delegation from Swinehouse . . . ethnic problems. And Anthony Hermeside from the Home Office is inviting himself to lunch . . .'

Coffin groaned.

'Yes, good luck, sir. I have all the notes you will need to brief you on him in the folder. Oh, and Hermeside doesn't drink.'

He departed in polite good order. He had arranged what he could, smoothed Coffin's path and now it was up to the Chief Commander.

Coffin drank his coffee, which was, as Paul had said, hot and strong, there was cream to go with it and a new sort of chocolate biscuit, all confirming once again that everyone knew everything and quite possibly more than could be known – rumour always magnified a story – and he was being offered comfort.

He drank some more coffee, gazing at a corner of the room where it seemed to him a part of his own mind was circling.

'Ever been betrayed?' he asked this self.

'Many times and oft,' Old Sobersides up in the corner, who seemed to know more about his life than he did himself, came back with. 'And you just have to get on with it.'

47

He had asked for a report on the body in Percy Street to be delivered quickly, and it was now on his desk.

The report, put together with speed by Sergeant Mitchell said:

The body is that of a white male, probably aged between thirty-five and forty. He was not dirty, he had not been living rough, nor was he undernourished. His hair, beneath the wig, was dyed.

Cause of death was a neat stab wound which had not bled profusely. We will know more about this when the pathologist reports.

It appears that he had been killed in the room where he was found. Blood traces, cleaned up but still to be seen, indicated this. Forensics are working it now.

Also, it is clear that he had walked there, wearing the clothes in which he was found. A video of him rounding the corner out of Jamaica Street shows him on the afternoon of the day within twenty-four hours of which he died. He was alone.

A first search of the rest of the house has turned up nothing except bomb-damaged furniture. Bed linen and towels in a cupboard in the upper bedroom, along with some old clothes.

A copy of the relevant part of the video is attached.

It was a blurred dark picture but one in which a figure, wearing jeans, swinging the Chanel bag over a shoulder, could be clearly seen turning the corner.

Good work, Mitchell.

He studied the picture again. Yes, there he was, centre picture, clearly shown. The end of the street was more blurred.

Well, that was it, for the moment.

Taking advice from his darker, grimmer self, Coffin did as he was told and got on with the job, following the appointments laid out in his diary and pointed to by Paul Masters.

Used as Coffin was to the dead times in an investigation when nothing seems to move forward, he found it hard. In a way, it was Inspector Lodge's case if the dead man was indeed his man. Equally, because of the involvement of Stella, Coffin ought to keep out. He did not intend to do so.

He worked through the day, keeping his head down to avoid the interested eyes and hints of sympathy, but his temper was not improved by either.

Paul Masters had accompanied him into one committee meeting to keep the notes.

As they entered this last meeting together, Paul Masters passed on one more message to the Chief Commander. He was sensitive to his chief's moods and knew at once that he would not be pleased at what he was about to learn.

The message was in a sealed envelope, but nevertheless, through his own channels, Paul knew what was in it.

'From Chief Superintendent Young, sir. He wanted you to have it soonest.' You might need a strong drink when you've read it, instead of this committee of ways and means.

Coffin went into the room, already full of committee members, took his place at the head of the table, surveyed them bleakly, muttered an acknowledgement, then opened his letter. Why is it, he was saying to himself, that even colleagues you liked and respected (not always the same thing by any means) turn into trouble when they become committee members?

He read the letter quickly. 'Thought you would wish to know that the dead man has been identified as Peter Corner, who was working undercover for Lodge. He had taken a job as office assistant and manager of the firm of builders repairing the house in Percy Street where he was found. He was identified by his underclothes, which had not been changed when he was dressed up as a woman. He had an invisible coded number, as is the rule, inside his pants.'

Coffin looked up from the letter. He could already tell that the bad news had been saved until last. 'Lodge has sealed off the room which Corner rented in Pompey Land, Spinnergate. He found some notes there in which Miss Pinero's name was mentioned.'

Damn, damn and damn, thought Coffin, even as he opened the meeting in a polite, calm voice.

Archie Young had scribbled an additional line or two himself which Paul Masters was not privy to since it had not been typed and thus was out of the chain of communication.

'Series of photographs of Stella, taken in a bar, in company with an unknown man.'

Damn again, so the dead man had been watching Stella. Of course, she knew a lot of men, met them in the way of business.

Old Killjoy, his other self, who had come along with him and was nesting in the corner of this room, said sceptically: So?

Still, if there was anything bloody to come out, he would rather Archie Young knew than anyone. Not sure about Lodge, though.

He became aware at this point that the committee was waiting for him to speak. He forced his two selves to fuse, and took up the duties of a chairman of a difficult committee which must get down to business.

It was the last committee of the day. He considered telephoning Archie Young, but knew, suddenly, he wanted to be at home. He collected the dog, who had spent the day with the two secretaries who were his devoted slaves, put him in the car with his briefcase and overcoat to make the short journey back to the old church tower which still dominated the Pinero Theatre complex.

He parked the car, dragged out the dog, who wished to stay comfortably where he was, and unlocked the heavy front door to his home. Because of security this was something of a complicated business.

'Stella?' He stood at the bottom of the staircase, looking up. 'Stella?'

There was no answer. Instead a kind of deadness as if no one really lived here any more.

Coffin sat on the bottom step, Augustus leaned against him, and they communed with each other on the misery of those left behind.

But life had to go on, as Augustus presently reminded

Coffin by letting out a low, hungry growl. It was his asking growl, and said, 'Food.'

'All right, boy.' Coffin got up. 'Don't know what I've got for you, but if all else fails we will go to eat at Max's.' Max had started with a small simple eating place not far from the old St Luke's church, but skill and hard work from him and his family of pretty daughters had given it great success, to which he added a restaurant and bar in the Stella Pinero theatre.

Max had, however, helped Stella to fill a deep freeze with meat and fish dishes so Augustus and Coffin shared a warmed-up chicken casserole. Then Coffin made coffee while Augustus retired to bed.

In the silence of the living room, Coffin took out the packets of Stella's letters. He opened first the collection which dated back to their earliest days together. Stella was a good, gossipy letter writer.

Will I find someone here, Stella, who is your dangerous friend? – Friend? I should not use that word.

He read quickly, seeking likely names: here were Ferdy Chase, Sidney Mells, Petra Land. These names came up frequently, not surprising really, he reflected, because in those days Stella had been a member of the Greenwich Repertory Company as had these performers.

One or two names, not to be associated with that group, but of whom Stella had gossipy stories to tell, came in: a man called Alex Barnet . . . a journalist, Coffin decided, and a woman referred to simply as Sallie, someone with the surname Eton, probably adopted. Actors always invented good names.

The letters were full of theatrical stories and jokes. The story of Marcia Meldrum at the height of her powers, screaming in fury when the bit of moveable scenery (Norman Arden was famous for his moveable scenery) rose up and took her wig with it. All right, she was famous for her thin hair, and her scalp had shone through, but her furious speech had gone down in theatrical history. And the tale of Edith Evans,

51

her youngish lover and the staircase, yes that had a wicked twist to it.

Was this why I kept them? he asked himself. No, it was because when I had them, I hung on to a bit of Stella, and I always had this feeling that she meant more to me than I ever did to her.

Where was I when Stella wrote to me? The letters had various London addresses, so from that he knew they came during the restless period when he was moving around from lodgings to lodgings. All in various parts of South London, he noticed. Not the best part of his life.

Then a long gap when the two did not meet – let's not go into that now, I am depressed enough – but it had been marriage, death and disaster for him. Stella had swum on the top of the water much better, making a success of her career, a short marriage but bearing a daughter, now a success in her own right, living far away and not much seen but in loving communication with Stella. Stella was better at human relations than he was, he reflected.

Another batch of letters. They were married now, but she still wrote when in New York or Edinburgh or on an Australian tour.

New names, but that was understandable because in the theatre you were friendly with the people in the play with you and then you all moved on.

Josie Evans, Bipper Stoney (what a name to choose, but a well-known singer), Heloise Divan. Marilyn and Henry Calan . . . yes, he remembered those, nice people.

One or two names hung around with Stella saying, And do you remember? Ferdy Chase, was one. Also Sallie . . . sex of the latter not clear. Coffin had assumed a woman, but now wondered if Sallie was not a man.

Stella just briefly mentioned names and meetings. Coffin knew he could run a check on these names.

Sylvia Soonest, Arthur Cornelian. Some of the names he remembered and could put a face to. Eton again.

Then he folded all these letters away and turned his mind to the photograph.

He knew he dreaded picking up anything of these latter letters but it had to be admitted that the doctored photograph did not show a very young Stella.

He forced himself to think about the photograph again: you could not see her face except in profile, and the curve of her back.

Fake, fake, fake, he said to himself. Come back home and tell me so, Stella.

The door bell rang, loudly, twice. It was Phoebe on the doorstep with a bottle under her arm.

'Came to see how you are. Had anything to eat?'

'I think so.' He tried to remember. 'Yes, the dog and I found something in the freezer.'

'Have a drink then. Not a bad wine, not the best claret in the world, but that would be hard to find round here. And this is, so my worldly friends tell me, drinkable.' She rolled the word round on her tongue as if she found it a bit of a joke. She looked towards him to see if he found it a joke, too. No, no laugh. 'We will drink this together and get really sozzled.' At least you will, if I can manage it.

They sat down together at the kitchen table in front of the big window which looked across the road to the old burying place now secularized into a little park. It was seldom used, too many ghosts for most people. The cats of the neighbourhood found it a good hunting ground.

The bottle of wine was opened and, after the first glass, Phoebe decided her old friend looked better.

'Now what would you do,' she said, 'if this was not Stella but another woman who was missing?'

'Oh, send people like you to find her.'

'And how would they know where to look?' She filled his glass again. They drank in silence for a moment or two.

'I suppose I'd search for an address book, or a diary. Take a note of bills, anything that might give a hint.'

She just looked at him.

'But it's Stella,' he protested. Stella's privacy, how could he invade it?

'If Stella is in danger – and I think that photograph on the dead man suggests she is – you have to find her.' She filled both glasses again, almost emptying the bottle. 'Can I help? Want me to do it?'

'No. Thanks, Phoebe, but no.' He stood up. 'I am probably going to hate myself for what I am going to do.' He held out a hand. 'Thanks for coming.'

In the bedroom, Stella had a pretty white painted desk, very small, where she kept her private letters, as opposed to the professional ones which her secretary at the theatre kept on file. Very few letters, but he put them aside to be studied. A postcard with a view of the Tower of London, a scrawl on the back which said: 'See you, love and remembrance, A.'

There was a blue leather diary with notes and reminders of engagements, mere initials which he could make nothing much of at the moment.

A big white card with letters in gold, advertising the Golden Grove Health Hydro, was tucked under the blotter but near to the telephone. The telephone numbers in neat gold print had been copied in large pencilled letters in the margin.

Coffin was aware of this trick of Stella's: she was short-sighted so that she sometimes wrote the telephone number she wanted out in bold letters to be seen while she dialled.

Worth a shot, he thought. It was late evening but they would probably answer. Wouldn't want to miss a booking.

'Good evening,' said a soft girlish voice, 'the Golden Grove Hydro. Can I help you?'

He introduced himself. 'I think my wife, Stella Pinero, is staying with you. Can I talk to her?'

There was a pause. 'But Mr Coffin,' the soft voice was plaintive, reproachful, 'she cancelled. You yourself rang to say she could not come.'

Coffin put the receiver down, only too aware that whoever had rung, it had not been him.

He dialled Phoebe Astley's number. He had to talk to someone.

54

PROFILE OF THE AVERAGE TERRORIST

There is not an average terrorist. Remember that fact.

They come in all shapes, sizes, ages and sexes. Do not think you will know one by the look in their eyes. You may live next door to one, or have sat next to one in the tube. One may be a friendly neighbour, or drive your local taxi. You could even have married one.

Do not believe that you will be able to read that face, whether it is one you love or hate. The face is a mask, the mask will not be dropped; love will not do it, nor hate, nor amusement; the wearer has been trained not to drop it. A terrorist who drops the mask is a dead terrorist.

As a genus they are not long-lived, owing to the hazards of the craft (Carlos Marighella, author of the guerrillas' *Minimanual* died young, shot dead). You will not find many old terrorists, although there must be some, probably sleepers, the hardest to spot. Occasionally a survivor, an ageing member, will be put into cold storage to be defrosted and brought up to room temperature if needed for use.

The terrorist may be a college graduate or relatively uneducated. But he or she will almost certainly be a person of some intensity. This might become apparent in conversation. Certain keywords like 'state' or 'nation' or 'police' might provoke reaction in the untutored terrorist. The trained one will know how to join in the majority view. On the surface. Any relationship will be on the surface. Truth need not come into it.

You will not know them by their table manners: if you ask them to dinner, they will not eat you. As far as possible they will have been trained to sink into the background. But this in itself is interesting to watch and may be a sign to make you alert.

Some terrorists are groomed to be front men. Shouters, these are called, and are probably the least dangerous of all, although this can never be certain. It may be that one of the chief functions of the shouter is to flush out your own sleepers.

Remember, there are no safe defenders of the faith, whatever the faith, yours or theirs. Conviction, whether inherited or taught, is always dangerous.

Alan Ardent

3

Coffin and Phoebe Astley met over a drink in Max's. It was late, but Max never closed when there was custom; he stayed behind the bar, serving their late meal and drinks himself and listening to the gossip. Except for Mimsie Marker, who sold newspapers outside Spinnergate tube station, he was the best informed man in the Second City.

'I didn't ring, so who the hell did? But the girl stuck at it, apparently keen to remind me of what I had not done.'

'So what will you do about it?'

'Don't know yet. Doesn't seem much point in banging on about it to the health place, any more than grumbling at the Algonquin. What she meant by booking in, I don't know.' Coffin was eating a ham omelette. He had found to his surprise that he was hungry. Phoebe had a large sandwich in front of her.

Max was watching them with interest from behind his long counter which was covered with a white linen cloth. He had been dealing with an exuberant wedding party, and was presently working out his profit margins while he kept an eye on Phoebe Astley and the Chief Commander, an old friend.

Phoebe put her hand on Coffin's. 'Look, don't worry too much . . . Stella is good at looking after herself. And she's a fighter.' Phoebe was one herself, and she recognized another. 'She'd fight for you, too. Perhaps she is doing that.'

'Think so?' Coffin finished his mouthful of omelette. 'What exactly do you mean by that?'

Phoebe took a long, thoughtful drink of coffee, then said:

'That photograph, however contrived, means trouble for Stella and, by transference, for you. And if she thought that, then she'd be out there doing something about it.' She took another drink of coffee and nodded towards Max, who came hurrying over with the pot, showing no sign that he wanted to close up for the night. Probably been reading my lips, Phoebe thought, and wants to know what is going on. She had long suspected Max of supplying news to the media. In the nicest possible way, of course – he was a nice man – but for money. Money and Max had a close and old relationship. 'That's all, just an idea, something or nothing.' Then she lit a cigarette.

'Thanks, Phoebe.' Coffin knew support when he heard it. And it was true enough, a happening like the dead body with Stella's bag containing that photograph would do no man's career any good. He hoped a lid could be put on the news, but while his close colleagues would probably keep their mouths shut, there was no hope the story would not get around. With embellishments. 'In a way, I hope you're right. But I wish she had not just cleared off. She could have told me where she was going.'

'She did.'

'But it wasn't true.'

'Give her a break. It's not much of a lie. May even be what she intended to do, until something happened. Came in the way. So maybe she tried the health place, perhaps to hide, and it didn't work out.'

Coffin gave her a measured look. Things must really be bad if Phoebe was being so kind. He thought about it for a moment. 'So what else have you got for me?' he asked.

'You could tell, could you? I must have a more revealing face than I ever knew.' She frowned. 'Something I picked up in the car park back at Headquarters . . . it's about the body found in Percy Street. It looks as if there is some doubt about the identity.'

'But I thought the identification as one of Lodge's young men was positive.' God knows that had been bad enough, but in a way, out of his hands.

'The clothes were identified,' said Phoebe. 'Not the man.'

Coffin said, slowly and heavily, 'There are, of course, many ways of identifying a man other than through his under-clothes.'

'You've got it. Once Garden got down to work on the body, he could see that it didn't fit any of the details provided by Lodge: age, body weight, length of bones, even hair colour . . . all wrong.'

'What is Lodge doing about it?'

'Archie Young has taken over, it no longer being entirely within Lodge's sphere.'

'It never was entirely,' said Coffin.

'No, well, you know how he is; he does rather grab, and he grabbed first time round, on grounds of security. Still is, of course, if you think about the mark on the pants. He's got a problem there.'

'Oh, yes. I was thinking of those pants,' said Coffin grimly. 'What about asking his chap?'

'That's what Archie Young said: "Ask him, perhaps he's given up wearing them." Bit flip. The Todger went total. Not easy to do apparently – ask, I mean . . . Peter Corner isn't around. Of course, they are a secretive lot in that outfit, not straightforward.' Like us, she meant. 'They take off, it seems, on their own little games. Still, those were his pants.'

'They came from somewhere and were put on the dead man. Alive or dead. Why was he wearing them? Where is the owner?'

'Odd, isn't it?'

'It's more than odd, it's bloody odd.' He stood up.

Phoebe drank the coffee which Max had poured for her. 'Don't go rushing off. Dennis Garden has closed up for the night, and the Todger has gone home in a huff. He likes to feel his feet on solid ground and he can't at the moment.'

'Then he shouldn't be in the job he's in.' Coffin sat down again. 'Has he gone to bed too?'

'I am not in a position to know that,' said Phoebe, 'but it's reported he said: "I am seriously disturbed".'

'And Archie Young?'

'Ah, well, he was more violent. A bit scatological, in fact.'

'Not like him.'

'Relieving his mind. He saw straightaway that it opened the field up: What has happened to the chap who owned the pants? Did he part with them willingly and, if he did, then why?'

'And who is the dead man and why did he die? Yes, that's another set of questions. But Lodge knows the identity of the original owner.'

'Oh, he does. And when he thought he was dead, that was one thing, but now he is missing and may be alive.'

Coffin considered. He could see that they were plunging into very murky waters, and although not unwilling to plunge in, for indeed it might become necessary, he did not wish to do so now and with Phoebe.

'But lowly workers in the field are not admitted to the knowledge of what that chap was,' said Phoebe sardonically. She, like many of her colleagues, had a sceptical attitude to officers like Inspector Lodge; it was thought that they were a dodgy lot. 'Of course, Lodge is only a kind of minder, keeps in touch with the boys in the field. I bet they don't tell him much.'

Coffin was silent, being privy to more secrets than Phoebe. He, too, had a side to his work which had touched a hidden world.

'But, of course, we have our own ways of finding out what we want to know,' said Phoebe, who had clearly got into her counter-irritant phase and meant to take him out of himself. 'And so the word is that his sleeper was working in the office of the building firm as dogsbody and office manager, and is now missing.'

'Better than being dead, I suppose.'

'Yes, but you see that's struck terror into Lodge's heart, because perhaps his man was not his man after all, or not totally, and has gone missing because he has been dealing the cards twice, if you see what I mean.'

'That's just guessing, though.'

'But intelligent guessing, which we are good at. To be

verified tomorrow morning by a call to the office. Finger-prints, that sort of thing. And where the chap lives. Going over everything with that toothcomb I never seemed to see around.'

She wasn't drunk, Coffin thought, but tired and letting words go to her head. Or rather her mouth.

'It's no joking matter.'

'Who's joking? I'm not joking. In fact, I am quite melan-choly about it all. I knew the chap. Not for what he was, of course, simply just as a good-looking chap who came my way.'

So he was good-looking, Coffin noted. 'How did you get to know him?' Not a question to ask Phoebe, who followed where her wind of fancy took her.

'He came round to talk about my bomb damage and we went out to have a drink. We planned to . . . well, never mind what we planned, that's off.'

'He might come back.'

Phoebe pursed her lips. 'No good. If he comes back and works for T. Lodge and Co, why is he cosying up to me, I ask myself. To find out what we know that he or his masters might like to know? Then again, if he is really working for the other team, the prospect of what he wanted from me is even worse. No, a straight up-and-down builder was all I was looking for.'

A faint, very faint, set of ideas were beginning to take shape in Coffin's mind. Let it settle, he told himself. See what happens. Sleep on it.

He realized with surprise that he might, after all, sleep. He paid Max, gave him a healthy tip, and saw Phoebe home. Or did she see him home? He could feel her resolute, sensible presence beside him as he drove home.

At the bottom of the stairs, he took a deep breath. The telephone was ringing; he moved fast up the stairs. It might be Stella.

But no. 'Inspector Lodge here, sir. Could we talk?'

He was unsurprised. 'Yes, I thought you might want to.'

'I knew you would guess, sir. I put up the act of being

willing to hand over the case to Archie Young, but, of course, I can't do that. Not entirely. He knows it, too. Pete Corner is my man, I must be interested. Those were his clothes . . . I have to find out how and when and why he parted from them. Also where he is. We have a system for keeping in touch.'

'I know.'

'He hasn't used it. He may have reasons – I hope he has – but if he doesn't turn up soon, then he has to be found. It's a bit of a problem. We have his clothes, but not his body . . . And that's apart from other complications.'

Who but the Todger would refer to Stella as a complication?

'Do you want to come round here and talk further?'

'I suppose I have said it all, sir. I shall be digging, of course . . .'

Digging was the word, and whatever he dug up, even if about Stella Pinero, would be in his hands, and those who controlled him.

'I understand,' said Coffin.

'Knew you would, sir. I can't help myself.'

Of course not, the Todger was only part of a network. As he was himself, for that matter. 'Better to have everything out . . . whatever.'

'There is something else: I have been a little concerned about Corner myself lately.'

He put the telephone down.

No Stella. But Augustus was asleep on the bed. He raised his head, muttered something, then went back to sleep.

Coffin sat on the edge of the bed while he thought about life. There was a smell of Stella's scent on the bed linen which even the furry smell of peke could not overlay. Coffin closed his eyes.

He was beginning to see Stella more and more as victim. He leaned back against the big square pillow, and closed his eyes.

The darkness stayed with him as he slept, but now writhed

and twisted in strange shapes. Every man's horror was upon him: he had lost his wife. Worse than losing a cat or a dog, a shade worse than losing a child? Nothing between them: he had lost a wife, had lost a child, he knew how it felt, but Stella was something more, she was part of his whole life, woven into the fabric.

When he woke into daylight, with the dog sprawled by his side, practically eyeball to eyeball, the presence of Stella had faded somewhat. She was still there, but more comfortably, as if she did not want to cause him too much misery.

It had turned warmer by the time he got to his office. He could see through the windows of this modern building where men in shirtsleeves were moving around, answering telephones, or watching flickering screens.

He hurried past, nodding a brief good morning to the outer office so he could get to work. Work would be his salvation, as it had been once before. It would not bring Stella back from wherever she was and for whatever reason, but it would make it easier to bear. A sense of her did not exist in this office.

There was plenty of work, not all of it connected with the bomb in the Second City. The day-to-day routine, which he had initially resented and performed badly, he had now come to enjoy. He was good at it too – or quick and neat, anyway, which counted as virtue. On a day like this, it was as good as aspirin and better than whisky.

The Second City was getting steadily more crime-ridden. In front of him he had a letter suggesting that something should be put in the water piped to families with a record. No recipe given. The front office ought to have filtered this letter out, not sent it in for his consideration. But perhaps they wanted to give him a laugh.

Then he read the signature: the writer was a distinguished member of the House of Lords. A tactful reply would have to go out to a man who was on one of Coffin's important committees, a man he might meet socially tomorrow or the next day, and who clearly had become exceedingly eccentric.

The thought depressed him but, hell, what did it matter?

Senility was nature's way of easing you off the scene, maybe allowing you a little amusement on the way while giving plenty of annoyance to your friends and relations.

He worked away quietly, dictating letters, handling telephone calls as put through to him, ignoring the voices from the outer room. Paul Masters seemed to be in good tongue.

It was still mid morning.

Then Phoebe rang: 'Archie Young and the Todger combined forces and made Dennis Garden begin work really early. He hated it, but did the job. He's just about ready to announce what he has found, cause of death and so on. The Todger and Archie are there now and I think they would like you to be there too . . . In the circumstances.'

'I'm busy.'

'Won't take ten minutes.'

'Are you sure you don't already know and can't tell me?'

'I am absolutely sure. I will come round and drive you.'

Dennis Garden received them all in his office in the University Hospital. It was a big new hospital and he had a big new office.

He looked pale, being up too early in the morning did not suit him, but he was freshly scrubbed and smelt of a mixture of disinfectant and verbena.

'Nice to see you, Chief Commander.'

No one shook hands. 'So what is it?' asked Coffin.

In a few short sentences Garden told them what would be in his report. He said the man died from a stab wound, but he had had a weak heart, so nature had helped, then he was beaten about the face, fingers cut off, and laid out afterwards. Dead about four days.

'Did he struggle?'

'Possibly,' said Dennis Garden. 'But he was not a healthy man, and he had been out on a cold night.'

'Are you suggesting exposure, then?'

Garden shook his head. 'He might have suffered from chilling, but he had taken a mixture of drugs beforehand. It all weakened him, though I agree, the absence of a struggle is puzzling.'

Coffin began thinking it out. 'So why was he got up like that? For a bet? For money? Someone picked him up? I wonder where that was.'

Archie Young cleared his throat. 'Near the Armadillo in Power Street probably, that's a likely spot.'

'A good guess,' agreed Dennis. He was subdued and quiet, not his usual manner of brisk confidence that God was in Dennis's heaven and all was right in his world. 'Not that I have any personal knowledge of the place,' he added stiffly.

Coffin wondered about that; he could imagine Dennis at a table there, quietly leading the band. 'But we are no nearer establishing identity,' he said.

'Not quite. He was known to me. We met occasionally. He'd been on the stage; nothing great, period drama, panto, that sort of thing. He liked dressing up.' As you live, so you die, Coffin thought.

'He went up for parts even now every so often – didn't get many. He had a tiny private income so he survived. As I say, I knew him socially. Di Rimini, he called himself. Not his real name; he liked play acting. If someone offered him money to dress up, he'd take it.'

Garden was offering an interesting suggestion: di Rimini had been paid to put on the clothes. Coffin could believe it.

Coffin looked at Archie Young. They knew Garden's ways socially. It depended what society you moved in.

'Would you call him a friend?' he asked bluntly.

'In passing. In passing only. A young friend.'

'But you knew him. So there was really no point in cutting off the fingers and rubbishing the face.'

'Of course, I can't say about that,' said Dennis stiffly. 'That's for your teams to decide. But whoever killed him could not have known that I had met him and that I would be doing the postmortem.'

Nor known that you could recognize his body even if his face was gone, thought Coffin cynically.

Dennis Garden met no one's eyes but twisted his lips wryly. There was not much more to be said. Promising a speedy official report plus photographs, he opened the door for them. Relieved, Coffin thought, to see them go. 'This is all off the cuff,' he said, as Coffin passed.

Coffin nodded. 'Of course.'

'Pity him being one of Dennis's boys,' said Phoebe, as they made their way out. 'Muddies the waters a bit. You could see Dennis feeling it.' She did not hide the satisfaction in her voice. 'He shouldn't mix it so much; one sex or the other, not both at once.'

'Really?' asked the Todger, something of a puritan. 'Difficult operation, I should think.'

'It can be done,' said Phoebe, smiling. 'No personal knowledge, of course.' She reined in the smile as she spoke to the Chief Commander. 'May I drive you back to the office, sir?'

'I am sorry about Dennis Garden,' said Coffin, once they were alone in the car.

'I'm not, I enjoyed it.'

'I could see you enjoying it.'

'He was rude to a friend of mine once.' The car was moving swiftly through the streets. 'Pity about the dead man, but he was going to die anyway. This way someone picked him and found a use for him. First time in years, I should think. Except for Dennis, of course.'

'You knew what Dennis was going to say, didn't you?'

'Let's just say that with the help of a friend who works in the mortuary, and a little intelligent guessing, I knew something.' She smiled. 'Might as well come clean: Francesco di Rimini, under his real name of Edward Bates, did a little work as a snout, as did my friend. I gather Bates did it more for the pleasure of nosing round and picking up scraps of info – which might or might not have been true – than for the money.'

'Might have been why he was killed.'

'Doubt it, don't you, sir? He wasn't big time.'

'Thanks for telling me.'

'Oh, you would have been informed. I just got there first.'

They had arrived and Phoebe parked the car neatly where he had but a few paces to walk to the main door.

Coffin was still thinking it all over. The puzzle remained: 'But why kill him at all? Why use the body, dress him up, make him look like my wife?'

'Ah, why indeed. To get at Stella?'

'Again, why?'

Phoebe transferred her car keys from one hand to the other then put them in her handbag. None so blind as those . . . she murmured to herself. 'To get at her is to get at you.'

Coffin digested this, which he knew already, so Phoebe was not being as clever as she thought she was. 'Well, it hasn't hit the news desks yet.'

'Not yet, But it will. The press and the TV will know soon, but Archie and the Todger will be sitting on them. Won't last. Be in the *Evening Standard* lunch-time editions, I expect. Mimsie Marker will be selling in the hundreds.'

'Especially if –' he stopped.

'There won't be a mention of Stella. Not at first.'

'No, I can't make up my mind what to do.' He smiled wryly. 'Can't send out a general search message, she'd kill me.'

Then he heard himself say loudly: 'I think she's dead. I think Stella is dead.'

'If there had been an accident, you would have heard by now.'

'I wasn't thinking of an accident.'

'Stella wouldn't do anything silly,' said Phoebe. 'She wouldn't kill herself.' She had a sudden picture of the vibrant, lovely Stella, of whom she had nursed some jealousy but nevertheless liked for all that. Besides, Stella valued her own appearance and even in death she would not damage it. A woman knew the strength of that feeling, thought Phoebe.

'Not suicide,' said Coffin. 'Murder.'

The loved ones of those who go missing fall into two groups: those who are convinced the dear one will come back even as the police are trying to get them to identify a dead body, and those who know from the beginning that the loved one is gone for ever. He could hear his own voice now, trying to bring reason to both parties, rational, quiet, useless words.

Coffin was surprised to find he belonged with the second group.

4

On the river near to Petty Pier stood a large house which the proprietor, Emmeline Jessimon, ran as a set of small service flats. The only service she gave was to change the linen and towels and tidy up once a week. Linton House had been run as a small hotel, but Mrs Jessimon had decided that one-room flats – self-catering, of course (she provided a minute kitchen unit with a tiny cooker and refrigerator) – would bring in a greater profit with less work. Money in advance, naturally. Two of the flats were occupied by lease-holders. One, an elderly widow called Mrs Flowers, was no trouble; the other was a tenant who came and went, as well as sometimes lending the flat, or so it seemed, to friends. This flat worried Mrs Jessimon. But on the whole it was easy work, she said to herself.

Usually this was true, and she had the help of the caretaker from the school round the corner, who helped with the boiler and the rubbish. True, he was on holiday at the moment (Bermuda, of all places), but she had his stand-in, a young chap called Vince. What a name for a man who cleaned out the drains in an emergency – if that was his real name; on occasion he seemed to forget, which made her wonder. Still he was nice, if silent, and she liked his help. But tenants had their own ways of making a nuisance of themselves, from falling asleep while smoking and setting fire to the sheets, to breaking such china as she provided. There was a notice in each apartment proclaiming CATERING ON REQUEST, but as one tenant, a theatrical on tour, had said: It would be a brave soul who faced Ma Jessimon's cooking. In fact, she just went round the corner to a Chinese takeaway.

On the same day that Coffin decided that Stella was dead, Mrs Jessimon (the Mrs was honorary) was checking up on the tenants in one of her apartments. First the quick let.

An interior monologue went on: Gone then. Luggage gone, clothes gone. Not that they had much. Fly-by-nighters, knew that the minute I set eyes on them. Can't fool me. Still, they paid for the week. Money in it for me. I might let it again. Change the linen, tidy up, check the fridge – don't want anything going bad in it. Remember the time that man left an uncooked rabbit in it? Thought it was a dead baby, I did. Perhaps it was, for all I know. Into the dustbin with it. Nothing there this time, not even a bottle of milk. Now milk, when not too stale, comes in handy.

Then she moved on to the next tenant, the permanent one, if you could call her that. She had been in. Paid for everything: milk, bread . . . She came with a man, but it was her that paid. You don't see that so often, even these days. I think men should always pay, it's what they are for. Lovely looking, she is. So was he. In a way. Younger than her. I suppose that's what she paid for.

No, I mustn't be unkind. He must have fancied her – kept his arm round her all the time. Must have been hot. It was a warm day.

Never heard them go. Not that it matters.

Could that be blood? Drops of it, on the floor. I'll never get that out of the carpet. Now I must be sensible, he probably cut himself shaving. Or she did . . . stupid to think otherwise. Don't want the police prowling round. It's her place. Not my responsibility. Tidy up, close the door behind you. Lock it. Quietly now. The tenant in number four likes to listen.

That's it, quietly down the stairs. You could fall and break a leg, you're so strung up. Never mind. A glass of sherry will do the trick. No, gin. It's a gin day. A gin and tonic, and a nice cup of tea and a rest. Then you can tidy up the room. A pity she couldn't do it before she left. It's a woman's job.

All that blood. A man should pay and a woman leave things neat and tidy.

Nor should a woman notice things better left unnoticed. I didn't notice the kitchen knife on the floor.

She came with a man, and she's gone with a man.

Across the Second City in the casualty department of a big, anonymous hospital, Dr Allegra, junior registrar, was so tired that he was talking to himself. Most of it was aloud and listened to by his patient; some, however, was a silent conversation in his head.

Lost a fair bit of blood, muttered Dr Allegra to himself. Bit more and there would have been real trouble. Don't think a transfusion is needed here. Just as well, since the hospital is short of blood. Funny thing to be short of: there it is pumping away inside everyone in the city, millions of pints, but you had to get it out, keep it sterile and spend money on it, then shove it into people. And money was short. Of course, if you were dying you would probably get blood. Better not to count on it, though. Three months as a junior reg had made a natural optimist into a cynic. He did not believe the patient's version of what had caused this wound.

Aloud, he said: 'This may hurt a bit, I shall give you a local, but you will probably still feel it . . . Yes, sorry about that . . . About a dozen stitches, I think.'

He whistled as he worked and went back to his own thoughts: Wish I wasn't so tired. I did make a bit of a night of it, but a chap needs something to look forward to at the end of the day with the blood and the needle . . . I don't think I'm cut out for surgery. Perhaps I might switch to psychiatry. Not doing a bad job here, nasty wounds.

Aloud, he said: 'Nearly done. I'll give you some painkillers . . . How did you say it happened? Accident?' Going silent again, he said to himself: Some accident.

'You'll have a scar there, I'm afraid.' You don't work in anything where looks count, I hope. He had the sense to keep that last comment to himself. 'Fade with time, you

71

know.' He didn't know, but you had to give hope: this was the most positive thing he had learnt as a doctor.

He stood back to study his handiwork; it looked good. He observed also some scratches on the hands, which made him even more sceptical of the 'accident'. Looks almost as if some-one had taken a bite, he thought, more than one bite, but he said nothing. Not then. Have to see the police later on, though . . .

The young doctor was not the only one interested in strange behaviour in odd men. Inspector Lodge got a telephone call from his vanishing 'sleeper'.

'Wondered where you were and what you were up to,' Lodge said.

'I've been taking an interest in Stella Pinero. I followed her; she went off in a car with a man − not willingly, I thought.'

'Well? Is she of interest to us?'

'Probably not. I tailed the car and traced them to a set of service flats. I couldn't get any information from the owner, an old biddy called Jessimon, although I have good access to her. After a day or two there, Stella Pinero left. I had to decide whether to follow her or the man. I followed her. She went first to the house of a woman who works in the theatre, and then home.'

'Go on,' said Lodge urgently. 'I want more.'

But the caller was gone.

Damn him, thought Lodge. Is he being straight with me? He would like to see me out and himself in, I know that much.

5

The Stella Pinero Theatre missed Stella. The performers in the playhouse missed her, the Theatre Workshop (always more notional than real since the area was used for many other projects) and the tiny Experimental Theatre in the old church hall missed her even more. Without Stella the whole complex felt a void. She gave it life.

'Not to mention money,' said Letty, Coffin's half-sister and a major contributor to the theatre's funds. She had flown in, talked to Coffin on the telephone, heard a more or less uncensored version of events, told him to toughen up and be a man (which he had taken badly), and come round to the theatre.

Now she was standing in Stella's office where unanswered letters were piled on the desk. 'Where the hell is Stella? Without her, I'm hurting.' Financially, she meant. Coffin had long ago decided this was the only way Letty could be hurt, since three marriages and possibly many other alliances had left her undented. Even financially she seemed to have many ways of replenishing the coffers: a successful lawyer, a banker and player with big money targets, this was the love of her life.

'We are very near the overdraft limit; it's one of the reasons I flew back from New York.'

New York this time, but it might have been Zürich or Johannesburg or Hamburg, wherever the money was moving.

Coffin's wandering, disappearing mother had deposited her children round the world like misplaced luggage. She had left Coffin in London, Lætitia in New York, and William in Scotland, where he, too, had gone into law. One way and another the law had claimed all three. It said something about their mother, Coffin thought: she had been beyond the law, so all her children had run for cover in it. Unconsciously, of course, not aware of their motivation, since their mother had never allowed them to know her. Disappearance was her theme. She had left her memoirs with Letty, perhaps trusting her business sense most. They were now with John Coffin, who struggled at intervals to make them into something that could be published. Such a life deserved fame, he had said to Letty, even if posthumous. Assuming his mother was in fact dead – nothing seemed certain about that lady.

'Stella will be back,' said Alice. Letty had seized on Alice, whom she did not know, as she arrived at the door of the theatre where a dress rehearsal of *Aylmer's End*, the next play in line in the Experimental Theatre, was just beginning. Alice looked a commanding and somewhat enigmatic figure. Not one to appeal to Letty. On Alice's side, Letty looked like a natural enemy.

'Who is in charge here?' Letty knew that since Alfreda Boxer, the theatre manager, had departed – to die quietly it was rumoured – there had been much shifting of management personnel.

'Stella interviewed another manager before she went away,' said Alice artlessly. 'But I don't know what decision she came to.'

'So there's no one?'

'We all help out. And Debby Anglin has been coming in as a temp . . . she's doing a degree at the university in business studies. And I've been helping as secretary, because since Jacky's boyfriend won a prize in the lottery we haven't seen her any more.'

Letty rolled her eyes. 'As I said: no one. Good job I'm here.' Why did Alice give her the impression she might as well have been talking in a foreign language?

Alice looked at her with envy: this year Letty's hair was a soft blonde with a hint, just a hint, of silver here and there;

she was wearing a brightly checked dress cut by a master's hands; and she was thinner than anyone had a right to be. Alice almost hated her.

Letty took from the desk all the papers she judged important, saying she would deal with them. There was a lot of her money in the theatre and she intended to save it. She gave Alice a questioning look. The plays? she was asking.

'There's always one on the stage and one in rehearsal and one on the go in the background – casting and that sort of thing,' said Alice, in her usual neutral yet edgy manner.

Letty patted her arm. 'Cheer up. Don't be nervous. Know what my first husband taught me? Never trust a man who is nervous. What has he got to hide? Applies to women, too. Act confident.'

'I feel nervous.'

'Stella will be back,' said Letty. Maybe without an arm or a leg – why did that thought flash through her mind? – damaged in some way, but back.

In the theatre bar, run by Max as she remembered, she saw a group sitting at a table drinking coffee. They looked up as she walked over.

'Letty Bingham.' She held out her hand. 'Stella's business partner.' She did not recognize any of them from past performances, but she knew that Stella's casts came and went. One of the girls had a face she had seen before, probably on television. They introduced themselves: Jane Gillam, Fanny Burt and a slightly older girl, Irene Bow. It was she whose face seemed familiar, and yes, Letty knew the name now, and she had been on television. Would be somehow, Irene had a televisual face if ever there was one. The two young men stood up politely.

'Michael Guardian, and this is Tom Jenks . . . We are both in *Noises Off*.'

'I am glad you've come,' volunteered Jane. 'We've felt a bit lost without Stella.'

'You're all doing fine.' Irene Bow patted her arm.

'It's all right for you,' Fanny said. 'You're only here for a few weeks or so of rehearsal time and then going off on tour, but we are going to be here for the next three months.'

There was a murmur of agreement from the two young men. Letty felt they were all watching her to see what she would say. 'I will keep an eye on things,' she promised. It was about all she could say, and perhaps not too convincing, but they looked relieved. 'I'll keep the money side in order, that I can promise. There hasn't been any special trouble?'

'Oh, no,' said Jane.

'Except for my dresser buggering off,' said Irene Bow.

'Old Maisie? She really only works for Stella. She wanted to do you, Irene, because she admires you so much,' said Jane, who had obviously appointed herself peacemaker-in-chief.

'Only she hasn't.'

'She sent a message saying she couldn't come in. She probably felt ill.'

Irene Bow laughed. 'Oh, well, I'm used to roughing it. Good job it isn't a costume drama, although some of the changes are quick.'

'I'll see what I can do,' said Letty, as she moved away.

On the way out, she stood for a moment watching the rehearsal of *Aylmer's End*, the work of a local author, and seriously doubted if this particular play would do. But who could tell?

The set was a sitting room with a fireplace, dead with no fire. A table with four chairs round it and three people mid stage. All wore blue jeans and identical checked shirts. One wore an apron, thus denoting sex.

'This place is a cesspit,' proclaimed the young actress who was centre stage; it was she who wore the apron. 'A sexist cesspit.' She took off the apron and threw it towards one of the men. 'Here, you wear this.'

'Shit,' said the actor. He left the apron on the floor where it had fallen, moved towards the fireplace and began warming his hands, 'I am not playing that game.'

Lesser Albee, thought Letty, would-be Wesker, a touch of the Osbornes. Perhaps Alice was right to be nervous.

She turned away. It was interesting, she thought, how quickly Stella and her company of players had been able to bring about that dusty, musty theatre smell of scenery and painted furniture in what had been not so long ago a church.

As Letty walked across the courtyard to her brother's dwelling in the church tower, she admitted that, absent though she might be, Stella was a professional and probably knew that everyone of the author's friends, enemies and relations (who might be the same thing) would come to *Aylmer's End*. She also noted with some respect for Stella's acumen that the play ran for only three days, and no matinees – the afternoons being reserved for readings from Shakespeare: *Hamlet, A Midsummer Night's Dream,* and *Twelfth Night.* 'Set texts for end-of-term exams,' she told herself. Yes, Stella would get her money back, and probably pay for the next generation of young performers whom she would employ in later productions. She was not adventurous, but, as her business partner, Letty could not be critical. Indeed, she was grateful that Stella was not the sort of producer to have those mad, original, four-o'clock-in-the-morning ideas that lose money.

All the same, she would have liked Stella to show up. Had she gone off on some sexual fling? No support from her brother for that theory; he would have none of it. With some irritation, Letty thought he would rather his wife were dead than unfaithful. Yet there was a lot he was not telling her. She did not count herself psychic, but she had much experience in lies and evasions – it was her job, after all. And Letty was convinced a man came in somewhere.

She paused at the bottom of the tower where her brother lived, wondering if he was there. Then she heard the dog bark, so she pulled on the bell till it rang loud and long. She was aware that many security cameras and spyholes protected the tower, thus Coffin certainly knew who was ringing the bell. No doubt he was looking at her.

She waited patiently till she heard Augustus bark again, from nearer this time, which heralded the approach of her brother.

'Ah, so you *are* here. In hiding?'

'Working at home.' He looked tired and drawn, but was

as neatly dressed as ever in well-cut trousers with a grey silk shirt.

'Same thing,' she said, pushing past him, patting Augustus on the head. 'I preferred the old dog, really. I like a dog who looks as though he has lived and Gussy here is a bit bland, aren't you, old boy? Right, right, you didn't ask me, and the old dog died. This one will do.' Augustus showed his teeth at her, not entirely amiably, as if he understood a judgement was being passed on him. 'I have been to the theatre, had a look round. We certainly need Stella there. I can do the money, but she has the flair. There's a play being rehearsed at the moment which will fall on its face if she isn't there to pull it together. I didn't get any clues as to why she had gone.'

'Her dresser, Maisie, might be helpful,' said Coffin, closing the door. 'But she seems to have gone to ground, too.'

'Not with Stella?'

Coffin shook his head. 'I don't think so. It seems she's taken herself off for a little holiday. She prefers to work exclusively for Stella, you see, so if Stella is not playing, she's free if she chooses – that's the usual rule. I've put Phoebe Astley on to finding her . . . Come on up and have a drink.'

Letty looked at him, raising an eyebrow.

'No, I'm not on to the whisky. I will have tea, the Englishman's ruin. You can drink what you like.'

She followed him up the stairs to the kitchen, where there was a teapot; she touched it to check: hot. 'I talked to a girl called Alice. She may have been keeping something back, I couldn't be sure. I suppose they have all been questioned?' She sat down opposite Coffin.

'They don't know where Stella is, or why she went off – I am sure of that. But Maisie may,' said Coffin, adjusting his feet so that Augustus could settle there with comfort to them both. 'Yes, she was close to Maisie.' There was pain in his voice. He had thought that Stella was close to him. Would she tell things to Maisie that she would not tell him? The answer seemed to be: Yes.

'I could go to see where Maisie lives, if you like?'

'No, leave it to Phoebe Astley,' he said, his voice heavy. 'It may need the official touch.'

In other words, thought Letty, you want it all kept under the official cover.

She poured milk in her tea and drank it down, then got to her feet. 'If I hear anything, in any way, of course I will let you know. Meanwhile, I must be off, usual address.' Letty maintained a smart Docklands maisonette, part of an old factory. It was one of her many addresses around the world.

'I know where to find you.'

'Shake yourself up and get out into the world again, that's my advice to you.'

'Thanks, Letty.' Coffin managed a smile. Letty always knew best.

'I will keep an eye on the business side of things at the theatre. You can rely on me there.'

He saw her down the stairs, with Augustus trotting behind. 'Like me to take the dog for a run?' she offered.

'No, thanks, Letty. I will take him, he's company.' Coffin leant forward and kissed her on the check. It was a rare embrace between them.

Letty walked round to where she had parked her car. She sat there for a minute, considering the Chief Commander's state. He's wretched. Damn Stella, what does she think she is about? She drove away angrily. Wait till I see her. If she ever did.

By the time Coffin and his little acolyte got to the top of the stairs, the telephone was ringing. He picked it up in a mixture of hope and fear.

'Phoebe Astley here. You on your own?'

'Go ahead, Phoebe, I'm on my own. What is it?'

'I thought you might have someone with you.'

She must be sitting round the corner in her car, using the mobile.

'My sister has just left.'

'Saw her car. Didn't know how things were between you two.'

79

Yes, you do, Phoebe, Coffin said silently. What you mean is that you don't like Letty, another female powerhouse like you are. How could you like each other?

'I haven't managed to see Maisie, and the neighbours weren't much help, although one of them said they had seen a man sitting in a car watching the house. May mean nothing. Others say they haven't seen her for some days, but they say she's like that: pops off to see friends, doesn't care about the garden, it can run wild for all she cares. They like her, though, a good sort if you're in trouble.'

'Is that all?'

'No,' Phoebe sounded troubled. 'She's worth digging out . . . Eden says that Maisie has been worried about Stella for some days.' Eden Brown worked in the theatre's costume room (among other tasks; she filled in where necessary and was happy to do it). She had once managed a dress shop in Calcutta Street in Spinnergate, and had fallen into trouble and been investigated by Phoebe Astley. Events had moved on and Eden had taken herself happily to work for Stella, whom she adored, and now shared a flat with Phoebe, both parties enjoying a cautious friendship. 'I'd like to have another look round Maisie's place. I might want to go in . . . check over the house.'

'Have you any solid reason?'

'No, just a feeling about Maisie. She might even know where Stella is.' And why, she said to herself; a question from which she knew the Chief Commander flinched, and from the answer even more.

'Before you do this, come up – I want a word.'

'Right now? OK. If you lend me the dog, I can pretend I am taking him for a walk while I have a prowl round Gosterwoood Street.' She took a breath. 'Just got to make another call on my mobile. I'll be up in a minute.' She did not wish Coffin to hear her call.

She made a call to Chief Superintendent Young: 'We're in action.'

The Chief Superintendent, who had also had a call to something of the same effect from Letty Bingham, nodded to himself. 'It's always the women who work the trick with him,' said Archie Young. He did not say it unkindly, for he liked the Chief Commander, but rather as one who states a fact.

When Phoebe banged on his door, the Chief Commander was ready for her. 'I'm coming with you, Augustus can stay here. I'll drive.' Don't want you doing anything illegal, he thought. But he did not say so aloud.

'OK, sir, if that suits you. You know where Gosterwood Street is?'

'Of course I do: parallel with Calcutta Street where Eden had her shop.'

Phoebe nodded.

'Let's go, then. Does she live there alone?'

'I believe so. It was her mother's house which she inherited.'

'They are small, those houses,' said Coffin thoughtfully. 'Pity the neighbours weren't more help.'

'They're a clannish lot round there. They dislike people prying. Can't say I blame them, really, but it can make investigation tough.'

'You had a look at the house?'

'Twice. First time I just stood there looking. Second time I rang the door bell and got no answer. Thought I might go back, third time lucky. I didn't know what to make of the house last time, to tell the truth. The neighbours said she might be away, but they could have been saying that to get rid of me.'

'They knew you were a police officer?'

'Knew me a mile away,' said Phoebe cheerfully. 'I had the feeling that Maisie might have been there watching from behind a curtain.'

Gosterwood Street, like Chislewood Street which ran behind it, nearer to the river, was a row of small, flat-faced houses, some brightly painted and well kept up, and others down at heel. Maisie lived in a house painted red and white, these being her favourite colours in which she had felt free

81

to indulge when her mother died, leaving her a sum of money in an insurance policy. Maisie had painted the house and bought a new bed, thus far her ambitions reached.

'Maisie's popular,' Phoebe said. 'They had an epidemic of scarlet fever down the street last year – wouldn't think it, these days, would you? But it happened, and Maisie went everywhere nursing the sick and helping them.'

'Didn't they go to hospital? There's one close, isn't there?'

'Not far. Some did, but others stayed at home and kept quiet about it.'

Coffin did not answer, he was already thinking about Maisie and what she might know about Stella. Their relationship was close, but exactly how much Stella would tell Maisie was a mystery. She had known Maisie a long time, they had worked together for years, and theatre people had strong bonds. But Stella could be reserved, she might not have said much, possibly not much at all. They might get nothing from this call, even if Maisie was there.

He parked the car in the only space available in Gosterwood Street, which was lined with battered old cars, few of which looked roadworthy. 'We will have to walk from here.'

'It's just down the road, the fifth house.' Phoebe had it clearly marked in her mind.

'Looks closed up,' said Coffin, as they approached.

'Can't tell, she could be in the back.'

'Do you really think so?'

'It's worth a try. Let's see what happens when I ring the bell. Loudly.'

Coffin watched her walk up the narrow path and ring the door bell. There was no answer. But Phoebe would not give up. She walked round the side of the house. 'I am going to look round the back,' she called over her shoulder.

'You think she's dead, don't you? Stella, I mean.'

'Fiddle. Of course I don't.' But although Phoebe did not say so aloud, she did think that Stella Pinero, the lovely, successful actress was dead. She only hoped that her husband had not killed her. 'I couldn't think that,' she said to herself. But alas, she could.

'Why do you think she's dead?' she asked herself as she rounded the corner of the house. 'I don't know. Just one of those terrible feelings one gets. Also, I don't believe Stella would go missing. Not her style.' She shivered. 'I feel as if a helicopter was hovering low over me.' But there was nothing in the sky.

There was a big black dustbin waiting to be emptied by the side of the house. Phoebe lifted the lid automatically. You never knew with dustbins. There was room for a body inside, but she did not expect to find one.

Coffin came up behind her. 'Empty?'

Phoebe held the lid back so he could see. 'More or less. There is a streak of something on the lid . . . could be blood.'

'Yes,' Coffin observed, 'but it may not be human blood. Nor is it new blood, it's dried and dark. Several days old. Forensics won't be able to do much with that.' The thought was not pleasing to him. 'Let's have another go at rousing Maisie.'

He walked back to the front door and rang the bell. The noise could be heard echoing through the house, but no one came. Coffin pointed: 'Streak of blood by the bell. Someone with blood on them rang the bell . . .'

Phoebe opened her mouth to say something but thought better of it.

'And don't say the butcher,' said Coffin.

'I wasn't going to. Butchers don't deliver these days.'

Coffin turned away. 'There ought to be more blood or less.'

'That's a terrible thing to say.' She caught up with Coffin. When she got a look at his face she thought: You have become a terrible person.

'If Stella is dead, there would be more blood. If the blood is hers, then Maisie knows where she is and I do not. But get the blood checked all the same.'

Bitter, too, thought Phoebe. 'I don't think there is enough blood, and it's too dry.'

'Bang on the door. Maisie may be inside.'

'I don't think so.'

He was already walking away. He drove back in silence,

but not to his home. He took them both to his office at police headquarters. Phoebe thought this was a marginally good sign; better to go there than sit alone in his tower.

He strode through the outer office where Paul Masters was working quietly, head down, in the little hutch he called his private office. He saw Coffin come in but said nothing.

Gillian was occupied with filing, and also kept her head down. The efficient Sheila was not to be seen.

Phoebe hesitated for a moment, met Paul Masters' eye, gave him something between a nod and shrug, then turned to go back to her own office where, as always, there was plenty of work waiting for her. He needs leaving alone, she said to herself.

He did not notice she had gone.

Coffin worked quietly on the sort of routine matters that bored him but went with the position; they occupied only the surface of his mind.

Paul Masters tapped on the door and came in quickly. 'Chief Superintendent Young would like to speak to you, sir.'

Archie Young was right behind him and in the room before Coffin could answer.

'Forensics have been over where the dead man lived. He had a one-room flat down by the harbour, Jamaica Place. Dennis Garden obliged with the address, he had visited him there. We would have got there anyway, of course.'

'I know Jamaica Place, it's an old warehouse.'

'That's right. Turned into dwelling places about ten years ago. Anyway, the dead man had lived there for three years or so. Francis di Rimini, he called himself. Edward Bates he was born. Did a bit of acting. Worked as a model. Drank a lot, lived a bit rough . . . Didn't mind who he picked up.'

'I get the picture,' said Coffin.

'Dennis Garden says he had been dead for several days when he was discovered. Signs of a struggle in the flat, so there was a possibility that he had been killed there, but the video set us right there. All the same, he was meant to be found.'

84

Coffin stood up. 'I want to see the flat.'

Archie Young nodded. 'Thought you might say that. I'll drive.'

No one stood on guard outside the flat in Jamaica Place, but a young policewoman was inside. She recognized the Chief Commander, saluting nervously.

Coffin smiled at her but said nothing. An open door led to the main room from which opened the small kitchen on one side and the bathroom on the other. Two white-uniformed forensic workers who were on their knees by the window rose politely as he came in.

He walked into the middle of the room where he stood looking around.

The room was plainly furnished and none too tidy, with the remains of a meal on the table where an almost empty wine bottle stood. The air was stuffy. A chair was overturned in one corner.

'A splash of blood on the back of the chair,' said Archie Young. 'More in the bathroom. Someone did some bleeding. Probably the dead man himself, shaving possibly. Garden says he was dead when his face was bashed in. He wasn't killed here, we have him on the video, walking down Jamaica Street. Pity we didn't have a camera on Percy Street, but that's economy for you, can't have them everywhere.'

'Yes, I know. So Garden thought he might have been picked in the street, and made use of.' Coffin was walking round the room. 'I'm not so sure, life is not usually so obliging. I wonder whether Garden might rethink the drugs side of it . . . Someone might have seen to it that he needed a fix and got at him through that.' Or just wanted him in the mood.

'I'll get him to check again. He won't like it, though.'

Dennis Garden was well known for claiming omniscience. Archie Young knew him of old, a hard man to convince of an idea he had not thought of himself.

'Even Garden can make a mistake.'

Coffin stood in the middle of the room. 'So the picture is that Francis or Frank or Ed Bates, or whatever he called

85

himself, left under his own steam, less conspicuous, then his face was smashed when he was moribund . . . some blood. The fingers were then cut away – that must have taken some doing.'

'Chop, chop.' Archie allowed himself a moment of flippancy which he at once regretted. It was all right for Garden to make jokes about dead bodies but not for Archie Young. Although, as he remembered, Dennis Garden had been quiet about this dead man, whom he had clearly liked.

'I wonder where the bits are, by the way.' Coffin was not smiling.

'A search is being made,' said Archie. Probably inside some pig by now.

'He was dressed in pants and jeans, clothes that must have been brought in on purpose. Oh, and a wig popped on his head and a handbag belonging to my wife tucked beside him.'

'That's the picture.'

'So he was ready to be found in the bombed building, all dressed up in the clothes that did not belong to him. Was it meant to be a joke on us?' Coffin gritted his teeth. 'If so, I'm not laughing.'

He went into the kitchen, where there was a mess of dirty dishes in the sink and the smell of generations of curry takeaways.

In the bathroom, one more forensic worker was standing by the lavatory. Even beneath the tight cap and buttoned whites it was clear that this one was a woman, young and attractive.

She looked at him gravely, then indicated a plastic envelope, the contents of which she had been studying.

'You were talking about the fingers, sir – I couldn't help overhearing . . .' she paused.

'So?'

'There is the tip of a finger in this bag; a little finger, I would say. It was tucked away behind the lavatory.'

Archie Young had come up behind the Chief Commander. 'What's it wrapped up in?'

'It seems to be a handkerchief, a woman's handkerchief. There's an embroidered initial S.'

Coffin had a habit of summarizing events in a case at a certain point, sometimes in a notebook, sometimes in his head. When in his head, he saw it like a blackboard with his own writing in large letters, headings underlined. He realized that it derived from the easel in his schoolroom of long ago. Did schools still use boards? He bet they still used underlining and listed points: one, two, three.

He was running over his mental headlines now as he and Archie Young drove away.

Maisie, that was his first headline. Maisie knew things about Stella that he did not. They had been friends, those two, for a long while. She trusted Maisie.

Why not me? was the painful question he could not help asking. The answer came quickly: because it concerns me.

Better find out what there was to find out about the blood on Maisie's door. By asking Maisie, if she could be located, how it got there. If she knew. People did not alway know what was in their bins.

Then there was the finger in a handkerchief with the intitial S on it. But not Stella's – never Stella. Put there on purpose to drag Stella in, he told himself savagely.

The underpants on the body aping Stella.

Stella, always Stella.

It was something more deliberate than a connective coincidence.

'It's like a Victorian melodrama,' said Coffin. 'The heroine's handkerchief turns up to incriminate her.' Archie Young made a sympathetic noise, but kept his eye on the road where the traffic was heavy. It was hard to know what to say. 'Plenty of people with the intial S,' he managed.

'I never see Stella with a handkerchief,' went on Coffin, his voice irritable. 'She's always leaving little bits of tissue about the place.'

Then Coffin started to laugh, not loudly but with genuine

mirth. 'What a fool I am! Good sense is coming back. Stella has been my wife for a long while now. She has learnt the rules. Whatever crime she committed, she knew not to leave so many clues around.'

'We'll find out who is behind it all, but it looks personal, sir. Either aimed at you or Miss Pinero.' Archie always had difficulty in knowing how to address Stella. He never felt happy with whatever he managed: Stella was Mrs Coffin and no doubt would be Lady Coffin quite soon, but she felt more like Miss Pinero. She would never, as Congreve had it, dwindle into a wife. Archie Young's wife was attending to his education and recently she had taken him to a production of Congreve's *The Way of the World*.

He watched the Chief Commander walk towards his front door. The tower was dark, but there were lights on in the theatre. Coffin looked tall and too thin; Archie wished the man had someone to come home to. Where was the dog? Distantly, he heard the sound of Augustus barking. Not as good as a wife, he thought, as he drove away, but better than nothing.

Coffin let himself into his tower and stood at the bottom of the staircase. There was a faint smell of scent on the air. He took a step forward.

Stella came running down the stairs. She was carefully made up, her hair looked newly washed and set, she was wearing jeans and a soft cashmere sweater which looked new.

'There you are, darling. Here I am back. How are you?'

He felt both relief, a powerful happiness, and a wave of anger. 'Where have you been?'

'At a health farm, darling. I told you.'

That's a lie for a start, Coffin told himself. She came right up to him and threw her arms round him. He held her tight. He thought she winced as he gripped her arms.

6

Young and Lodge, who had a tactful, remote relationship as men who handled tricky jobs, were drinking together in the bar favoured by the Second City's top-ranking CID officers. Without being friends they had a quiet respect for each other, although Archie Young would have preferred not to have the Todger on his patch. But in the present situation, the ways things were with bombs and terrorists around, he recognized the necessity of someone like Lodge and that perhaps they were lucky to have him and not one of the rougher boys. There was a look about their eyes that he did not like: seen too much, heard too much, done too much, trust no one, it said. And, in consequence, I don't trust you, Archie said to himself. Liking did not come into it. There was certainly this side to Inspector Lodge, but he kept it hidden better. (As also to the Chief Superintendent himself, but deep, deep down.)

The chosen pub, the Sevastopol Arms had earned its name because of its position. There, in a straight line across the river, but not visible because of the buildings that were in the way, stood the Woolwich Arsenal in whose sheds had been forged the guns and armament that went to the Crimea. The Sevastopol was an old dark brick building, deceptively small from the outside and larger within. It had defied being modernized and brightened, remaining sombre but comfortable, which pleased its own peculiar clientele who did not want dancing, music or karaoke, but did want excellent beer and good whisky.

'What do you make of Miss Pinero?' Lodge kept his voice

down. He had been introduced to Stella, he had seen her act, but he knew that there were reservations about her in the Second City Force. She was treated with a certain formality since it was felt it distanced the Chief Commander from what was viewed in some quarters as an awkward relationship. She brought trouble, didn't she, from her different world?

'Lovely lady,' said Young, loyally.

'To look at, yes.'

'She's generous and kind,' Archie persevered.

'And?'

'I didn't know too much about her life and interests till recently. My wife's a pal of hers.'

'We know a touch more now,' said Lodge grimly.

'That photograph was a fake.'

'Oh, yes, we're agreed upon that. But she is there, in the picture. It does suggest she has some strange friends. Or has had in the past; the picture of her looked a mite younger than she is now, so, an old friend.'

'They don't have to be friends,' said Young stoutly. 'Or even known to her. Actresses have a lot of photographs taken, matter of business, and hand them out. Publicity and all that.'

'If she wasn't away, we could ask her.' Lodge stopped short of using the word question. You did not talk about the Chief Commander's wife except with care.

'Sure,' said Archie. 'Like your chap. Not nice for him having his pants used that way. Not nice at all.'

They looked at each other in silence.

'Point taken,' said Lodge. He got up to go to the bar. 'My turn, I think. Same again?'

Archie nodded. He was breathing heavily, as if he had been running. He was aware that Inspector Lodge had access to information that he did not have, and he suspected that John Coffin also knew more than he had talked about. Sat on all the right security committees, didn't he? Damn the woman. If she ruined the boss, he, Archie, would want to kill her.

90

The Todger came back with two glasses, together with a sandwich for each of them. He put them down carefully, then sat down himself. 'I'll come clean with you. I am worried about my man's probity. Checks in when it suits him, tells me something, mentions seeing Miss Pinero . . . then he's off again. Silence.'

Telling me this, because he knows it's what I want to know, thought Archie Young. Of course, he knows we are worried sick about the Chief Commander's wife. I don't want her to be dead, but, by God, if it would make things easier, I might be up to doing it myself. Then he laughed. Probably not, though; there are things you will do for a mate, but not kill their wife for them.

'Does that mean you think your chap is a doubtful security risk? Working double?'

'We don't know. Have to consider it, though.'

'Don't you always?'

Lodge allowed himself one of his rare smiles. 'Yes. In fact, there is probably a check running on me now.'

'Oh, you are a lovely lot,' said Archie Young, drinking deep. 'Let me know if I'm included, won't you?'

'Couldn't say if you were, but always count on it, that's my advice.'

Archie looked at him over the top of his glass and saw that he was not joking. 'What a world. I've been told that the most useful terrorist is the one in the humblest position. Not noticed, you see, but noticing everything. I suppose sex comes into it, too: men are probably more useful than women.'

'Not always,' said Lodge. 'Drink up, I've got to get home. My wife expects to see me some time.'

'Mine is away,' said Archie Young. So Lodge did have a wife; he felt faintly surprised. 'On a course. Got her own career. Mind you, I respect her for it.'

'Good for you.'

'Wouldn't matter if I didn't, she'd still go ahead. She'll end up in the House of Lords, I daresay, with a life peerage – if they haven't all been abolished by then.'

'Would that make you Lord Young?'

'I shall have to think about that.'

Lodge stood up. 'I'd better get off.' He was not enjoying working life at the moment and it showed.

'Funny business for both of us,' said Archie Young, trying to be helpful. 'Miss Pinero being dragged in, whether it's her fault or not, is a bugger. And for you . . .' he paused, wondering uneasily what it was that he and the Todger both knew.

Lodge shrugged. 'Delicately put.'

'It's a delicate matter.'

'Certainly is.'

'Seems almost a manufactured performance, putting on an act,' went on Young, 'using Miss Pinero, using your chap's underwear, cutting off the fingers of the dead man, and yet choosing someone who is identified without trouble.'

'A queer sort of show,' said Lodge.

'Show?' said Archie Young, raising his eyebrows. 'Yes, good word, show it is.'

They had placed their mobile phones on the table in front of them like twins. Now one began to ring.

'Yours or mine?' said Lodge.

'Mine,' Archie Young sighed. 'Hello?' He listened, all the amusement leaving his face. 'Right, I'll be there.' He pocketed his telephone, then turned to Lodge. 'That show we've got on the road, another character has joined it: a body's been found.'

7

'Let's go upstairs.' Coffin released Stella from his embrace and gave her a little push towards the winding staircase. 'Up, and we can talk.' And you'd better make sense, because I am in no mood to be played with.

Mixed with the sheer physical relief of having her back, the joy of seeing her, mixed with these was anger. He didn't want it there, was half ashamed of it, but there it was: a black streak winding through the joy.

'I ought to get round to the theatre,' Stella said. 'Business talk, you know.'

'We'll talk first.' He put his hand firmly under her elbow and propelled her upstairs.

She spoke over her shoulder breathlessly as they went up the stairs, not resisting their progress but a touch reluctant. 'I really should go to the theatre first, you know. There must be all sorts of problems and so on that need sorting out, even if I wasn't away very long.'

'Long enough,' said Coffin.

Stella smiled. 'Not that long, darling. But piles of stuff on my desk, you must have seen it, messages from Alice – she's being very helpful, you gave me a friend there.'

'Did I?' He did not want to talk about Alice.

'I ought to be checking the accounts. Naturally I can't leave the money side to Alice.'

'Letty is doing that.' They had nearly reached the level of the kitchen.

'Oh.' Stella did not sound quite pleased.

Oh, yes, thought Coffin. Come on, my lady, I want to know where you have been and why.

One more turn of the staircase brought them to the large, light sitting room. No one had been thinking about Augustus, but he had his own methods with Coffin and was now first into the sitting room. When he got there he turned round to face them, his tail wagging.

'Hello, Gussie,' said Stella, bending down to pat him. 'How's he been?'

'Fine. With me all the time.'

'He always is.'

Coffin pulled up a chair. 'Sit down, Stella.'

'Don't order me about.'

'I'm not, Stella, but you look tired. In pain, too, I think, from your arm. Yes, I noticed.'

Without a word Stella sank back into the armchair. 'Aren't you going to sit?'

'Presently.' He walked about the room for a minute, pacing up and down, then he drew another chair towards her, leaned forward and took both her hands in his. 'What's up, Stella? Where have you been? Why did you lie about where you were going?'

'Not exactly a lie. Just a change of plans.' Her voice was nervous.

'Oh, come on, Stella, you can do better than that.'

She put her hand to her head. 'I can't think.' Her sleeve fell back, revealing a white bandage, badly applied.

Coffin looked at it, took in its appearance, but said nothing.

'I really think I should go across to the theatre, even if Letty is there. Very decent of her, I know how busy she is.' She looked at her watch. 'The curtain will have gone down if I don't hurry and they will all have melted away. You know what they are like.'

'I know,' said Coffin, somewhat grimly.

'Letty will have gone, surely, but Alice Yeoman will be there.' Stella stood up.

'How's she doing?' He wanted to know.

'Not too bad. Bit of time off here and there.'

'Not ill, is she?'

'No, just a spell of menstrual trouble,' said Stella, with the insouciance of one who had never let that sort of thing trouble her. Actresses couldn't, could they? You went on regardless.

'Let's talk about something else. I don't think you are ready to tell me where you have been.' Stella gave him a wide-eyed, shocked look. 'Do you remember that blue Chanel handbag I gave you?'

'Of course.'

'Where is it?'

Stella frowned. 'I don't know what this is about . . . I suppose the bag is in the dressing chest where I keep my good bags. You gave me this one, and I treasure it,' she said, defensively.

'Go and get it, please.'

'What is all this?'

'Just get it, please.'

He went to the window to look out while she went to the bedroom on the next floor of the tower. From the window on this side he could see across the road to the lights in the old churchyard, now a park, not so long ago the scene of a murder. Augustus came to lean heavily and lovingly on his left leg.

The wait was long enough to make Coffin wonder whether he ought to go upstairs to join Stella. She hadn't looked well. He was angry with her, but he loved her, the two strands came together strongly in his mind, the one fuelling a fire in the other. Damn you, Stella, he thought.

Presently he heard the door open behind him. 'You were quiet.'

'No quieter than you.'

'I wouldn't be singing at the window.' Augustus stood up, scenting disharmony; it did not distress him, as his proprietors may have thought; he found it interesting, even exciting, but a dog had to know where to position himself. 'Did you find it?'

'No. It's not there. I must have left it somewhere or put it away somewhere else. But . . .'

Coffin interrupted her: 'Any idea where?'

Stella stopped short with what she had been about to say. She was visibly angry. 'What is this? Why does it matter? I am just back, I'm tired, I want a bath and a drink . . . It could be in the theatre, I might have left it there. Alice Yeoman will know, or Maisie. If I left it there, then one of them will know.'

'Go and look. Please.'

'Why the hell should I?'

'I will tell you when you come back.'

'I'll go later. I need to wash, have a drink –'

All the anxiety and anger inside Coffin rose within him: his hand went up, he was as near as nothing to hitting Stella in the face. He had never hit her or any woman. All the violence inside him, and there was plenty, was repressed, controlled.

He took a deep breath.

'All right, I will tell you now: while you were away, missing, out of touch, so that I did not know if you were alive or dead, the body of what appeared to be a woman with hair your colour, about your size, wearing jeans and a shirt such as you wear was discovered in a bombed house in Percy Street. The corpse's face was bashed in and the tops of the fingers cut off. By the side of the body was a Chanel handbag with a photograph of you inside it. Not a nice photograph, Stella: you appeared to be eating human flesh.'

He stopped talking, out of words, out of breath. Augustus sidled away.

Stella said nothing, but she threw out her right hand as if to steady herself.

'I almost hit you, Stella.'

'I know.'

There was a silence. Augustus shifted himself uneasily round the room.

'I'll go,' she said. She did not look back. Augustus began

to trot towards the door, looked at Coffin and thought better of it. Stay here, dog, time to be prudent.

Coffin watched her go.

He was troubled. Why, oh why, this insistence that she had not been gone long? More than a day, Stella, more than you want to admit. She would have to answer questions soon.

The theatre was quietening into silence. The curtain had come down both in the Stella Pinero Theatre and the smaller Experimental Theatre, but the bar and the restaurant were open and would be until midnight; it was a private club when the performance ended, Max knew his customers. In addition, there were always a few people hanging about backstage to talk to friends.

No one recognized Stella as she made her way quietly backstage; she was wearing jeans and dark spectacles with her hair drawn back. She was a beautiful woman and always would be, but everything about her – hair, eyes and make-up – was deliberately soft tonight as if she had turned off an inner light.

It was quieter here in the recesses of the theatre than in the bar, probably because those of the cast of *Noises Off* who had not fled home were in the bar themselves. The Theatre Workshop was dark this week, and the Experimental Theatre, as she remembered was doing *Aylmer's End* together with Shakespeare to music with help from a local school. That would be long since over.

Irene Bow, Jane Gillam, Fanny Burt, Michael Guardian and Tom Jenks, all of whom had been in *An Ideal Husband*, were also in the current production.

Irene Bow was probably not far away because there was a trace of her scent on the air; her passage through the theatre front and backstage was usually marked by a whiff of her current favourite fragrance. They changed but were always strong and expensive, a bit like Irene herself, as Tom Jenks had said ruefully, having been one of her short-term lovers. Probably all the time he could afford, his friends had said.

97

Yes, there was Irene at the door of her dressing room talking to Alice Yeoman. Nothing scented and expensive about Alice, who wore tan trousers and a soft linen shirt. No make-up, and no scent.

'Who is that shouting . . . ?' Alice was looking around her.

'Oh, you're always hearing shouting,' said Irene impatiently. 'Here's Stella.'

They greeted Stella with pleasure and surprise. Since little gossip or speculation about her had reached the theatre, all was normal as far as they were concerned. In Irene's case, this meant she was thinking and talking about herself and her part.

'Oh, Stella, you can help here.' Irene fixed her large eloquent eyes (hadn't one disgruntled lover called them 'pop eyes'?) on Stella, who, having had a painful few days and facing the prospect of further unpleasant hours ahead, reflected that if she had been captured by a remote Indian tribe, kept hidden in a deep cave and now just released, Irene would still have come forward with a complaint about her dressing room.

'Irene's not happy about her dress,' said Alice, her voice calm.

A frown flickered across Irene's face which both the other women could read: she did not like a junior member of the cast to call her Irene, though she was forced to admit that it was done now. But she could let them see how she felt, delicately, quietly; she could get the message across.

'There's a good deal of running around in the first act, indeed all the time, and that dress, besides making me look like a sweet pea, is too tight. I have nearly split the seams as it is,' she said, in her lovely, rich voice. Ophelia lamenting Hamlet could not have grieved with more eloquence.

'Irene's so slight, too,' said Alice in a level voice.

'Who made the dress? Was it made here?'

'Yes,' said Irene. 'Here.'

Ah, there's the rub, thought Stella. Irene wanted one made by her own designer, if she has one, and if she hasn't then I bet she is in the process of getting one as a prestige symbol.

Just for a moment, Stella managed to forget her own anxiety. 'Get them to let it out,' she said promptly. All right, I've annoyed you, Irene, but so what? This is my theatre. She turned to Alice. 'I may have left a blue Chanel handbag over here. Have you seen it around?'

Irene bounced away down the corridor, knocking into Mick Guardian.

'Came back for my car keys . . . If they aren't here, then they're lost. Any chance of a lift?'

Irene ignored this. 'Stella is hopeless, getting worse. Losing her looks too, getting quite skeletal.'

Not your trouble, old love, thought Mick. You're going the other way, putting on weight. Could you be pregnant? But no, no embryo could nest happily inside Irene.

He passed on, found his car keys in his pocket, and made his way back to the exit.

Stella and Alice Yeoman were looking for her blue handbag. It was not in her dressing room, all neat, tidy and empty, not in her office, not even in the wardrobe room where no one was around and which was not so neat and tidy. Never was.

'Wouldn't be here,' Stella said.

'You never know. Maybe someone saw it around, thought it belonged in here, tidied it away. Is it important?'

'Yes.'

Alice frowned. 'I think I did see it, but I can't remember where. What about asking Maisie?'

Stella said, in a low voice, 'She's having a few days off.'

'Oh yes. So she is.' Alice looked thoughtful. 'I'm sorry, Stella, I'd like to help.'

'If you can't, you can't. If it turns up, let me know.'

'Yes, sure. You know, we had a lot of people backstage lately. Guided theatre tours, several of them in.'

'Brings in money.' Money for the theatre complex was always on Stella's mind. Letty's too.

'If someone saw the bag and said, "Oh that's Stella Pinero's," and it happened to be a fan of yours, they might nick it.'

'Or even if they just liked the look of a Chanel bag.'

Alice nodded silently.

'Right. Well, thank you, Alice. I will be in tomorrow. Plenty to do, I guess.'

'Miss Bingham has been in.'

It was a probe, and recognized by Stella as such: Alice could tell there was something going on and wanted to know what it was. For her part, Stella could tell the girl was studying her face, taking in the tension, trying to read it. She had probably noticed the bandage wrapped round her forearm, even though her sleeve was drawn over it, and wondered about that too.

'I expect the Chief Commander is pretty busy, what with the bomb – or was it bombs? And the murder. If you've been away, you might not have heard.'

'I had heard.'

'What a thing. I think there's a lot in it we haven't been told about, keeping it quiet. One of Professor Garden's boyfriends, so the word is.'

Stella shook her head. No answer was the best answer.

When she got back, Coffin was drinking coffee and watching television. Pretending to, more likely.

'Not there,' she said. 'But Alice Yeoman thinks it was once around. May have been stolen, may still be there. She will let me know.'

'She's reliable,' said Coffin, absently. He was her patron and must put in a good word.

'Letty seems to have been around.'

He didn't answer but got up and walked towards her.

'What would you have done if I had hit you, Stella?'

'Hit you back.'

Coffin looked at her and laughed. 'Good girl. I do love you, Stella.'

He put his hand on her arm, and stroked the bandage. 'Now, tell me how you got that, and what you have been up to.'

'It goes back a bit.' She turned her head away.

100

He moved her chin, gently. 'Look at me.'

'You know how it is with some actresses – a fresh lover with each play; it's almost expected. I've never been quite like that . . . but all the same . . .'

'It happened?' he prompted, still gently.

'Yes, quite a few years ago, before you came back into my life. He was – is – a lot younger than me. I suppose that was part of the attraction, I was flattered.' She stopped, speech was difficult. 'Pip Eton, that's his name.'

Coffin looked at her with love and sympathy. 'Go on.'

'It really didn't outlast that season at Chichester. Shortly after that you and I started seeing each other again. Well, we had already started to meet – you came down to Chichester.'

'I remember.'

With some pain, Stella said: 'I think now that may have been a factor in Pip's attraction to me. He may have been told to take me up.' She stopped. He could see she was having difficulty in coming out with it.

He decided to help, even if brutally. 'You mean he had his eye on you because of me?'

She smiled at him, and he saw that he had given her what she most wanted: a moment of relief. 'I didn't see it then, but yes, looking back, yes, it probably was . . . He liked me, though,' she added quickly. 'I could tell, he was a good actor, but not that good.'

She stopped again, so he gave her another prod. 'Go on. I suppose it was hot and strong while it lasted?'

Stella sighed. 'It was; short, though, I went to London and then on tour and forgot him. Well, more or less. Our paths didn't cross, and though I thought he might seek me out, he didn't. I went on to Australia.'

'What did he do?'

'He dropped out. Did a bit of telly, nothing much, and then nothing at all . . . I think now he was under orders.' Another pause which, this time, Coffin did not interrupt. 'Then he telephoned me.'

'When?'

'About a month ago . . . can't be sure of the exact day. He

101

left a message on my answerphone. Then he telephoned me at the theatre, spoke to me there.' She plunged on. 'Not loving, nothing like that. Quiet, but . . . I don't know what to say: threatening, but quietly, so quietly that I didn't grasp at first what was happening. No, that's not true, I did, but I couldn't believe it.'

'Threatening what?'

'Threatening that if I did not do what he wanted, he would sell photographs of me to the media.' She looked at him piteously. 'I want you to believe that these photographs were doctored . . . I was in them, yes. Pip did take some photographs of me, he was good, but these – ' she shook her head.

'And what did he want you to do?'

Instead of answering directly, Stella said: 'I always knew he had a political side.'

She looked at her husband and read his expression. 'You're not surprised.'

'Your name had come up.'

She covered her face with her hands. 'Oh, God. So you knew.'

'Not all of it. Not as much as I hope you are going to tell me.'

'He intended that I should be a channel to you, that through me he could both feed you information and gather it.

'I wanted to get away and hide, just for a little while. That's why I told those stories about where I was going. Confusing my trail. But I didn't get that far: Pip was outside when I left, he got me in his grip.'

'What do you mean by that?'

'I mean, he pulled me to his car and drove to where he lived, a rather nasty flat in a road off the main road leading through Spinnergate towards the City. I could see where we were going, he didn't attempt to stop me seeing. I was a prisoner, or at least I felt like one and I certainly couldn't get away easily. He said he would not let me go until I had agreed to do what he wanted.'

'Which was?'

Stella shrugged. 'To spy on you, to let him spy on you and all your dealings with any terrorists. Stupid of him really, since I could say yes and then go away and renege on it. I didn't say yes.'

'How long were you there?'

'I don't know. I got a bit confused about time, as if I'd been drugged . . . I was given food and drink. I think there was someone else there . . . man or woman, I don't know, but I am sure I heard low voices. Then he started to threaten me. I thought he was going to hit me, so I hit him first.'

'You mean, you had a fight?'

'A sort of scuffle. No, it was more than that. He was wearing a shortsleeved shirt and I bit his arm.' She sounded puzzled, as if she wasn't sure what had really happened. 'I suppose my teeth were the only weapons I had. He had a knife and my arm got hurt, and I think he got stabbed too in the scuffle . . .' She sounded puzzled again. What had happened? 'There was blood . . .'

Coffin said, 'You aren't talking like yourself, Stella. More like a badly written play.'

'If I am, then it's because it is the only way I can talk about an experience that seemed unreal to me. It was real, I suppose. I knew that when I hit him.' She was frowning. 'I think I got hold of a knife; I seem to remember it was a bread knife – you know, the sort with a jagged edge . . .' She saw Coffin looking at her with a frown. 'I was a fool to let him get me into his car, but the truth is I can be gullible sometimes, act without thinking. I did so then.'

He saw she was trembling, and he put his arms round her. 'It's over, Stella. So what happened then?'

'He shouted and went out of the room. I daresay it was painful, I meant it to be. He was gone a long while. I may have gone to sleep, I have wondered if there was some dope in the tea he gave me. Then I realized I was on my own, the flat was empty, so I left in a hurry in case he came back. I walked down the road, and soon I had an idea of where I was.'

'But you didn't come straight back here?'

'No, I was near where Maisie lived. I went there and she tidied me up and gave me a cup of tea . . . I came home then.'

'I shall have to get hold of Pip Eton. He's not your friend, Stella. I don't know if he knew the man whose body we have, but he certainly provided the photograph found with him.'

The telephone rang at this point, and Augustus leapt away in alarm.

'He doesn't like sudden noises,' murmured Stella.

'He's going to have to get used to it,' said Coffin, as he picked up the telephone. He listened for a moment, not saying much. 'Right, thank you. Let me know if and when you have an identification. Cause of death, too, if you don't know it already.'

He turned to Stella. 'There's another body.'

Stella made a surprised noise. 'They don't alert the Chief Commander for every body found, surely?'

Coffin was silent for a moment. 'This one is different. I think I shall have to go and look at it.'

It was late evening, but a fine, bright one with a moon, and the body was not far away.

Stella watched her husband depart with foreboding. All those things I am going to have to talk about that I would rather keep quiet, she thought. She could see her face in a looking glass on the wall and knew that it needed rebuilding.

Actresses could disappear and come back as someone else, and now was the time for her to do this. If she could manage it.

She knew she was going to have to answer questions, even if so far she was being handled with kid gloves, but the time would come when the gloves would be off. She thought of Archie Young and knew he would be getting ready for her.

8

This one was different.

It was a fresh body, not long dead, that much was clear even to the first person who found it that evening where it was nestling in an alcove outside the old St Luke's Church, presently a theatre.

That first viewer was the theatre security man, Luke Locker by name, who was taking his usual end-of-performance look around. He did it in a relaxed way, since except for the odd drunk and the occasional pair locked in lovemaking in the shadows (which he tactfully ignored), there had been no trouble. His wife was away and, not being able to afford Max's prices, although Max could be generous with the odd sandwich, he had been living on fish and chips. He was just meditating whether, if you kept eating fish and chips, you ended up smelling like a fish. Fried at that. Was that sexy or not? His wife had been away some weeks, so his mind ran along those lines.

What he saw ahead of him, lit up by his torch, awoke him from his comfortable fantasies.

A guy?

But no, it was not November, nowhere near Guy Fawkes' night, nor did this figure have that jolly, jokey look of a good Guy. Sinister, this one.

At first he had thought the figure was leaning against the wall of the alcove between two buttresses of the former church. After a closer look, he decided the right word was propped up,

He drew nearer and saw flesh. It might be one of those

acting kids putting on a performance. They did such things, but this time . . . he shook his head. Although he did not like actors, he had observed that they did not fool about with their craft.

He made himself take another look. He put out a hand to touch the face under the paper hat . . . Then he jerked back.

'Bloody hell, a deader!'

He could just make out the writing on a card pinned to the chest, and what he read there made him even more uneasy.

The theatre manager and the big girl, Alice, took over the telephoning, and he waited by the figure until the police arrived, being careful not to touch.

First a patrol car, soon followed by a detective sergeant with a woman detective.

Then the SOCO team.

Then the police surgeon to certify death but not to move the body till the pathologist and the forensics had done their bit.

There was quite a crowd now, sidelining Luke, who was obliged to hang around because they were going to question him later. He knew one of the uniformed police. He had been at school with her. A nice fat girl she had been then. Now she had thinned down into being big and muscular. Elspeth Butt.

He sidled up to her. 'Funny business.'

The body was by now lying on the ground being examined by the police pathologist attended by the police surgeon. The pathologist was a man Luke did not know, but did not think he would like if he did. He noticed the man was treated with great politeness. Did someone call him Dennis? Or was it Sir Dennis?

'Funnier than you know.' She hardly looked at him, too intent on watching the pathologist, who was making a delicate first examination.

'Yeah?'

'Not the first body we've got.'

'I heard.'

A burst of laughter from a trio of her peers interrupted anything she might be going to say.

'And *whose body are you*?' one of them sang out, while the others roared with laughter.

Then fell silent.

'It's the big man himself,' said the singer, falling silent as the Chief Commander came into the light.

Coffin looked down at the figure. It was dressed in a jacket and kilt, but both were made of newspapers, cut and pinned. Coffin studied them, observing the dates to be various. A paper hat sat on the dead man's head, looking indescribably jaunty. The man's face was partly obscured by the newspaper, but enough was visible to see he was not old. A thinnish face with dark hair.

A big label with printed letters was fixed to the dead man's chest; A PRESENT FOR STELLA, it read.

'I see why you called me in,' said Coffin. A photographer had stood aside politely as he arrived. The SOCO officer was dusting the wall of the alcove for fingerprints, muttering to himself that there was nothing to be got from rough stone.

'Thought you'd want to see.' Archie Young stepped back so Coffin could get a closer look. 'The MO said he's been stabbed, as far as can be observed. Whether he died from this wound is not clear yet, but he will do a proper examination when the photographer and the SOCO are through. We don't want the newspapers removed yet and there may be other injuries.'

'Any identity?'

'None at the moment. I expect we will get something soon. There was a crowd from the theatre buzzing round him when he was found. They had been eating in Max's restaurant. None of them identified him. Max doesn't know him either. Wouldn't expect it, really.'

Coffin met Archie Young's eyes and did what was required of him. 'I have to tell you that Stella is back. I can get her down to have a look; she may know him.' He nodded at

Young. 'Do you mind if we don't go into this in detail now?

Young nodded, thinking: You might be suprised how much we all know about you and your wife's movements. 'I don't like the way her name is cropping up lately,' he said. 'Seems all wrong, somehow.'

'You can imagine how I feel.'

'We'll get it sorted out, sir. You know how it is: when you're as well known as she is, your name gets dragged into all sorts of dramas.' He was trying to choose his words carefully; he was more moved than he wanted to show.

Coffin looked down at the body. 'Why the skirt? Mean anything, do you think? See any symbolism?'

'I think a kilt – let's call it a kilt – is simply easier to make out of paper than trousers. It's all mad, I don't think we can describe this killer as sane.'

'But why the paper at all?'

Young shook his head. 'Your guess is as good as mine. It might mean something or nothing, according to how mad the maker of the clothes – if you can call them that – is.' To himself he thought it was just another way of getting at Stella Pinero. Like the message. He looked at Coffin: 'I hate to ask, but . . .'

'Yes, well, as I just said, Stella must be asked whether she can identify the body.'

'I don't suppose she'll be able to, but you never know,' said Young. 'Anything she might come up with will help.'

'She may have something to tell us.' She is going to have to talk, he told himself, regardless of whether either of us likes it.

Archie Young looked at Coffin expectantly.

'She will tell you herself,' said Coffin. He looked at the body again. A thin, tanned face under the paper hat. 'Is there a wound on the arm?'

'Yes, professionally dressed from the look of it. Possibly in a hospital. But the MO has only had a peep so as not to disturb the wrapping.'

'It hasn't been examined then?'

108

'No, not yet. For now, the cause of the wound or whatever is unknown.'

'I wouldn't be surprised if it was a bite,' said Coffin. Or several bites, he added gloomily to himself. Young looked at him in surprise. 'In that case, the identity of the man can be established quite soon. Stella had better come down straightaway; she hasn't got far to come.'

Stella had showered, got into jeans and a silk shirt, and restored her appearance. One thing about being an actress, she thought, it does teach you how to create a face. With lipstick, cream rouge and eyeliner, she had made herself look like a lady ready to face the world. Perhaps a lady who'd had a shock recently but had come through and was prepared for the next one. Not exactly a tough lady, but a lady on guard.

She took the summons to view the corpse with apparent calm. 'Right, I'll come now. If you think I can help.' She walked down the staircase, out of the door, and swung left into the quadrangle that fronted the theatre.

The area had been screened off while the dead body itself, after being carefully photographed in situ, had been lowered to the ground for examination before being carried away. Otherwise it had not been disturbed.

A policewoman ushered Stella through. 'This way, if you please, Miss Pinero.'

Coffin stepped forward. 'Sorry to drag you here, Stella, but I think you can help us.' He spoke without looking anyone in the face. 'Stella will, of course, tell you anything you want to know.'

Stella nodded without speaking. She looked down at the dead face. She read the notice saying that this was a present for Stella and shuddered. 'Yes, I know who it is. I know him as Pip Eton.'

'Was that his real name?' asked Archie Young.

'I don't know. He was an actor. Actors have many names.'

Somehow, Inspector Lodge had sidled past the screens to be among those present. Late as it was, there are always people around in the theatre so that an audience was half-formed, although kept back by the police. Stella could see the tall figure of Alice, with Max and one of his daughters edging forward. Max caught her eye, moving his head in something between a bow and a nod. Alice stared straight ahead as if she couldn't believe what she saw. The girl who stood next to her, one of the wardrobe staff – a dogsbody called Frankie as Stella remembered – was laughing. Theatre people were not like the rest of the world.

Stella knew she had to say something to Archie Young.

'I know his name, I can tell you a little about him, I wish it were otherwise.' She paused, and took a deep breath. 'But how did he get killed and why is he dressed like that?'

No one answered.

Coffin said: 'You'll have to tell him the lot, Stella. And we had better do it in our own sitting room. Come up, you two.'

Stella looked at him. 'I'll go first and make some coffee. Can I have your key? I didn't bring mine.'

She was thinking as she climbed the stairs ahead of the others. Tell a straight story, she told herself. Archie Young will believe you, but Lodge may be difficult.

She made the coffee carefully, taking her time. She heard feet pass on the stairs, then she carried the tray up. Voices were talking quietly in the room ahead.

She listened for a moment. He's already told them everything; all I need do is answer any questions.

They were sitting waiting for her, with Augustus sprawled across Coffin's feet.

Good for you, boy, she thought. 'Good dog,' she said aloud. Augustus looked at her steadily with his round black eyes. He liked Stella, who was kind to him, but he preferred Coffin. There was something about his smell that suited Augustus, whereas Stella's smell was lighter and sweeter. Augustus knew a few words if not many, and one of the words he knew was 'dog' which he applied to himself.

Stella hesitated at the door, then Coffin stood and came over to take the tray. 'Thank you, love.'

'You're ready for me?'

He nodded. 'I've run through what you told me.'

'Thank you.'

'I thought you would prefer it.'

Stella poured the coffee and handed it round. 'Well, you know all now, all I can tell you. It's hard for you to believe, but I don't know who killed Pip or when it happened, except that I didn't do it.'

'Never thought it for a minute,' said Archie Young. 'You did well to hold out the way you did.'

'He was stupid to think I would help.'

'He didn't know you as well as he thought he did,' said Coffin.

'He wanted me to be a channel through which he got information . . . Unluckily, I was wild in the days when he knew me.' She looked at her husband. 'You wouldn't have been proud of me then. Not the wife for a leading police officer.'

'You're a different person now.'

'It had been a long while,' said Stella. 'I daresay I have changed.' She smiled at her husband.

Inspector Lodge had received his coffee in silence. Now he spoke: 'He's not known to me, not under that name,' he said. 'But he must be in the records somewhere. Fingerprints, photograph, and so on. We'll find him, and then we can move on to who killed him and why. You say you did him some injury?'

'Yes, but not enough to kill him.'

'Nasty business.' Lodge drank some coffee. 'Hard to understand the reasoning behind propping the chap up like that, dressed that way.'

'And leaving the message for me,' said Stella. 'It frightens me.'

'As it was meant to do,' said Lodge. 'Nice coffee.' He finished his cup, replacing it on the tray. 'He's a frightener, this chap, that's what he is.' He thought about it. 'Or was.'

Stella said: 'He had changed . . . that's how it felt to me.'

'As it happens,' said Coffin tersely, 'he is dead.'

'Not long dead, so the police surgeon thought at the first

111

look,' Archie Young put in. 'Matter of hours. Not killed on the spot, though. Probably killed by the stab wound, but he couldn't be sure at that point. He had other wounds, made earlier so it seems. That would be when you had your struggle . . . And you don't know where you were taken and detained?'

Stella shook her head. 'No, I was bundled in the car, I saw the way at first, down towards the Spinnergate tube station, but then we shot into a maze of side streets . . . I suppose I should have tried to remember more.'

'And when you escaped?'

'I found the main road, and got on a bus . . .'

She knows more than she is saying, he decided. 'You would have been confused,' he said in a soothing voice.

He was talking for the sake of talking and he knew it. To see the pain on the face of the wife of your boss and find it mirrored in the eyes of the Chief Commander himself made it a very embarrassing occasion, but questions would have to be asked; he had put off talking to Stella long enough.

He lowered his eyes: they had to work through this on their own and come out the other side. If they could.

To his relief, his mobile phone rang. He looked at Coffin, who nodded. 'Take it.'

Archie listened. 'From the office,' he said, then handed the telephone over to Coffin. 'Here, see what you make of this.'

Coffin nodded. 'Phoebe? Yes, go on, I'm listening . . . Where did you get this?' He kept his eyes on Stella's face as he talked. Other people do have miseries as well as me, he thought, I must get over this on my own. I am in love with her, but I don't believe she is in love with me. Not any longer.

He put the receiver down, still looking at her. I remember happiness, he told himself. Well, let her hear this, see how she reacts.

'Phoebe Astley had had a call from a friend who works in Summers Street substation. A doctor from Paget Road Hospital walked in with a report. A patient came in . . . said he had been attacked by a strange woman whom he did not know. She had bitten him, then knifed him. No, he had not attacked her back. No, he could not understand it, thought she must be mad. After he'd finished treating the man, the doctor asked him to wait, wondering if he should report it, but the man cleared off before he could stop him . . . After a bit the doctor thought he ought to refer the incident to the police. Which he did.'

'And it got back to us?' said Lodge thoughtfully.

'Phoebe's young friend is bright. And I'm sure that Phoebe has been making discreet soundings here and there. I'm not surprised she should come back with information, she does.' Perhaps he wished she had not come back with this particular titbit.

There was silence in the room. Then Archie spoke.

'Our dead body. He had a recently stitched wound.'

'Looks like it,' said Coffin.

'Pip Eton.' Stella bowed her head. 'I suppose he would go to a hospital . . . It's not true what he said, you know, the way he describes what happened. I was hurt by him . . . I suppose I did hurt him back. Did the doctor believe him?'

Coffin's face relaxed into a smile. 'As a matter of fact, no. Thought he was a liar.'

Stella said, 'Thanks, I feel like crying.'

'I think the doctor was puzzled by the wounds, and by the man, although he kept a professional silence.' Coffin looked at his wife.

This is a private conversation, thought Archie Young. I shouldn't be listening.

'You should have gone to hospital yourself, Stella,' said Coffin.

'I was bleeding, I'm a good bleeder,' Stella said, with melancholy pride. 'I went to Maisie, she tidied me up. She did a first aid course once.'

Inspector Lodge was studying the Chief Commander's face. 'Is that all?'

Coffin withdrew his attention from his wife. 'No,' he said slowly. 'Something else the doctor had to say: he thought that the patient had someone waiting for him . . . Apparently he went to the window to look out and saw him again . . . walking with someone, he thought, towards a car, but he was called away at that point so could not be sure.'

'Could he see who?' asked Lodge.

'Not from what Phoebe's heard,' said Coffin, a trace of reluctance in his voice.

'Sex? Man or a woman?'

'Seen from the back: tall, wearing jeans, probably a woman, could have been a man.'

Lodge looked at Stella. No one could call her tall, nor manly.

'Astley did well,' said Archie Young, rising to his feet. 'Got contacts all over the place and they work for her, I've noticed that before.'

'She's going round to the hospital to see the doctor herself.'

'I shall go too, although I don't suppose the doctor will have much to add,' said Lodge. 'But this man Eton seems to come into my territory.' He turned to Stella. 'I should like to talk to you again, if that is all right?'

Stella nodded. 'Of course.'

'I shall be present,' said Coffin quickly.

'Welcome it, sir,' said Lodge.

He was punctilious, but his very politeness set a division between them.

Both Young and Lodge refused Stella's offer of more coffee as they left.

'What do you make of that?' asked Archie Young, as they walked across the courtyard to where the police activity continued; SOCO were still taking photographs.

'God knows.'

Lodge walked on in silence, then he said: 'You realize that the killer must have come from the theatre?'

Archie nodded. 'I had worked that out.'

'I suppose it would be quiet enough to do a bit of killing there?'

'In certain places, if you knew your way. I think so, yes.'

'Of course, he might not have been killed there.'

'No.'

They walked on, nearly up to where the police unit was working.

'Terrorism doesn't just come from outside,' said Lodge heavily. 'It's inside, too. Do you understand what I'm saying?'

'I think so.'

'Has to be so in this case if the Eton chap – if that was his name, probably not his only one – was involved.'

Archie Young did not answer.

'If you learn anything I ought to know, you will tell me?' Lodge went on.

'Of course.'

Lodge nodded. 'We aren't much liked, my sort. I can understand it.'

They had come up to the brighly lit enclosure now.

'What's the woman Astley like? I haven't had much chance to get to know her. We will never be buddies. My sort and her sort don't understand each other easily.' He smiled wryly.

'Good at her job.'

'I got that. I don't find it easy to work with women, but I can see I shall have to.'

'Phoebe is easy.' In some ways, while in other ways she was not, being immensely protective of her own territory, but the Todger could find that out for himself. 'She's done some good work. Very good work.'

As it happened, Phoebe was ahead of them, talking to one of the workers. She nodded as they approached. 'Hi.'

'You came through with some interesting news,' said Archie Young. 'How did you get it?'

She shrugged. 'Luck. My friend had passed the word, and then I was in Summers Street station talking to one of the CID sergeants; he was there when the doctor came in, the hospital where he has a clinic is a street or two away: Paget Street. The flat in Jamaica Place where the first dead man lived comes in the same precinct, so I've been in and out checking on this and that.' She was carefully vague. One did not give too much away. 'It was just a guess that this body had anything to do with the doctor's story.'

'We don't know for sure that it has,' said Archie, 'but it makes a good guess. Miss Pinero was able to add something.'

Phoebe stared at him alertly, and then turned towards Inspector Lodge, who was looking down at the paper-clad corpse.

'Not my man, anyway,' he said. 'That's a relief, I can tell you.'

'Did you think it would be him?' Archie Young was surprised.

'Always expect anything in this job. It's a theatrical business.'

'Yes, well, the theatre comes into it somewhere. He may even have been killed here. He was almost certainly undressed here and dressed again . . . On the other hand, perhaps not. Mustn't take anything for granted. I can see you've noticed what the newspaper is.'

'Yes,' said Lodge. 'We can all read, can't we?'

The Stage.

Stella said: 'Did you notice that he almost asked for your permission to cross-examine me?'

'He'll be correct.' Coffin was quiet. 'But it will have to be done.'

'I'm sure of it. You'll be there, anyway.'

'I will.' He patted the sofa. 'Come and sit down, Stella. I want to say something.' Yet he found it hard to get started. 'Two men, killed for reasons we don't know. One was a friend of Dennis Garden, and the other . . .'

'I knew him, and I thought I'd be the one that was killed, not him.'

'Why was he left like that? That's a question to ask.'

Stella shook her head. 'I didn't kill him. I wouldn't leave a message naming me. You do believe me?'

'I believe you, Stella, but there is a link with the theatre . . . you saw what he was covered up in – I won't say "dressed"?'

Stella looked at her hands. She was quiet for a minute,

then she said: 'Yes, with pages of *The Stage*. You would need more than one copy to dress a man.' She raised her eyes to her husband. 'We had quite a pile of back numbers in my office. I think they may have been used.'

'And you can't remember where you were imprisoned?'

Stella shook her head.

She knew that this denial would not hold for ever. In time she would talk, and answer questions.

Coffin would start probing, then Archie Young, then the man Lodge.

She began to think of what she would say. She usually had her best lines written for her, but this time she must write them herself.

9

Those two great and dissimilar institutions the Police Force and the Theatre have one thing in common: loyalty. Whatever criticisms are spread within their ranks (and there is as much of that as anywhere else) are contained within it. Some may seep out and be picked up by outsiders, and the press is always on the lookout for something, but sticking together is more admired than gossiping beyond the walls.

Thus when Stella Pinero went into work the next morning no one reminded her, although they were all thinking about it, that she was under suspicion for two murders. There was plenty of police activity, but no one mentioned either killing to Stella. All were pleased to see her, possibly the more so because it meant that Letty Bingham would not be omnipresent. Letty's commanding ways were not popular in the St Luke's Theatre community, which preferred Stella's more relaxed rule.

Alice, not as tidy as usual, greeted her with what was almost a smile from a young woman usually solemn of face. She was there as a protégée of John Coffin, which sometimes seemed to weigh on her, so although always polite to Stella, she was reserved, cautious. Stella herself wondered if the young woman disliked her, but that seemed too harsh a judgement on someone who worked so hard and whom she herself had tried to claim as a friend. 'She's unknowable,' Stella once said to her husband. 'Just shy really,' he had answered. 'Her father was a good copper, her mother was a bit of a wild one, so I've heard. Both dead, of course.' Stella had said: 'She's not wild.' Which was true, for Alice was

118

solemn and quiet, so much so that her fellow thespians, although liking her, wondered whether the theatre world was the right life for her. She didn't mix; when she did go out for a drink with the others or joined them for a snack in Max's she was almost wordless, although showing herself to have a sharp sense of humour when she did speak. The current speculation among the company was that she was a bastard sprig of the Chief Commander's and found her position embarrassing.

Stella did not know of this speculation, of course. 'I'm glad to be back at work,' she said simply to Alice.

Likewise John Coffin, who had walked into his office to be greeted politely by Paul Masters and handed a folder of papers. Several of these contained reports on the two murders. But there were other events in the Second City calling for the attention of the Chief Commander: an armed raid on a big bank in Spinnergate with one guard badly wounded; a fire raging in a railway tunnel, and the study of the two bombs.

Coffin had risen early, leaving a note for Stella and taking Augustus with him. After giving the dog a quick walk in the park across the road, he had put him in the car to wait while he talked to the police on duty outside the theatre complex.

The body had been taken away, but the forensic squad were still at work and looked like being there for some time.

'Apparently happy, with a base of sadness,' was Paul Masters' judgement that day on his chief. He liked Stella Pinero – you couldn't help it, she had such charm – but if there was to be a division of loyalties, then he was John Coffin's man. Had to be.

There had always been what Paul thought of as a 'streak of silence' in Coffin, when he put on his official face and you got no further. He thought that this face was set firmly in position now.

'Can't blame the man,' he muttered to himself as he went back to his own desk. The two secretaries looked at him curiously, waiting to see if he would say anything, pass any comment, and when he did not they went back quietly to their own work. Silence was the only thing just now.

But nothing could stop their thoughts. Sheila had a friend in St Luke's. They're all talking about the body in the theatre, wondering how anybody could have put it there with the place milling with people, let alone strip the man's clothes off and get him dressed the way he was.

Coffin, too, was worrying away at this puzzle, although he knew miracles, even black ones, could be performed in the theatre.

Coffin worked through his papers, dictated a couple of letters, and answered several telephone calls. He did not want to talk to anyone and was glad not to have to. He and Stella had shared a bed but otherwise had not communicated; he hoped it was a loving silence, though he had his doubts. Love on his side, if mingled with a touch of anger, but what on Stella's?

Slowly, he had to admit that there was a part of Stella's story that he did not believe. She was not telling the truth.

So events were fizzing away inside him. Eventually he telephoned Archie Young, who was not available, and then Phoebe Astley, followed by Inspector Lodge. All of whom were denied him, and for whom he left terse messages.

'Probably together, deliberately keeping out of my way while they work. I suppose it's called tact,' he decided morosely.

He waited, working on quietly, seeing those people who had appointments with him, later taking a polite lunch with a visitor from abroad who might have been from outer space as far as Coffin was concerned.

Paul Masters witnessing the tight control the man was keeping over himself, became increasingly concerned about him. Paul was anxious on all levels, but he did not know what to do about it.

So far, neither Young nor Lodge nor Astley had rung back. Paul had made discreet enquiries himself to discover that all three were out of touch.

He did not accept this as natural, nor did he think the

Chief Commander accepted it. For some reason they were keeping their distance.

Stella Pinero telephoned, but Paul had to say that the Chief was out giving lunch to a distinguished visitor from abroad but would be back soon. Did she wish to leave a message?

No message.

Stella picked up a note in his voice and bit her lip. She could imagine what was being said about her. She knew how much Coffin was admired and respected, so if she was thought to have harmed him, she would be pushed out into the cold. Nothing would be said, of course, but she would shiver. 'I was only going to tell him about the *The Stage* newspapers, but he probably knows already.'

Her mind went back to that morning. She had awoken to find her husband gone, having left her a pot of coffee and a note on the table telling her not to worry. Fat chance, she thought, I am all worry.

Then she had picked her way through the police lines, being checked at intervals, and explaining who she was and that she was on the way to work. She was far from sure the identification helped, but it certainly aroused interest.

She turned away from the telephone, and stared down at her desk while admitting to herself that she felt frightened. No new feeling, of course; she was frightened before every first night, sometimes before every performance, all actors knew the feeling, but this was different. Much more sharply personal.

Alice put a cup of coffee down in front of her. 'Brought you this.'

'Thanks.'

'You look as though you need it.'

She took a sip. 'You've put sugar in.'

'You want the energy.'

Stella sighed. 'You aren't wrong there.' I never had you down for a sympathetic soul, she thought, but you are offering it. 'I see the returns are holding up. Last week, anyway.'

'Been nearly a full house most nights.'

121

'That's good.' She stared down at the papers in front of her. 'I'm worried about the coming week.'

'It's the same show.'

'I know.' What she did not say – though both knew what she was thinking – was: But what about the murder? Murders really, and my name involved.

Alice said: 'Bring more people in, I bet.' She started to move away.

'If they can get in. It's like a fortress, or haven't you noticed?'

Stella drained her coffee cup, then stood up. 'Hang on.' She went over to the set of shelves which was usually loaded with scripts, books, folders of this and that, and dusty collections of old newspapers. *The Stage* had a space to itself. 'What became of all the old copies? Where are they?'

'I thought you'd know.'

'Tell me.' Stella was short with her.

'The police came in, had a look round, and took them away. All that were left . . . A lot had gone already.'

'Why wasn't I asked for permission?'

'No one said anything to me, Miss Pinero. They just came in, one in uniform and one in plainclothes – CID, I suppose – swept through and took them.'

'I suppose everyone is being questioned?'

'I haven't been done yet. I think they started with Max's staff. Of course, Jane and the others don't come in until later, so they will catch them then. As far as I can see, the police are just working their way through.'

Stella nodded. 'My turn will come.'

'Shall I take your cup?'

'Bring me another one, please, Alice, so I can get my strength up. I think I can hear police feet outside, and it makes me feel weak.'

Alice laughed; she did not believe Miss Pinero was weak.

'I hope we can open tonight. I will have to be firm about that.'

'I think Miss Bingham has fixed that.'

'Oh, has she? Is she in?'

'I think she was. She may have left; she said something about Geneva and then New York on the phone.'

Leaving me in it, Stella thought.

'How could someone have got the body to the alcove without being seen?' said Alice.

'Oh, Alice, when you have worked in the theatre longer you will realize anything can be done. People either don't see or don't take it in. They expect things to be moving round . . . there are plenty of trollies and such like that are in use all the time. The killer used one, I expect. Daresay the police will find out which. And not that difficult . . .' she shrugged.

Alice shook her head. 'I don't know. I still think it's strange that no one noticed. I mean, someone killed, people around and not noticing. Of course, the corridors were quiet.'

'A year or so ago a schoolgirl was raped and murdered in a roomful of her friends and they slept on.'

Alice absorbed this, her eyes darkening, and nodded sadly. 'Does point to someone in the theatre, though.'

'That I do not dispute.'

Kind of her not to name me, thought Stella. Perhaps she is shouting my name inside herself. Or perhaps not. She's being loyal to the Chief Commander, who got her this job, and behind him she is being loyal to her father who got killed while working for that same Chief Commander.

Their eyes met: dark brown and deep blue.

'Your mascara has run a bit on the right eye, Miss Pinero,' observed Alice. 'You don't mind me mentioning it?'

Stella took out a tissue and went to the big looking glass on the wall. 'No. Thank you for telling me.'

'I know you like to look immaculate.'

Stella smiled but said nothing as she dabbed at her eyes. You know I have been crying, she thought. You know I'm in pain, mental and physical. She touched her arm, I ought to have gone to see a doctor. Maisie did her best, but I don't think it was enough. I hope an infection doesn't set in. I don't suppose he had AIDS.

Supposing he did?

Oh well, the postmortem would show all.

Alice said awkwardly, as if she did not believe what she was saying, 'You know we're all your supporters here.'

'Thank you for saying that.' Even if it is not true. She finished repairing the damage to her face; it was amazing what a bit of make-up would do, for your morale as well as your looks. She began to feel more cheerful as she retouched her lipstick and gave her lashes a fresh brush of mascara. She was an actress, after all. 'I am playing to my face,' she said, staring at her image. 'That looks better, so that's how I am.'

'Oh good.'

'Let's hope it lasts longer than the lipstick.'

'You can always put more on,' said Alice, in a serious voice.

Stella gave her a quick look to see if she was being laughed at, but no, it did not appear so. Unless Alice was a better actress than she suspected. You always had to take that into account. Life in the theatre made you a cynic.

She shuffled the papers on her desk. 'Back to work.'

'There's a fax from Miss Bingham there, I put it on your desk just before you came in,' said Alice, 'saying she has got to go to Geneva but will be back this evening.'

Stella found it, and read it. Miss Moneybags herself in operation; Geneva would be a natural landing ground. 'Darling Stella, just to say I have to attend a business meeting in Geneva, flying out and back this evening, late. Don't worry and look after yourself. Love from Letty.'

I suppose she does like me, thought Stella. I have never really been sure. But then, do I like Letty? Admire her, yes, respect her, yes, and fear her a little, too.

Let's face it: I'm jealous of her influence on my husband. Oh, well, if he gives me the elbow, she will have him to herself.

But I won't think about that. 'Thanks, Alice.'

Alice took her dismissal with a slight smile, disappearing down the corridor along which she saw Jane and Fanny advancing. 'She's there, free and in need of cheer,' she said to them as they passed.

Jane waved her hand in reply without saying anything.

She was friendly to Alice in a distant kind of way but did not regard her as a real inhabitant of theatreland.

'She's so broadshouldered and hefty, I always wonder if she's a lezzie.'

'Doesn't necessarily go with body size,' observed Fanny mildly.

'Well, there's something. Don't like her, you know. Don't trust her.'

Fanny smiled. 'You don't trust many, Jane, love, not even yourself.'

'Not even myself,' agreed Jane seriously. 'I question every move I make when I'm on stage, it's valuable. So when I do anything, I know it is *right*.'

'You take yourself too seriously, love. Lighten up. Anyway, you've got this wrong. Alice is not a lezzie, she has a man; I've seen them together. Roughish, I thought he looked, if that interests you. You always say you are interested in human nature.'

Jane bowed her head, as if she knew it, but knew it was the burden of great talent. Within ten years, Fanny was to win an Oscar and be lauded as a spontaneous and natural actress. And where was Jane? No one knew. Acting in repertory in the Channel Islands, someone at dinner at the Garrick said. Or was it in the Byre Theatre in St Andrews?

Stella was pleased to see them. 'Things to talk about,' she said briskly. 'As you know, the university drama society is mounting the next production but one in the small theatre.' She looked down at her notes. '*King Lear*, ambitious of them but there you are.'

The big theatre would be blank for a week, then the next production for Jane and Fanny and Tim would be J. B. Priestley's *An Inspector Calls*, this being both fashionable now with the intellectual element from the two local universities of the Second City as well as drawing in the cheerful medium-brows who simply wanted to be amused.

The three women were talking it over when Tim came in. 'Hi, there, Stella, nice to see you. I say, this is a business: a dead body of our own. By golly, I'm glad I was already in my digs with my landlord to testify.' He grinned. Tim made no bones about where his sexual tastes lay. Dennis Garden himself was giving him a room. And more – as Tim constantly let all his friends and enemies (he had some of those too) know.

'No one could ever call you reticent, Tim,' said Stella. 'Come on, to work.'

'Let's hope we are all around to perform,' he said, sitting down.

'Someone will shoot you one day.' Fanny gave him a push.

'Can I smoke?'

'No,' cried Jane, whose vocal cords were sacrosanct.

'OK, OK,' laughed Tim, who had no intention of smoking anyway. 'Only asked to annoy.' He looked at Stella and got a smile in return; she knew very well that he was deliberately, and kindly, offering himself as a person she could laugh at.

Dennis must be doing the postmortem at this very moment, he thought, so I might be the first to know exactly how the chap died. But no, Dennis is too professional.

It so happened that the University Hospital in Paget Street where Dennis was indeed at work, was also being visited by Phoebe Astley and Inspector Lodge.

The main building of the hospital was a depressing grey stone block which had started life as a Municipal Public Health Hospital, then been absorbed by the National Health Service and raised to the status of a university teaching hospital. Many smart new buildings had been added. The interesting thing was that it had always been a good hospital and much loved by the people of the district who had been born there and sometimes died there.

Now it was modern and up to date; only the smell which floated out of the walls of the oldest part of the building and which no disinfectant could mask spoke of its ninety-odd years of history. And it lived on the usual knife edge.

Astley and Lodge walked in through the entrance hall side by side. They had agreed to come together to track down

126

and then interview the young doctor who had treated Pip Eton. Phoebe was out of temper with Lodge, who had kept her waiting.

Before seeing him park his car and going out to meet him, she had occupied herself first in discovering the name of the doctor she was interested in and had then passed the time reading the memorials to past members of the hospital killed in all wars since the turn of the century. At least one war had taken place in a faraway country of which she hardly recognized the name, part of an empire long since passed away, but a tribute, certainly, to the pugnacity of the medical staff of old London. 'Suppose I ought to have known that,' she thought, as she strolled past the marble and brass memorials. 'They haven't changed: show them a fight and they're in it.'

She toured the lobby again, avoiding hurrying nurses and speeding doctors with coats flying. No memorials to the Falklands Campaign or the Gulf War . . . too soon, perhaps. They were political souls, here in the Second City, and might not have approved of either enterprise. In the old days it was King and Country and that was it. The last two campaigns had been professional affairs, of course, volunteers not needed.

She was still thinking about it as she went to meet Inspector Lodge. He was all apologies. 'Sorry to keep you waiting. I was held up by a telephone call, you know how it is.'

'I used the time to find out the name of the doctor who was on duty in the outpatient clinic that evening: Dr Allegra. He's over here from South Africa, finishing his training. He's here now, which is lucky for us.'

'Busy, I suppose?'

'Sure to be, but we can break in.'

'Does he know we're coming?'

Phoebe nodded. 'He will be expecting us. Follow me, I know where to go.'

Lodge followed her in silence down a corridor to a long room filled with people, emergencies of one sort or another – a broken arm, a possible poisoning, a sick baby: there were two of those, one crying, one deadly silent – waiting their turn to see a doctor. A polite young woman at the desk said she would ring through to Dr Allegra, if they wouldn't mind waiting.

Since there were no seats left, they leant against a side wall.

Lodge seemed gloomy. 'Ever had an investment go wrong?' he asked.

'Never had an investment.'

'In a person.'

Phoebe looked at him in surprise. 'Ah, that . . . Well, the usual number. Happens to us all.'

'My man – the one I had planted in the building firm, remember?'

'The missing one?'

'I've heard from him now. Once . . . Don't know now if I can trust him.'

'What are you saying?'

'I don't choose these chaps that work with me, I'm just a channel. They do the dirty work, but you have to trust them. I don't know now. He says he is working on someone important, the real thing.'

'The murderer? Or the bombers?'

'I suppose so – both, the claims, connected,' said Lodge doubtfully. 'If I can believe him.'

'Did he name anyone?'

'No, that's part of my worry. He wasn't explicit. I could have done with a bit more detail. More concrete, if you get me.' He sounded regretful. He likes that man, Phoebe thought.

Phoebe had her eyes on the young man who was coming towards them with a professionally harried look. He held out his hand.

'Inspector Astley? I'm Dr Allegra . . .' He had a slight South African accent, rather attractive to Phoebe's ears, as indeed he was himself, being tall and fair and nicely muscular. All assets appreciated by Phoebe.

She shook his hand and let Lodge introduce himself, which he did promptly.

'Not easy to talk here,' said Allegra, surveying the noisy, crowded room. 'And I don't have a room of my own – too junior – but there's a kind of common room.'

The room to which he took them was long and empty with a few soft armchairs and a table with a coffee machine on it.

'Like a coffee?'

Phoebe accepted it, while Lodge shook his head.

'So he's dead, this chap?' said Allegra. He shook his head. 'I knew there was something wrong there.'

'How do you know he's dead?' asked Lodge gruffly.

Allegra was surprised. 'Is it a secret?'

'We haven't released his name.'

'Word gets around. It's that sort of place. A gossip mill, that's what it is. Everyone was talking about the corpse in the theatre ... pretty weird, it sounded, and I thought: "That's my guy." I'd been worried about him, there was something not quite right.'

'Go on,' said Phoebe.

Dr Allegra looked hopefully at Phoebe. 'I don't suppose you smoke?'

'No.' A lie but what else to say to a doctor?

He sighed. 'You are wise; my case exactly, but if you had wanted a cig, then I could have had one with you.'

Judging by the smell in the room, his colleagues were not above lighting up as the need took them. He saw her looking at a half filled ashtray and smiled ruefully.

'Yes, walking wounded we are here.'

Lodge found this interplay tiresome. 'So, what is it you have to tell us, Doctor?' He made the word 'doctor' sound like a threat.

Dr Allegra looked down at his hand, stretched his fingers, then retracted them, causing Inspector Lodge to draw in his breath irritably.

'I'm really trying to be straight about this, say what I observed. I thought he was a thorough liar, and although he had a nasty wound I did not think he was telling the truth about how he came about it. He seemed unclear about whether he had been bitten or stabbed. I thought he liked the drama of a bite. There were certainly two serrated, macerated wounds. But I thought they were knife wounds which had been . . .' Here he hesitated, '. . . touched up, but not by teeth, another knife or scissors, Yes, scissors might have done it, and they could have been self-inflicted. Whether this was so or not . . . I thought he had been wounded but done the rest himself. Self-wounding, a known thing. After thinking it over, I decided to report it.'

'By that time, you knew of the murdered man found in the St Luke's Theatre?'

'I did. Word gets around, like I said.'

'The postmortem will give us some idea on the wounds. It wasn't the wound that brought him to hospital that killed him, of course.'

'No, what I saw was not life-threatening. It might have got infected, but I stitched and swabbed it. I think it hurt.' There was a touch of satisfaction in Dr Allegra's voice, clearly his patient had got across him. 'There was something else: he didn't say he was going, and while I went to get some dressings for him to use at home, he made off.'

'Not polite,' said Phoebe.

'No, and then, a few minutes later, I saw him getting into a car. He was laughing. To himself, I suppose,' Allegra added thoughtfully. 'Although I think he had someone with him . . . a man . . . Couldn't see . . . I didn't care for him. Capable of putting on an act.'

'Well, he was an actor,' said Phoebe.

To himself Lodge added: And also, if we are to believe another performer, a man capable of violence, threats and of having terrorist connections. Did he believe that 'other performer', as he called her? His inner jury was still out on that one.

Paul Masters took several calls both before lunch and after, explaining to all callers that Coffin was out entertaining an important visitor but would be back later. Yes, he assured both Lodge and Phoebe Astley, their messages would certainly be passed on. And, no, he did not know why the Chief Commander was not answering calls on his personal mobile. As far as he knew, it was working.

'Doesn't want to,' was what he said to himself. He knew from past experience that Coffin was capable of ignoring calls when he chose. 'Wants to think.'

And plenty to think about, he mused, as he sat back to his own work. Himself the survivor of several unhappy relationships, he reckoned he could have given the Chief Commander a tip or two on how to handle Stella Pinero. Tougher, rougher, would have been his advice.

'I wonder where he is, though,' he said aloud. 'Nothing in his diary.' Not that Coffin always followed the rules and let you know where he was, but Paul Masters usually had a better idea than most.

Sheila Heslop looked up from her word processor. 'I know where he is. I saw him as I came back from lunch.' Sheila had taken a late lunch because her mother was visiting her. 'Speeding along the road towards St Luke's Theatre. I live that way myself. He was going so fast he nearly knocked an old chap off his bike. I think he slowed down after.'

'Sure it was him?' It did not sound like the way the Chief Commander usually drove. 'I bet you were driving pretty fast yourself.'

'Recognized the car,' said Sheila, returning to her work. 'And I was going quite slowly, as it happens. I had Mum on board and I was dropping her off at her favourite shop. You don't drive fast when you've got my mother on board. It was the boss all right. Reckon he's in a mood?'

Paul did not answer.

Coffin had done more than slow down, he had pulled over and switched off the engine. 'I could have killed that man,' he told himself. He knew he was capable of violent moods, but he thought he had disciplined himself out of them after the disasters of his middle years. Apparently not; anger was still there inside him, like a stream running deep and only waiting any opportunity to burst out.

His mobile phone had rung several times as he had driven from the smart restaurant where he had given lunch to the eminent French policeman where their talk had been quiet and secretive. Each time the phone sounded, Coffin had ignored it. Now, parked by the kerb with the traffic roaring past, he made an outgoing call.

For a time, he thought he might not get an answer. Try the theatre then, perhaps she was there.

But then a hoarse voice shouted back at him. Nothing had ever succeeded in convincing Maisie that you did not need to shout over the telephone.

'Hello. Who's that?'

'Maisie, you know who it is: John Coffin.'

'Oh, didn't recognize your voice.' She was not unfriendly, merely surprised. 'You sound different.'

He did not believe her, but ignored it. 'Anyone there with you, Maisie?'

'No, only me and the old cat.'

'I want to ask you a few questions.'

There was a hoarse murmur.

'How long have you known Miss Pinero?'

'Oh, ever such a long while.'

'Since when? When did you first meet her?'

Maisie said hoarsely, 'I don't like to talk about Miss Pinero when she's not here.'

'I haven't got time to muck about, Maisie. Just tell me when you first met her.'

He could hear heavy breathing across the line; whether it was the cat or Maisie he could not be sure. 'Come on, Maisie.'

Maisie sighed. 'I don't like talking about Miss Pinero on the telephone. I'd rather do it face to face.'

'No time. When did you first meet?'

'I don't know why it matters, sir, but she did a season in repertory at the old Spinnergate Theatre. I was working there. We got on, and it was just about when her career

132

took off . . .' Coffin could hear a kind of shrug. 'We stayed together.'

'And she lived in Spinnergate then?'

Maisie thought about it. 'I believe so,' she said at length. 'As far as I know.'

'It would have been a long way home each night to the flat she had in Blackheath,' Coffin pointed out. 'And she had been earning well. A film and TV work.' Unconsciously he was revealing the eye he had kept on Stella all those years they were apart.

'I don't know about that, sir,' said Maisie. 'Not my business. I think I ought to go now, the cat wants to be let out.'

Coffin took pity on her. 'Yes, it's all right, Maisie. I have asked and you have answered. You've told me what I want to know.'

'I have?' said a disturbed voice.

Coffin heard a scuffling noise as he finished the call: it might be the cat, if Maisie really had one, or Maisie herself.

Coffin drove on to St Luke's. He did not go to his own apartment in the tower; he knew he had a better chance of finding Stella in the theatre itself. He parked the car, got out, and felt as if he had Gus tumbling out after him. One day he would have to train Augustus to stay at home alone, but he never seemed to have the time. There was one good thing about Augustus, he never got lost, he was always right behind you. Coffin could almost hear his snuffling breath now. He was not a barker, and only rarely a fighter, but he was a heavy breather.

He walked in, looking for Stella. In mid afternoon a lull had descended upon the place; he was aware of a rehearsal taking place in the small theatre, and of distant voices here and there, but otherwise the place was quiet. Stella was not in her office, nor in the manager's office, neither was anyone else. Eventually, he was alerted by Augustus, who had run on ahead and was now barking joyfully in the wardrobe room. This was a suite of three rooms and Stella was in the first. On her own, pensively studying a long dress.

'Pity Donna Karan doesn't do stage clothes,' she said, with a sigh. 'Or does she? Not that we could afford her.'

'Stella . . .'

She swung round. 'Oh darling, I didn't realize it was you, I've been trying to get hold of you.'

'Oh, good. Any special reason?'

'Just to talk to you. Touch you.' She came up and kissed him; he did not return her kiss.

She drew back. 'You aren't very responsive.'

'You'll find me responsive enough at the right time.'

'It's known as empathy,' she said coldly, taking a step away. 'I think you've lost it.'

He ignored the remark. 'What have you got on your feet? Flat shoes, good. You can walk in those.' He took in what she was wearing. 'Jeans and a cashmere sweater. That'll be warm enough, I think. It's not that cold, and we shall be walking fast.'

'I am not going out, I'm busy here, there's a lot to do.'

'I'm taking you for a walk.'

Stella was silent. Then: 'You're serious.'

'It's very serious for me.'

'Where are we going?'

'Let's go outside and start walking.'

Stella picked up her big shoulder bag and dropped it over one shoulder. It was heavy, her bags were always heavy. Then she said nothing until they had gone through the corridors and out of the building. 'Can't we drive?'

'No, it's a walk – a walk of discovery – and you are going to find the way.'

'Is this a game?'

'Call it that if you like. My game.' Coffin's game.

10

Stella withdrew her arm from his grasp, which had been firm, almost hard. 'Where are we going?'

'Just walk on, my love.'

'Am I your love?' Was it a question?

'You will always be that, Stella.' But his tone was quiet, more determined than passionate, as if she had fallen into a part in a play which she could not now walk out of. I signed that contract, she told herself, mustn't forget it.

She walked on in silence, along the busy Spinnergate main road with buses, lorries and the battered old motor cars which the district specialized in passing them at speed.

They came to a crossroads where they stopped. 'Which way?' she asked. She looked at her husband's face: expression not promising.

'I want to get to where you were taken that night.'

'But I don't know.'

'Memory is a strange affair: I think as we walk along you might find you do know the way. Or can remember bits. Will you try?'

'I suppose so. But I think it's a waste of time.'

'You came along this road when you escaped from your captivity, you must have done, because Maisie lives down there –' he pointed to a side road. 'So which of these four roads did you come down?'

Stella thought about it, then she pointed. 'It must have been the left turn. Yes, I seem to remember looking across the road and seeing that oak tree.' She pointed to the large oak, now shedding its leaves, on their side of the road. 'I think I got on a bus.'

'Right, let's go down that road. Heaverside Road.'

'I don't want to. If you are playing a game, then I am not.'

He took her arm firmly in his. 'Onward, Stella. You do remember this bit of your journey? Of course, you could lie to me, but somehow I don't think you will.'

'Why not?' She was walking briskly if reluctantly, half dragged along.

'Because you know I will know, I will read your face. I am the professional here, Stella. So you may decide to keep silent. That won't work either: I shall see your eyes. You will look where you do not want to go.'

'All right. Yes, I do recall this bit. Damn you.'

He ignored this. 'Let's walk on. You might enjoy it if you give yourself to it.' There was a certain irony in his tone.

Stella let herself be taken along. 'I used to feel safe with you, it was one of your attractions.'

'I always wondered what was.'

'I don't feel safe now.'

'Oh, you're safe enough,' he said cheerfully. 'Safer than you've ever been.'

'I hate you in this mood.'

'It's not a mood, Stella, more a state of mind.' His tone was polite, formal.

They had passed two turnings on their side of the road, ignored a pedestrian crossing leading to a row of shops down Pedders Street, a narrow street at right-angles to Heaverside Road, and were heading towards Spinnergate tube station. Coffin drew Stella's attention to this.

'We've gone beyond Eliot Street and Patten Lane . . . you didn't want to turn down either of those?'

Stella stopped dead. 'I wasn't thinking, just walking.'

'Ahead is Arrow Street. Does that ring a bell?'

She shook her head. 'I don't know what you mean.'

A bus came down Arrow Street stopped a little beyond Eliot Street.

'You must have got off that bus you spoke of somewhere

around here, then walked to Maisie's. You remember that?'

'Yes, of course I do. I recognize where we are, naturally.'

'So let's go down Arrow Street.'

Arrow Street was a long, narrow thoroughfare, heavy with traffic. On one side there was a terrace of new houses, and on the other were two megalithic blocks of flats. It was a respectable but dull street. Another red bus was already appearing at the end of it with a lorry of frozen food passing on the other side.

'Not a street I like,' said Coffin. 'Had a couple of nasty murders down here a few years ago. Shouldn't let it influence one's feelings about a place, but somehow it does. I can see the blood on one of the victims still: a small child. Beaten then burnt. Only half-burnt, though, so there was blood and charring on the body. I remember hoping that the kid had been dead when the burning started. You wouldn't remember the case.'

'I don't.'

'The other case was even nastier. In that flat over there –' He pointed towards the top floor of the first block. 'Some poor sod is still living in it. Wonder if he knows what went on there. I daresay. I doubt if the neighbours would have spared him the lovely knowledge.'

He put his arm round her. 'Let's get on . . . If we go down Arrow Street . . . it is straight as an arrow's flight isn't it? . . . you are bound to remember where you got on the bus and that will give us a clue to where you must have walked.'

'I do remember . . . it was at the end of Arrow Street.'

'Coming back, is it? Memory is like that . . . patchy. You think you have forgotten, and then suddenly, there it is in your mind, all fresh and clear. Let's go on down Arrow Street; not worth getting on a bus. Getting tired?'

Stella shook her head. 'No, I am not tired.' Many things: disturbed, even angry, but not tired. Some emotions drive away fatigue.

'We can take it slowly.' As they walked, he went on talking. 'You know this part used to be all part of the Shambles

. . . where the cattle came in off the boats and were slaughtered. In the days before refrigeration, of course.'

'I didn't know that.'

'No, why should you. I never like to think of all that death handed out . . . mass killing. Must give a feeling to a neighbourhood.'

'You're not talking like a policeman.'

'I'm not all policeman.'

'Or perhaps it's just part of your technique . . . I haven't seen this side of you before. Well, I wouldn't would I?'

'Technique?'

'Yes, to unsettle a suspect. And, as a matter of fact, it's working,' she said angrily. 'I can't bear to think of all those sheep and cows.'

Coffin laughed, his mood lightening. He took her hand.

'And don't say you love me for it, I'm not in the mood.' But she did not take her hand away.

Suddenly their feelings towards each other seemed to have changed. 'She's going to do it,' Coffin told himself. 'She's going to show me, tell me.'

But they were both wary as they walked the length of Arrow Street.

Coffin wondered if he had been right to tell her about the Shambles. Not true, he had made it up on the spur of the moment, but it seemed to have worked.

'You didn't bring Augustus, after all,' she said.

'No, he's not a good walker over a distance. Prefers the car.'

'So do I.'

'I thought it was better this way. You sweep past things in a car; on foot, noises and smells bring back a memory which you might otherwise not have picked up.'

Smooth, Stella thought, very smooth. Perhaps he really believed what he was saying. Things were going to come out, she could tell. Impossible to keep quiet any longer. Stupid of her to have tried.

'For instance,' he went on, 'see that man over there?'

She looked; the man was well dressed in a dark suit, carrying a briefcase and what appeared to be a copy of *The Times*. 'Businessman of some sort. Lawyer, accountant? He looks prosperous.'

'Oh, he is: he runs the local outfit of prostitutes.'

'He's looking at you as if he knew you.'

'He knows me, all right. As I know him. He may acknowledge me or he may not. Depends on business.' Coffin was watching the man with some interest. He was going across to a man sitting in a car, he addressed him briefly, then moved away. 'I didn't know there was a contact there, but there is, although I don't think my friend was glad for me to see it. I guess they would have talked longer if he hadn't seen me watching.'

'Who is the other man, then?'

'He is a banker. I shall have to think about it, he may be putting money in. Better than Lloyds or the Stock Exchange, much safer. Provided you know the right people.'

'I suppose he does.'

'That's what I will be thinking about. My friend thought I might be one of the right people once, if the correct amount of currency changed hands. Well, he learnt otherwise.' Coffin sounded amused. 'Now, see that woman across the road?'

'The one who has just come out of that rather nice house?'

'Yes, and you're right, it is a nice house.'

The woman was beautifully dressed in a pale suit, with a flow of blonde hair. A crocodile bag swung from her shoulder.

'What do you think she is?'

Stella gave her a knowledgeable look over. 'She's not an actress, but . . . I don't know, she's a performer of some sort.'

'I'll say she is. She belongs to the stable of our friend now disappearing down the road.'

Stella was surprised. 'Upmarket for Spinnergate.'

'Fifteen years ago you would have been right. Now . . .' he shrugged. 'Since the City moved in not so far away, prices have risen. Of course, the girls come and go, it's an ageing profession.'

'So is the stage,' said Stella, with feeling. Without meaning to, she quickened her step and marched on down Arrow Street.

'A walk down Arrow Street is never wasted.' Coffin caught up with her. 'Here we go.'

Arrow Street ended in a small open space with a traffic roundabout in the centre; China Street forked off to the right and Kettle Street to the left. Both were lined with small pleasant houses and shops. It was one of the nicer residential areas in Spinnergate.

Coffin looked at his wife. 'Which way appeals, Stella?'

'I think I remember the pedestrian crossing,' she said nervously. 'Into China Street.' She looked along the road and then at Coffin. 'We may be getting close.'

The Pelican crossing changed from red to green and they crossed the road in silence.

'Let's take it slowly now, so you can look about you, see what clues you get. It was dark when you were taken there?'

'Yes.'

'But daylight when you escaped?'

Stella thought about it. Then she nodded.

'But you were in a state of shock, so not noticing as well as you might be. Still, let's see what happens. Even in the dark there are smells. There may be a smell in China Street that reminds you of where you were.' His voice was grave and serious.

He's playing this game better than I am, Stella thought. It's nearly over, anyway. I know that. I can tell that he knows it, too. Why are we both playing it to the end? Her answer came at once: because I am frightened. I will have killed something. Trust, I guess, or worse. What could be worse, but love, of course.

They were passing a baker's shop which proclaimed that tea and coffee with pastries were to be had all day and every day.

'Could we stop here for a cup of tea?' Stella pleaded.

'I was going to suggest it.'

'Were you?' Was that good or bad for her? She found herself all the time now trying to formulate an assessment.

'Well, perhaps that is an exaggeration, but it did cross my mind. You look tired and we don't yet know how far we have to go, do we?'

'No,' said Stella, in a hollow voice.

The baker's shop smelt pleasantly of fresh bread. Perhaps they permeated the air with some special scent, thought Stella cynically. Nothing was baked on the premises.

But the little room at the back where the tables were laid with fresh cloths and real flowers was welcoming. She sank down on a straight-backed chair while Coffin went to order the tea.

'Can we not talk?' she said when he came back. 'Or simply be quiet?'

'Two Indians, milk and some lemon for you, is that all right? Silence? Why not? Although the woman who took the order seemed to want to talk; she knows you, I think. Saw you in the theatre, I suppose.'

The tea, when it arrived, with a plate of shortbread biscuits, was served in blue-and-white china; it was strong and hot. Stella drank thirstily.

She noticed that Coffin, never as fond of tea as she was, drank slowly. Too many cups of canteen tea as a young copper climbing the ladder . . . and occasionally falling off, he had added with a wry smile; he could always laugh at himself.

The wall behind Coffin was covered with a large looking-glass in which she could see herself. She could also see the woman who ran the shop. She was a large, plump redhead with a friendly face but sharp eyes. Those eyes were now looking at Stella.

Stella realized that the woman was trying to catch her eye. She looked down at her tea to avoid the contact. How hard it was not to look up and see.

She sipped some tea. Come on, woman, she told herself. If this is a game, you can play it too. You make the rules, too. Damn it, you're an actress.

She lifted her head to give the woman a radiant smile. She saw Coffin looking at her.

'Never discourage a fan,' she said, still with a smile.
'"No talking" is over, is it?'

'Yes,' Stella stood up. 'Just give me a minute while I go to the cloakroom.' She passed through the shop, had a quick word, still smiling, with the woman behind the desk, and disappeared. She was not gone long.

Coffin was waiting for her outside when she came through the shop.

'Are you sure you're up to this? You want to go on?' he asked her gravely.

She nodded, walking forward. 'Come on, it's this way, I think.' She turned to look him straight in the face: 'As I remember.'

There was a cul-de-sac off China Street called Fish Alley. An unpromising name for a group of pretty apartments over-looking the river.

At the entrance to Fish Alley, Stella halted. 'Down here, I think.'

'Sure?'

She nodded towards a dark shop on the corner. 'That shop is a coffin-maker's . . . not many of them left now, most coffins are mass-produced. I couldn't forget that shop, could I?'

Coffin considered that it was the first time he had ever considered his name – a good Kentish name – an embarrassment.

There was an aged, worn inscription on the glass which read: COFFIN MAKER TO HIS MAJESTY KING GEORGE III.

'Can that be true?'

'Shouldn't think so,' said Stella, 'but it's very imaginative. They are imaginative round here.'

A wizened little old man's face peered at them through the dusty glass. He smiled and waved.

'George III,' said Coffin, waving back. 'Or does he think I am?'

'I don't think he's sure.' Stella could see the old man's intent, cheerful, battered, old face. 'He seems to know you.'

'Very likely he does, my face gets known for what I am.

142

Let's admit it: we are both well known in our different ways. Hard to hide.'

Stella nodded. 'I know where I am now. I remember.' She pointed. 'On the right. That small block. It's the middle flat. I remember running down one flight of stairs.'

'I am pleased. It's very helpful to know where you were held and where Pip Eton was living.' Coffin sounded positive, as if he had got what he wanted. He smiled at his wife encouragingly. 'Clever Stella, I knew you would come through for me. We must let Archie Young and Inspector Lodge know.'

So we must, thought Stella dismally, all of them must know and come tramping around. She felt suddenly weary, as if she was being walked over herself. 'Is that it? Can we leave it there? Walk back. Or ring for a cab, I am a bit tired.'

Coffin would have none of it. 'No, Stella. Now we have got this far, we must look over the place, check it out. Not touch things – forensics will want to do that – but verify it really is where you were held.'

Fish Alley, near to Petty Pier, was quiet with a few cars parked along the kerbs; a woman was pushing a pram along the road, and a mongrel dog, tail up, trotted cheerfully behind her.

'Lead the way, will you, Stella?'

She hesitated, then walked forward slowly. It was coming, it had to be, she saw that the truth was arriving.

'It's called Linton House, I see.' Coffin was following her. 'A grand name for a modest establishment.' He was studying the numbers listed on the wall in the entrance lobby. 'Must be number 2A. No name given. Understandable, I suppose. Incognito is the name of the game.'

For the first time, Stella understood that he was as nervous as she was. 'A flight up,' she said.

As they mounted the stairs, a woman put her head out of a ground-floor flat. 'Thought I heard voices. Nice to see you, Miss Pinero.'

Stella smiled and nodded. 'Mrs Flowers, here I am.'

'I heard you here yesterday.'

'No,' Stella shook her head. 'No, not yesterday.'

'Oh.' Mrs Flowers sounded surprised. 'Thought I heard someone up there above.' She started to withdraw backwards through the door. 'Oh, well, you know how it is. It's an old house, the floorboards creak all the time.' She gave a jovial laugh, a wave of the hand, and closed the door.

'Old gossip,' said Stella. 'Used to watch what went on.'

'She sounds useful.'

'Oh, yes, send your police questioners in. Make her day.'

They had arrived outside the door of 2A. Coffin surveyed the neat grey door with its shining brass bell. 'I suppose we shall have to break in. No problem, I've done it often enough in the way of duty. I remember once I had to break into a house where there were five people dead around a dinner table.'

'It won't be necessary to break in,' said Stella, lips stiff and her throat tight. 'I have a key.'

'You took it with you when you left? Cool of you, Stella.'

She did not answer, but put the key in the lock, turned it twice, then pushed the door open.

Beyond the door was a small hall, carpeted in soft grey, the walls painted white. Light streamed in through the open doors of the sitting room on the right and a bedroom on the left.

'Smells empty,' said Coffin. 'No one dead here, anyway. You can always tell by the smell.' He closed the front door behind him, then stood looking at Stella.

'Honesty time,' he said. 'You knew this place before. If you were taken here, it was not by chance.'

Stella did not answer. She put her hand to her throat. She looked into her husband's eyes and saw something there that she did not wish to see. In their long and difficult relationship, sometimes on, sometimes off, he had shown her anger, but behind it she had always seen love. Now she saw a kind of opacity. For the first time, she could not read him.

'Honesty time,' she repeated. 'That's a good line.'

'Stop acting, Stella.'

'Sorry, can't help it. You're frightening me.'

144

'Even that is acting.'

And he was right.

Stella shook herself as if she were trying to throw out one persona, the actress, and get back into another, her own proper self. She led the way into the sitting room. 'Let's go and sit down.'

The sitting room was a long narrow room with windows at both ends, it was a room which looked as though it was basically tidy and in good order, but over which disorder had marched. A cup and saucer on the floor, an overturned chair, empty beer cans all around.

Stella righted the chair before sinking down on the chintz-covered sofa.

The action was, as she saw herself, a dead giveaway, if one were needed.

'You own this place, don't you, Stella?'

'Yes.'

'I would have known anyway. It smells of you, Stella. You didn't know that, did you? How could you? But I can tell.'

'I hope it's a nice smell,' she said, playing for lightness.

'Now I want to know all about it – and the truth, mind.'

'I don't know where to start.'

'Not at the beginning, not why you own this place or since when or what you do with it – that can come later.' He saw her wince. 'Tell me exactly what happened that day you packed your bags and announced you were going to several places where you never went and probably never intended to go.'

That is how he talks to a suspect, Stella thought. But then, I am a suspect. 'I did intend to go to the health farm. But Pip Eton was waiting outside. He grabbed me and made me drive to here.'

'And why here?'

Stella licked her lips. 'I didn't know it, but he was living here; had been for a few days, I think, maybe longer.'

'And how did he get in?'

'He had a key . . . I had given him one, years ago.'

Coffin nodded. 'So, years ago, you gave a key to Pip Eton

145

– I won't ask why – and he kept it. Right? And, without you knowing it, he let himself in and began living here. Is that right?'

'Yes, but I don't think "living" is the way to describe it . . . He was just here. Using the place.'

'For what?' And, when she did not answer: 'I must know, Stella.'

Reluctantly, she said: 'I think he must have used it as a kind of base, a meeting place for people like himself . . .'

'Terrorists.'

She bowed her head. 'I didn't know. I only learnt what he was, what he had become, when he entrapped me, trying to make me turn informer on you. I refused then and I always would have refused.'

Coffin nodded without saying anything.

'But you have a secret life of your own which you did not tell me of. I didn't know that you had a part on a hush-hush committee which he called ATA1. He told me that, not you.'

'Secret information. It's just work, Stella, part of my job.'

'I would never have let him use me. He had been trying for ages, much longer than I let you know. I just laughed him off at first, I didn't think you knew anything secret. I was wrong about that, you had your own secret life. In the end, he tried force, he attacked me. I just defended myself.'

'I believe you. But you owned this place, you knew where you had been taken, even if by force, and you knew Pip Eton – rather well, I suspect, Stella.'

'In the past,' she said quickly. 'All in the past.'

'Lodge isn't going to like it. I can't say I do myself, but I'm glad you have told me everything.'

He walked to the window and looked out. A quiet street scene. 'You didn't keep much of a watch on this place.'

In a much louder voice, Stella said: 'Since my marriage to you it has played no part in my life. I have lent it to various friends, not many, and that was all. It was an investment now, a place I might sell when it suited me.'

'It wasn't that all the time.'

'No. Performers have their own stresses, a quiet place,

146

where I could take . . . yes, a lover, helped me to unwind. But not since you and I met again, never.'

'You never took me there.'

'No. Can't you see why? You were serious.'

Coffin smiled. 'All this took some getting out of you.'

There was a pause.

'You knew . . . you knew all the time, everything.'

'I admit it. That secret side of my life informed me as a matter of course. You can imagine how I enjoyed it. Naturally it was done in a very tactful way; they didn't come out and say, "Your wife is in contact with a very bad character indeed, a chap on our wanted list", but I got the message. I wanted you to tell me. I needed you to tell me yourself.'

She covered her face with her hands. 'I feel terrible.'

He came back from the window where he had been standing to sit beside her on the sofa. 'I've had my own ups and downs, you know: nearly chucked out of the Force once. I was in limbo for a bit, and then on a kind of approval.'

'Will you have to resign now?'

He didn't answer, but stood up. 'Let's have a look over the flat. Forensics will have to come and check it out.'

'There's only the bedroom and the kitchen, besides the bathroom,' Stella explained.

'Kitchen first.'

The kitchen was small, with a compact white refrigerator and shining sink. The whole room looked unused. Coffin swung open the refrigerator door and a waft of cold air came out, but except for a carton of stale milk, it was empty. There were crumbs of bread and a wrapped loaf by the side of the electric cooker and two teabags in the sink in company with a dirty mug.

He looked in the rubbish bin which held a few beer cans and a bottle that had contained whisky.

'Someone was here, but not doing much eating,' he said. 'Let's see the bathroom.'

A quick look showed a bloodstained towel slung over the handbasin. Coffin looked but did not touch.

'Bedroom now.'

147

This room was dominated by a large double bed. It was tidy, but when he pulled back the duvet the undersheet was tousled, as if someone had been sleeping there.

'Your lodger,' said Coffin.

The dressing table was tidy and unused except for a comb with hairs in it.

'Careless fellow,' said Coffin. 'You should always take your hair with you.'

A cupboard covered both walls, but it was empty except for a tweed jacket.

'Not mine,' said Stella.

'Belonged to the chap who left his hair and probably his blood behind. Forensics will tell us.'

'Pip,' Stella was clear. 'The blood isn't mine, I didn't touch a towel. The towel belongs to the flat, though.'

'Good,' said Coffin lightly. 'Something established.'

Stella sat down on the bed. 'Wait a minute, I've been thinking, I was a fool not to see it. You didn't need me to lead you to this flat, you knew. You knew that as well as the rest. You probably had a key.'

'No key and I didn't know which flat, just the general neighbourhood, but I did know you had something here . . . Lodge doesn't know, nor Archie Young.'

'That's a comfort,' said Stella bitterly. 'But then they are not privileged with your confidential, special information. I mean, they are not in your game, are they?'

Coffin had bent down to look under the bed, his foot had caught on something. He drew out a carrier bag.

'What's this?' He drew out a crumpled cotton shirt stained with blood, pale blue jeans, and a jacket, also bloody. There was a bright cotton skirt and toning blouse as well.

Stella looked. 'Those are mine, I recognize them. How did they get here?'

'How indeed?'

'I gave them to Maisie to give to the charity shop she works in.'

'Then we shall have to have a word with Maisie, shan't we?' said Coffin, his voice grim. Somehow he did not make it a question in which she could share. 'Do you trust her?'

'Yes, and yes.' Stella sounded bewildered. 'She's been my dresser on and off for years. We're friends.' She paused. 'More important, do you trust me?'

'Always and for ever,' said Coffin. He held his arms out. 'And you have to trust me. We may have a bad time, both of us, but we will get over it. No promises, but I think so.'

Stella lifted her head. 'Kiss me.' She sank slowly backwards under the pressure of that kiss on to the bed.

'I can think of better beds,' he said. 'What's happening here?'

'Always a tendency to fall in love with your leading man – in films more than in plays; the script demands it,' she said nervously.

'Are we playing lovers because the script demands it?'

'No. You know that.'

He raised himself. 'Then let's go home, we have a better bed there.' Besides, forensics would be all over this one. Even in a moment of love he remained the policeman. 'You will have to take those clothes off, in case they have traces, and I am afraid they will want to go over all your stuff, things you might have worn or brought here.'

'I don't like that.'

'It will happen. Mine today as well, I expect. Nothing can be overlooked.'

Stella realized once again, this time with an even sharper pain, what she had done to him. 'We are both in it, aren't we? I have dragged you in . . . I'll do anything you want.'

'Just co-operate. And don't try to be clever. Remember, they're clever too.' He added: 'I'll ring for a car to collect us.'

'No, let's walk. I would rather.'

'Not too tired?'

'No.'

Coffin hesitated, then said: 'There is something for me to say. I owe it to you to tell you something of what I've been involved with these last months.'

Stella looked at him without speaking.

'I was a member of a committee vetting security. Top-level

149

stuff. Spying on friends and colleagues. Treat it as a game, I was told.'

'And who were you watching?'

'I can't name names even to you.' Especially to you, because you were one of them. I was to watch Inspector Lodge and Sir Fred, who was no doubt watching me, Pip Eton – yes, his name came forward because of you, I knew about him, Stella. Also one person who managed to stay in the undergrowth and is a murderer.

'Not a nice game.'

'No, well, that's it? Still want to walk by my side?' Stella nodded. 'Thank you.'

As they emerged into the street, Stella said: 'I've remembered something . . . There was someone else here besides Pip. I heard another voice . . . There was a woman.'

What a lot was packed into that period when you were drugged, Coffin thought sadly.

11

Nothing in Coffin's life ever went as planned, a process he had long learnt to expect but was often surprised by all the same.

Even before he and Stella got to St Luke's, while they were still walking towards it, a police patrol car stopped and hailed him with relief.

'Sir, sir, they're trying to get you. I was told to look out for you . . . thought you might be walking the dog,' here the driver saw Stella and gave her something between a bow and a salute. 'Afternoon, ma'am.'

Stella smiled and took a step aside. It so happened she knew the driver because his wife worked in the theatre box office and he was a regular attender with surprisingly highbrow tastes.

He held out his phone. 'Do you want to use it, sir?'

Coffin looked at Stella with a smile and shrug, before picking up the phone. Paul Masters answered at once, relief in his voice.

'Glad to get you, sir.'

'I wasn't out with the dog.'

'No, sir, of course not, the dog's here, you left him with me, lying on my feet this minute.' In fact, he had had the pleasure of the dog's company all the morning. Briskly, he went on to report that there was a riot down at the Spinnergate Docks.

'Well . . .' began Coffin.

'Of course, it's being handled by Inspector Dover of B unit, but I knew you would want to know.'

'How big a riot?'

'Mini, sir. However, the media are there.'

'Damn!'

'Yes, sir, but it's not why I wanted to make contact.' Paul Masters drew breath. Distantly, Coffin could hear him politely requesting Augustus to get off his feet, please. 'Sir Fred is on his way for a meeting with you, he will be here in about twenty minutes.'

'Ah,' Sir Frederick Mantle was a prominent figure on the secret committee on which Coffin served. In fact, Coffin had the idea that Sir Fred was a member of the even smaller committee which controlled the larger one. There were always rings within rings, in his experience.

Paul Masters was not privy to all the secrets of Coffin's life, but he certainly knew something of the part played in life and circumstances by Sir Fred.

'What about Inspector Lodge?'

'On his way too, sir.'

'I'm on my way,' Coffin assured Paul. 'Keep Sir Fred happy if he gets there before I do.' A last thought: 'Get hold of Chief Inspector Astley and tell her I want a word.'

'Will do. She was asking for you earlier, sir.'

Was she? Coffin thought. What had she got about the death of Pip Eton or possibly the earlier victim, the one with fingers cut off and no name?

Coffin refused a lift in the patrol car, and turned back to Stella.

'Crisis?' she asked.

'A small one. Nothing to worry about.' Or so he hoped, although one never knew with Sir Fred. 'But I shall have go straight back. Can't linger.' And he gave her the smile she loved most: gentle, full of humour and self-knowledge.

She slid her arm through his. 'Let's enjoy the walk back.' She asked no questions, she had been his wife long enough to know that was something you did not do. 'Tell you what: I'll try and have a word with Maisie. Find out what she knows about the clothes under the bed. Can't believe there is any harm in her, she's such a good old thing.'

'I won't forget what you say about hearing a woman . . . If we get the chance, I will ask you to identify a voice. But think about it . . . as a professional used to the nuances.'

'I shall. I think it was a woman.'

Coffin nodded and kept quiet his conviction that good old things like Maisie could get up to a surprising number of little wickednesses if they felt like it.

They parted at the corner of Madely Street near to the police headquarters and within easy distance of St Luke's.

'I won't come any further with you,' said Coffin to his wife.

Under the interested eyes of several of his colleagues driving past in a van – on their way, he supposed, to the small riot – he gave her a brief kiss, then followed this up with a much longer kiss. A relieved and happy Stella responded with an enthusiasm that further delighted the happy band en route to subdue their fellow citizens of Spinnergate. Stella, of course, knew exactly what she was doing. While not always acting, she was never quite not acting. She waved her hand to him and strolled away, making a good exit.

She thought to herself: I will have a straight talk with Maisie and sort things out. She had never yet been in a situation where she could not 'sort things out' and it had not occurred to her that this time perhaps she would not be able to. She would telephone and let Maisie know she was coming. Yes, that would be wise.

She looked ahead to St Luke's and the theatre complex which lay just around the corner.

Coffin called first into the viewing room where banks of screens showed the live pictures from the cameras set on the tops of roofs over the Second City. They commanded all the main streets and street corners. He looked at one street corner which was crowded with moving figures, on their way to the riot, no doubt. A van was turning the corner, the cameras were swivelling to follow.

The sergeant in charge of the room said that they had been asked to keep a check on that van.

Coffin watched for a while, then went away to the meeting in front of him.

Coffin found Inspector Lodge already waiting for him in the outer office, with Phoebe Astley lounging in a chair by the window. Phoebe was in jeans and a tweed jacket – as Stella had once said, 'She has the legs for it' – while Inspector Lodge was darkly clothed in anthracite grey. Both of them stood up as he came in.

He acknowledged them with a nod and a wave towards his own room. 'Go through, I'll be with you.' Then he turned towards Paul Masters. 'How's the riot going?'

'Pretty nearly tidied up, sir, But you can see for yourself on the TV.' He pointed to one of the screens across the room, where, the sound off, a figure could be seen against a background of men and women waving flags demanding ACTION AGAINST THE ENEMY.

Coffin winced. 'No, thank you. And Sir Fred?'

'Telephoned through. His car is held up in the traffic – the riot, you know, but he will be here shortly.'

It was always the way with Sir Fred. He was always arriving shortly and leaving shortly after that. A man of high motives and much mobility.

'Buzz when Sir Fred touches ground here.'

'Right, sir.' Paul Masters was wearing one of his brighter suits that day, he was never one for the dark outfit, his spell in the uniformed branch must have been a severe trial to him, and today he was in cream and tan. Coffin had named it his defiant suit and wondered whom his efficient, ambitious, but aggressive young assistant was battling with today. Probably Coffin himself, he thought, as went into the other room.

He sat down quickly at his desk, tidy as usual, with all papers neatly stowed away. The problems to be dealt with were there, though, even if hidden in the drawers or in files.

'Phoebe, glad you are here. I want you to do something for me.' He sat down and scribbled an address. Linton House, Fish Alley. 'Check over this place. Take a team in – forensic,

154

the lot – and see what you get. Come back to me. Quietly.'

Phoebe stood up. 'Right, I'm off. Can I have a bit more information?'

'When you discover the name of the owner you will understand.'

She looked at him, frowning. 'You know.'

'I know.'

He's dumping me into something, Phoebe decided, he's done it before. But fear not, friend, I will fight my way out.

'I want you to come at it cold, form your own impression. You may get a surprise.'

'Shock is the word that comes to mind,' said Phoebe. 'I wonder why?'

'What did you want to see me about?'

Phoebe considered. 'You know I've been working on the copies of *The Stage* that were used to wrap up the corpse? They match with those left behind in the theatre. The fingerprints on those found on the corpse were very smudged. But one or two were clearer . . . they matched with those of Miss Pinero.'

Silence. Inspector Lodge kept his face expressionless.

Coffin did not quite manage this, but he was calm.

'How did you get her fingerprints?'

'She supplied me with them yesterday.'

'Very sensible of her.'

'Not surprising to find them on the newspapers, they were from her office.'

Coffin sat in silence for a second, then he said: 'You have the address. Go to the flat on the second floor.'

Phoebe nodded. 'I'll be off then. Sounds like work. Don't tell me you've got a body waiting for me.'

'No body, but there may have been one there. I'm not sure about that.'

She raised an eyebrow. 'Our boy dressed up in paper clothes?'

'Could be. Find out for me. And nothing, as yet, for the media.'

155

So it has to be Stella Pinero again, Phoebe decided. 'I'll be on my way.'

She slid through the door as a buzz and a noise in the outer office announced the arrival of Sir Fred.

Grey-suited, small, plump, almost smiling all the time but never quite making it a broad grin. Stella, on meeting him once, had said that she would cast him as Dracula any day.

'Apologies for being late.' Sir Fred set great store on being punctual. 'Came through a bit of trouble on the way here,' he announced with satisfaction.

'Under control,' said Coffin.

Sir Fred continued looking at him, eyebrow raised.

'Two rival football teams, basically.' With added elements from all over the Second City, but he was not going to mention that. Coffin was reluctant to explain at all.

'Bad, bad.'

Coffin could feel his teeth grinding together as he bit back his irritation. He understood that the ability to create this irritation at will and thus weaken a protagonist was a valuable skill of Sir Fred's, but he did not relish being the victim.

So he smiled. 'Let me give you a drink. Whisky?'

Sir Fred was well known to like a certain malt whisky, so his answer would be revealing. If he said no, then that would be a very bad sign indeed.

There was a pause. It was ended by Sir Fred: 'Thank you, Jack.' No one called Coffin Jack. 'A little, thank you.'

Coffin got up to go to the armoire which Stella had picked up on a tour of France and brought back (at vast expense) for him.

'Neat,' said Sir Fred. 'Never water malt. Ice yes, water no.'

'I haven't any ice. But I could send for some.'

'No matter, no matter.'

Coffin turned to Inspector Lodge: 'The same for you?' Lodge did not refuse. Finally Coffin poured himself a drink, making it a careful, small one; he needed all his wits about him with this pair.

Then he sat down to study the two men; he was pretty sure that they had been discussing him already. It would be in character for Sir Fred to do this and for Lodge to listen, nodding sagely. Coffin found he was getting crosser with every minute that passed. He ranked much higher than Lodge, but it seemed that in the different world of security, Lodge had the pull.

So Coffin drank, kept a still tongue and waited for Sir Fred to utter. That gentleman was taking his time, which again irritated the Chief Commander, who was thinking of Stella.

Sir Fred put down his glass. 'I have admired you, Coffin, you know that.'

Do I? Coffin asked himself silently. I hadn't noticed it. Aloud, he said: 'Thank you.'

Obviously Sir Fred was getting ready to add a rider to his last remark of praise.

'But,' he began, 'you are too close to all this . . . your wife, you know. I think you should step back.'

Coffin did not answer. He was not surprised, but even angrier. He took a drink, offered some more to Sir Fred who accepted and to the Inspector who refused. Coffin leant across to fill the glass. If he trod on Sir Fred's toe to do so, he did not care.

'I understand what you're saying.' Coffin paused in pouring the whisky. He saw with pleasure that Sir Fred was sweating. Lodge looked cool enough, damn him. 'But I don't think I can, and for the very reason you suggest that I should: my wife.'

He put down his own drink, largely untouched, and stood up. It was a spontaneous movement of protest, no threat intended, but Sir Fred pushed his chair backwards quickly. Lodge coughed.

'Now, now,' Sir Fred said. 'Don't take it amiss what I say. It's in your own interest, my dear fellow. And Stella's. Keep out. Let others take over.'

Coffin looked straight at Lodge.

'No, no, not necessarily our friend here.'

'Inspector Lodge is involved too,' Coffin pointed out coldly. 'He has Peter Corner. Missing.'

'He's been in touch.' Lodge spoke up quickly.

Coffin decided it was his turn to stand on his dignity. 'Has he now? I was not informed.'

'You would have been. I tried to contact you today, this very afternoon, but you were out of touch.'

Coffin briefly admitted the truth of this to himself while still not forgiving Lodge. Then he saw a flash of expression on Lodge's usually impassive face . . . He cares for that man, Coffin told himself. God, how could I not have seen that about Lodge? He and Corner, not a relationship, almost certainly not, but he is attracted. Well, I never.

Lodge swivelled in his chair, then took out a handkerchief to blow his nose. He had given himself away, and he knew it. Sir Fred was watching, no surprise there. So he knew. There were no secrets in the world they both moved in. No doubt this side of Lodge was used.

'We will talk about this later,' said Coffin, in a voice that offered no promises.

He turned to Sir Fred. 'I think there is something else, sir, isn't there?'

Sir Fred finished his drink, carefully setting down the glass so that it should not mark the polish of the table at his elbow. 'Clever of you to see it. Always knew you were a clever chap.'

Coffin waited.

'It concerns the first dead body. Di Rimini, or Bates as he was rightly called. By this time, did you or did you not know that he was a police snout?' Coffin nodded, unwilling to reveal what he knew or did not know. Keep Sir Fred guessing. 'No doubt you are surprised about my part in this, but I am obliged to have contacts here and there.' He did not glance towards Lodge, who was sitting still. 'Even if it flushes out people like Bates, the snout. Not much used and not much use either, as far as can be ascertained. He was not a man over-blessed with friends who confided in him, but he was a drinker. Mostly, I believe, he drank on his own.' Sir Fred looked a little sly, as if he knew that Dennis Garden counted as a friend. 'But he picked people up, or sometimes was picked up himself.'

Come on, Coffin muttered, get on with it. Don't swither.

'You know we can't choose the contacts we work with.' Sir Fred gave a seraphic smile.

'What are you working round to?'

'A person who drinks in the sewers of Spinnergate – joke, dear boy, one of our contacts, but we can't use the best people – informed us that di Rimini, also known as Eddy, had said he knew that a terrorist was at home in Spinnergate and was very close to the top man himself. I quote.'

Coffin said: 'Who is this man who passes all this on?'

'Did I say man?' said Sir Fred smoothly.

'From all I have learnt of Bates or di Rimini, call him what you like, he was not the sort to confide in a woman.'

'Well, frankly, our contact seems to fit either sex.'

'Two drunks talking together,' said Coffin. 'What reliance can you put on that?'

Sir Fred stood up. 'Look, it's no good us quarrelling, we won't get anywhere that way. I pass it on to you to think about what it suggests.'

Coffin stood up, too. 'Oh, I see all right: that di Rimini – I prefer that name, I think – was not just picked up off the street as someone who could be killed, dragging in my wife, but was killed because he had dangerous knowledge.'

Sir Fred nodded. 'It's worth thinking about.'

'Did he have names to offer as well?'

'No names.'

Coffin turned to Lodge, who had risen also. 'And what about your man? Has he got this story too?'

'No, or if he has then he hasn't reported it. He simply says he is working on a good lead.' Lodge sounded uneasy, which Coffin noted. Everyone was uneasy in this bloody case.

He turned to Sir Fred. 'Thanks for coming, thanks for telling me, but as you can see I am not going on holiday to the South of France. I am not getting out.'

'Never thought you would.'

'It may be taken out of my hands, of course. I see that. But the story about my wife knowing a suspected terrorist was passed on to me some time ago, so I have had time to think about it. Stella did not kill either di Rimini or Pip Eton. And for that matter, neither did I.'

'Never thought it for a moment.'

'Or had him killed.' Which is what you might have done yourself, you old sod, in a similar position . . . Except that Sir Fred would never get into any position of personal peril. That you could count on.

Sir Fred was actually smiling, although Lodge was as grave as ever, the perfect secret servant.

Coffin suddenly felt good. I got the better of that round, he thought.

Such moments can be dangerous, because that is ofen when life wipes out the joke.

As he got himself through the door, Sir Fred said: 'For what it's worth, I don't think Miss Pinero was meant as the contact.'

'Message from Miss Pinero, sir,' said Paul Masters, through the open door. 'She can't talk to her dresser, Maisie, the woman isn't there.'

Coffin sat at his desk, silent, troubled. You're never where you think you are, he thought to himself. The ground moves beneath your feet.

Because he had his secret, he had his own game, one he had entered into – what was the word? – obligingly.

He thought about it with sadness.

Get back to thinking about Stella, he told himself. Poor Stella was part of the game and she did not know it. He had used her, which was one of the reasons he must forgive her for Pip Eton.

He thought about the Production Room in the basement of his own police building, the room in which were stored all the artefacts which had had a place in crime: a blood-stained jersey, a six-pack of Coca Cola, and rows of radios and clocks. Each item, neatly packaged in a plastic bag, label-led and recorded in a register, lay on the steel racks which rose to the ceiling.

The copies of *The Stage* that had covered Pip Eton would

be there, stored away in safety, like the clothes from Francesco di Rimini. Unless Phoebe had kept out those newspapers which had Stella's fingerprints on them.

Unlucky Stella, he must get her out of this trouble, although at the moment he was unsure how to do it. It would come though, because it had to. A bell was ringing faintly in his mind, which was a good sign because a physical symptom often accompanied a genuine idea, he had noticed.

He had found that he got ideas from a study of the objects which had figured in a crime. Somehow the mind was acted upon by the touch of a piece of cloth, a leather bag, a dried bloodstain on a shirt. It was as if you had been there yourself at the scene of the crime. He never expressed this idea to his colleagues, who would have found it fanciful.

But he knew what he had to do first: go to see Maisie and ask her a few sharp questions about the clothes she was supposed to have given to a charity shop but which had turned up under Stella's bed in the flat. 'Maisie as a priority, then the Production Room.'

The clothes themselves would end up in their plastic bag on one of those steel racks in due course, no doubt. The whole room was a bit like the property room in the theatre, only here all the plays were over. Dead and done with.

Before setting out, he rescued Augustus from his hiding place under Paul Masters' desk, put on his leash and walked him to the car. 'Sorry to see him go,' Paul said, watching them. 'I like the little chap, and I think he's beginning to like me.'

Augustus obligingly wagged his tail, although Coffin knew well that this meant nothing more than a general pleasure in being a dog.

Coffin appreciated the company of Augustus because he could talk to him and get no answer back, and he enjoyed this in a world which so often returned a reply he did not want.

'Get in the car, boy. You're coming with me on a visit. We won't be taking Stella, and yes, that is where she sits, and you won't be getting out of the car.'

Augustus settled down on the front seat. He was too short to see out of the window, but he liked the motion of the car. He was aware of Coffin's voice droning on in his ear, but he paid no attention since none of the magic signals like walk or food were coming through.

Traffic was heavy as the evening dark drew on. It was getting dark earlier now, summer was over, autumn well advanced, you could feel the distant march of winter.

He spoke to Stella on his car phone. 'I'm on my way to speak to Maisie. She may be home by now.' She had better be there. 'How are you?'

'Better for the afternoon with you. But busy. Letty is in control, more or less. She's marvellous with money.'

'As we know.'

'As we know. Letty is cross but working fast; Jane is trying to make me build up her character, which I won't do, it would throw the play out, and Fanny is being sweet. Alice has migraine and is away. Everything pretty much as usual.'

She did indeed sound happy. It was wonderful the way she bounced back. Theatricals had to, probably, with such an up-and-down life.

There was one more call to make. 'Archie? How's the riot?'

'A load of nonsense.' The Chief Superintendent was tired and irritated. 'Someone just wanted some publicity. Got it, too. We shall all be on the TV news.'

'I want you to go to Linton House in Fish Alley. It's off Arrow Street.'

'I know where Fish Alley is.'

'Flat on the second floor. I think it may be where Pip Eton was killed. I have sent Astley there, but it's for you, too.'

Archie Young grunted a reply. 'We have the Ferguson and Giner Eccles fraud tidied up. Two arrests; the courts may muck it up, but we've done our bit.' The Chief Superintendent had not been involved in the riot at the docks, that had been handled by the uniformed branch, B unit, and CD (Crowd Control and Disperse) unit in particular, but he had his own problems of which this big fraud case was one. The

162

di Rimini and Pip Eton murders were just another case, even if an interesting one.

'I hear there's a floater turned up by the Great Harry Dock,' he said. 'But the word is that it's a suicide, so not one for us. Right, I'll get down to Fish Alley, but Astley's efficient, she'll have it all organized.'

'I want your eye on it.'

'Right, right.' Young was well up on the saga of Stella Pinero, as indeed were all his colleagues. As one wag had said, you'd have to be living up a tree in Greenwich Park with the birds not to know. Stella was admired and liked, but was also the subject of intense speculation and gossip.

'The place belongs to my wife, long lease, dates back to the days before St Luke's. Keep it as quiet as you can.'

Young said, 'Right, right,' again. He hung on to his telephone until Coffin broke the link. Bugger all, he thought, he deserves better.

12

Coffin had driven to where Maisie lived. He was studying the house with some interest. This time round he wanted to see what Maisie had made of the place. You could tell a lot about a person from what they did to their home, and he needed to understand Maisie. He could see that she cared for the place, the paintwork on the door and on the window frames was red and white, and looked to be new. Or if not new then washed recently. The curtains on upper and lower windows hung crisp and fresh. Yes, Maisie was a good house-keeper. He hadn't taken that in last time, now he did.

The house also looked mildly prosperous. How much did dressers earn? Not a great deal, he imagined. Possibly Maisie had other resources. It was worth thinking about. In Coffin's sad experience money was always worth thinking about. The most unlikely people had their little secrets here. In his own family, his sister Letty probably had more than one secret and not so little either. He had none, partly as a matter of professional ethics, but also because he had never had any money to speak of. He did not despise money-makers like his half-sister Letty, but it was not his style. Or luck, he might have said. He did not despise money-makers, he just was not one.

He walked slowly down the narrow garden path, pausing to study the door with its brass knocker and brass bell. The trace of blood was still there, by the door bell. Coffin rang the bell.

No answer.

He waited, then rang again. He could hear the bell ringing

in the hall, but no one came. So he tried the knocker; experience had taught him that householders often came to a hearty series of knocks because the neighbours could hear it.

He knocked several times more, then drew back to look at the house.

All right, Maisie was out. She might be at the theatre, but Stella wasn't performing, so it was not one of her nights and Stella had not been able to find her there. As always now when the image of Stella appeared, he felt anguish. Since she had come back into his life, he had known great joy, but he seemed to have become sensitized to other emotions; happiness, misery, he felt them all more keenly. It was as if being with Stella had peeled a layer of toughness from him.

He shook himself like a dog (had he picked this up from Augustus? – a sardonic underthought) and went back to hammer on the door. If the bloody woman was there, he would flush her out.

This time he rang the bell and banged on the door all at once. It made a satisfying noise but did not produce Maisie.

But the front door of the adjoining house opened and out popped a woman. She stood on her doorstep and demanded to know what was going on. 'Enough to wake the dead. My husband works nights and he needs his sleep.'

As if to support this, a tousled head appeared at an upstairs window. 'Bloody noise. Shut it, will you.' He left his wife to carry on.

'It's no good banging on the door like that. If Maisie doesn't want to open the door, she won't.'

Coffin explained mildly that he needed to talk to Maisie. Had she gone away?

'No, not her, she always gets me to look after the cat when she goes away. Anyway, she's there. I saw her come back from shopping and go inside.' The woman marched back to her door.

From above came a shout: 'Bang again and I'll get the police in.'

'I am the police.'

The woman swung round, walked over and stared at him. 'Yes,' she said after consideration. 'You could be, you've got the look. Bit old though, aren't you, to be on street work?'

'We don't all get the promotion we should do,' said Coffin.

'That's true enough,' said the woman. 'Look at my husband: twenty years in that place and nothing to show for it except a bad back.'

A voice from the window called out: 'Stop gassing, Ena, and come back in. I want my tea.'

Ena gave a shrug and turned away. 'Try the door,' she said, over her shoulder. 'Maisie doesn't always lock it behind her.'

'And you ought to know, you cow,' called the irate voice from above before drawing the window down with a bang.

Lovely man, thought Coffin, as he returned to the front door with whose appearance, down to the last scratch on the paint, he now felt thoroughly familiar. Still, who knew what Ena was like to live with?

He hesitated for a minute, then took hold of the brass handle. It turned, the door opened.

Coffin stepped inside. He was careful and had not made much noise but no one shouted, 'Who's that?' at him. He looked around him: a small hall carpeted in red, a door to the left, and another at the end of a short corridor. A staircase rose sharply in front of him. Break your neck on that if you didn't step carefully, he thought.

'Maisie, are you there?'

He opened the door on the left, put his head round the door, and stared in to a tidy sitting room with a round table in the window, four upright chairs covered in red velvet and a sofa of the same. There was a television set against the wall.

All ordinary and quiet enough.

Only one odd thing: the television was on, but with the sound turned down. Coffin stared at the mouthing face of a woman with a froth of bright red hair. He thought he knew the face, which was that of the hostess of a chat show. The camera moved to take in the ranks of the audience, some of whom were laughing: the red-haired lady had made a joke.

People did leave the television on with the sound off; he had done it himself if the telephone rang or someone called unexpectedly.

There was a teacup on the little table by the sofa; Coffin touched it: cold.

It was hard to be sure on this carpet, but that looked like a stain by the door, a drop, a blotch. He bent down to touch it, one delicate flick with a forefinger.

Blood.

Perhaps it was already too late to be calling Maisie's name.

He walked down the corridor to the kitchen, only to find it empty. There was a milk jug by the kettle which still had a trace of warmth in it. Hot not so long ago, he thought.

Moving more quickly, he went up the stairs. The door was open to the bedroom. A chair was turned over and the telephone pulled from the table to the floor, where it lay quietly, no longer making the scream some telephones make when disturbed in their sleep.

He must find out how long it took for a telephone to go quiet after it had been knocked from its hook.

Without realizing he was moving, he found himself standing in the bathroom.

There was blood on the floor, blood in the bath, blood where Maisie lay with her head backed against the wall. Blood on a small bundle of tabby fur.

They needn't have killed the cat as well, he thought.

He looked down at Maisie's body, then he knelt for a closer look, being careful not to touch. She had been stabbed in the throat, that was where all the blood had come from. It was all over the bath and over the carpet. There must have been blood on the killer and hence downstairs.

It looked as if Maisie had been stabbed either in the bath or dropped into it, and that she then struggled out and got as far as the window.

It looked, at first glance, as though Maisie had not fought her killer. She was a sturdy, strong woman who could have put up a fight, of which there was no real sign.

167

Coffin walked down the stairs and out to his car where he used his telephone to call Paul Masters.

'Paul, get hold of Archie Young. He's probably in Fish Alley with Phoebe Astley, but he'll have his mobile on.' And curse him if he hasn't. The Chief Superintendent had been known to turn it off. 'And get him down here. There has been another murder.'

He gave the address and asked for the back-up crews of SOCO and forensics as well as the police surgeon.

'I will be here.'

He got out of the car, to find Ena and her husband on the pavement waiting for him. They advanced side by side, shoulder to shoulder, towards him. He was surprised to see that Ena was younger than she had seemed, while her husband, now wearing jeans and a white shirt, was not such a rough as he had looked when shouting out of the window.

'It's Maisie, isn't it?' Ena was fierce. 'What's happened? She's dead, isn't she?'

'Now, you don't know that,' said her husband, putting his arm round her.

'Shut up, Stan.' Ena turned her head to get a look as the first police car swung round the end of the road. 'Something is up, anyway, and I think it's Maisie.' She began to march towards Maisie's house. 'I'm going in to have a look. Maisie was a friend and I want to know.'

'Don't go in,' said Coffin, putting a restraining hand on her arm. 'Leave it.'

Ena swung round. 'She's been murdered . . . done in.' She had tears in her eyes. 'Poor cow.'

Her husband came up to her and took her by the hand. 'Come on, love, back into the house.'

'I want to know.'

'You'll know later,' said Coffin. 'I shall want to ask you some questions.' It was amazing what different faces people could put on. A few minutes ago Ena had been aggressive, angry, with a husband who had seemed surly and ill-tempered, but now here was a woman mourning a friend, being comforted by the sympathy of her husband.

168

What an old fool I am, he thought to himself. I ought to know that by now. Don't I do it myself, change my face to suit the circumstances?

Two more police vehicles had arrived. From the first, a white van, came the forensic team, and from the second, the tall figure of Archie Young.

Coffin took a pace towards him. 'You made good time.'

'Got the message, came straight away. Left Astley doing her stuff in Fish Alley.' He looked at the Chief Commander with well-contained curiosity, wanting to know how Coffin had found the bloodstained clothes in the flat, and what was to be made of it all. How did it fit with the double murders? He was assuming that the two killings were connected; that was the working assumption of the investigation. Could be wrong. And now there was this new death. And, once again, there was Coffin, discovering it. 'Another body?'

'Yes, Maisie Evans. She is, was, dresser to Stella. I came round to ask her about the clothes . . .' He stopped talking.

Archie Young waited, before saying: 'Would I be right in thinking you mean the bloodstained clothes in the flat in Fish Alley? And before we go any further, let me say: the accepted opinion is, yes, Pip Eton was killed there. Fingerprints and traces of old blood that can be matched with his, or we hope it will. Also on the clothes which you mention.' He was brisk and businesslike; this was a difficult situation for him.

'Yes, Stella was there with me when I found them. I had got Stella to admit that this was where Pip Eton had held her.'

'It's her place, isn't it? So you told me,' asked Young, bluntly, his eyes on the front of the house where a stream of police officers was now passing in and out.

'Yes, I know it and you know it. Stella thought it was a kind of secret. She had lived in it once; now . . .' he shrugged. Let Archie think what he liked. 'She let friends use it in a casual kind of way.'

'Casual,' nodded Young thoughtfully, stopped by a sharp look from the Chief Commander's blue eyes.

'Damn you, Archie. I am speaking to you as a friend.'

169

'Hearing it as one,' said Archie.

'But you are police as well, I know that. I just don't want Stella prejudged.'

'I like to think I am a friend of Stella's,' said Young with dignity.

'Her flat, her clothes, with blood on them. That's not so good. She told me these were clothes she gave to Maisie to take to a charity shop. I came round here to talk to Maisie myself – and found her dead.'

'Right. I've got the picture.' And a nasty one it is, thought Archie Young. All this, and her fingerprints on the copies of *The Stage*, it was beginning to mount up.

Coffin nodded. 'Whatever you are thinking, so am I. And I'm even more disturbed, you can believe that.' He moved towards the house. 'Let's take a look inside.'

Side by side they moved into the narrow hall. They were both big men, so that there was not much space. Coffin's shoulder knocked at a picture on the wall which fell to the floor.

Young picked it up, a romanticized picture of a cat family, mother and three kittens. 'Nice picture. She liked cats.'

'Yes,' said Coffin shortly. 'There's a cat upstairs in the bathroom with her.'

Young gave him a sharp look.

'Yes, dead too. The killer was not a cat lover.'

The police surgeon had finished his examination of the body. He stood up, took off his white rubber gloves, and nodded. 'Stabbed in the throat. Tore into an artery, accounts for all the blood, must have come spurting out.'

'How long dead?'

'Not long, matter of hours. Could be less. Rigor only just setting in. She's hardly cold.'

Coffin nodded. If he had been a bit quicker, then he would have met the killer.

'Looks as if she was stabbed in the bath, where she may have been pushed, and then managed to stagger to the window.'

'Does look like that. So she didn't die straight away?'

'No, although the killer may have thought she had. Who found her?'

'I did, less than an hour ago.'

Dr Marriot, the police surgeon, who knew Coffin, pursed his lips. 'This is pure speculation, and I wouldn't like to go into court without a better check, but I think it was not much before.'

'And the cat?'

'I haven't inspected the cat, and I'm no vet, but I make a guess it died soon after. Poor beast, just got in the way, I suppose.' He knelt down to take a look, prodding the little corpse with a gentle finger. 'Stabbed, like the woman.'

Dr Marriot prepared to depart. 'I've done my bit: it's for the pathologist and the forensic lads to get on now . . .' He looked round the room. 'She struggled a bit, I guess. Not a lot, though. Think she knew who killed her?'

'Very likely,' said Coffin, who did think so.

'What was the motive? All right, don't answer. You don't know.'

The doctor got himself out of the room in a good-humoured way.

'So why do you think she was killed?' Archie Young asked Coffin. Any real motive, he was asking himself, or just some nasty murdering bugger?

'I think she was going to tell me who she gave the clothes to that we found. I don't know how the killer knew she was going to do this, but I think that was the motive.'

'Maisie may have warned the killer herself.'

'Wish she could speak now.' Coffin moved towards the telephone which was still on the floor, awaiting the full attention of the photographer, who was still busy with Maisie, and the forensic team who were looking for scraps of this and that and dusting for fingerprints. He looked at the bedtable. 'I see she has an answerphone.'

Archie Young studied it. 'No calls waiting.'

'Sometimes you can hear an earlier call if she hasn't wiped it off but just let the tape run on. I've done it myself.'

'Haven't we all?'

'Let's listen.' Coffin put a handkerchief over his hand to tap the buttons.

Quietly, a voice was speaking. Coffin felt his neck stiffen.

There was a certain amount of noise from the comings and goings of the SOCO outfit and the forensic team gradually working their way round the house.

'Turn it up louder,' requested Archie. 'I can't hear.'

A moment later, for the Chief Commander's sake, he regretted having asked.

Stella's voice could be heard speaking softly. Coffin said, without much expression, 'I'll turn it back.'

Stella said: 'John will be coming round to speak to you, Maisie. I won't be coming myself, but you know what to say.'

There was a pause while Archie Young first looked away out of the window and then straight at Coffin.

'She couldn't have done it better if she'd tried for years, could she?' said Coffin, in a no-expression voice. 'But it was spontaneous. I wonder if we have it all? Didn't quite finish.'

'It doesn't mean anything, you can ask her.'

You bet I will, thought Coffin. Before I strangle her myself. 'Let's see what Maisie's last call was.'

'She may not have the last call check on her phone.'

'She has,' said Coffin. 'And guess where she dialled? The theatre.'

He met Archie Young's embarrassed gaze, and shook his head. 'Let's go downstairs.'

I suppose I could always shoot myself, he thought, and then he began to laugh. Oh Stella, Stella. What am I going to do with her?

Archie Young heard the laugh. He was glad the boss felt like laughing.

In the hall, Archie saw that the picture Coffin had knocked down was on the floor again. Two of the forensic team were there, Jem Sider and Al Jansem, he knew them both.

'Oh that's down, is it?' I knocked it down earlier. It's awkward, seems to stick out.'

'Yes, and I know why. You didn't look at the back.'

Jem showed the two men the back of the picture on which was taped a large brown envelope.

'Get it off,' said Coffin, 'and see what's inside.'

'Might be a bomb,' Jem was a joker. He had it off and handed it to the Chief Commander. 'Wait a minute, sir.' He held out a pair of white rubber gloves.

Coffin put on the gloves, and opened the letter. It might very well be a bomb, but if so it was likely to be of an emotional nature.

Inside was a thick wad of twenty-pound notes.

'Not a bad place to keep your savings,' said Jem, 'when you live round here where you might be broken into. Who'd think of looking behind a picture?'

Outside in the street was Jack Lowerly, the local CID inspector who would be handling the case. He looked awkward, if not surprised (since he had been well alerted), to be confronted with the Chief Commander and the Chief Superintendent. Both men were liked and respected, but rank told. You watched out, and checked how you were doing.

A darkened ambulance was waiting at the kerb to take Maisie's body to the mortuary where it would be given a careful examination by Dennis Garden. Since this seemed a safe observation, he said: 'Be getting the deceased off, sir. The Prof will be taking a look, but I don't suppose he will have much to add. Clear enough how she died.' Lowerly allowed himself to go on as his audience seemed to be listening. 'A real tragedy, a nice lady. My wife worked in the theatre for a while, in the office, and saw a bit of Maisie.'

Coffin nodded.

Lowerly, always a talker, went on: 'We're trying to locate the next of kin, but no luck so far, a solitary lady, her life was the theatre. Would Miss Pinero have any idea?'

'I'll ask her.'

'There will be a bit of money, I expect. My wife said Maisie liked to turn an honest penny.'

'Robbery doesn't seem to have been a motive for her murder.'

'So I gather, sir.' A foxy look came over Lowerly's sharp-featured face. 'There will be money in it somewhere.' He decided he had done well, and was moving away before he fell into trouble.

'You're a philosopher, I can see, Inspector,' said Coffin. 'But with murder there has to be something else as well as money.'

Lowerly left wondering whether he had done well or badly after all.

Coffin and Archie stood by the Chief Commander's car; Coffin shrugged.

'All the same, he wasn't far wrong,' said Young. 'Not always a straightforward motive for a murder, however much we try to show there is.'

There's no need to listen, he said to himself, watching his chief's withdrawn eyes. I'm only talking for the sake of talking, as I guess Lowerly was too – and making a better job of it than I am.

Coffin had heard him, because he gave him a wry smile. 'You and I know that sometimes there isn't a motive for murder – not a credible one – and that all we have is a killer and victim.'

'More than one killer, do you think?'

'Forensics ought to be able to utter on that . . . fingerprints.'

'If any.'

'If any. Body traces, fibres . . . There's always something if you look hard enough.'

Archie thought that you sometimes had to look mighty hard, but he kept quiet.

'I think just one killer, but that's a guess.'

'You're usually a good guesser.'

'Thank you. Experience, really, I suppose . . .' He paused. 'I have had a high-level warning to keep out of it.'

Archie, to whom all things were soon known, had heard about Sir Fred's visit.

'Stella will have to make a statement. And I would like

her to make it to you, not Astley. Lodge will have to be present, I suppose. It's his territory.'

'Right.' Archie Young recognized that in certain circumstances Inspector Lodge had to be accepted as important. He did not much like the man, but he understood that it was not Lodge's game to be liked.

Coffin said quietly: 'If Stella is seriously involved, I shall have to go.'

Archie was later, when he talked about this to his wife, to feel ashamed that his first reaction was where would it leave him? He had had John Coffin's support all the way through his career. They had worked together as a team, with Archie respecting the flair and intuition (not to mention plain luck) of his boss. With him gone, what would happen to Archie? His wife, robust and practical as ever, had poured him a large whisky and told him to grow up and be a big boy. He had not been quite sure what she meant by that, except a strong feeling she supported the Chief Commander, but women were always on the side of John Coffin.

Except possibly the one he had married. What was Stella Pinero up to?

He said goodbye to the Chief Commander and went back into the murder house. Then he rang Phoebe Astley on his mobile to tell her what was going on and to ask her about Fish Alley. He listened without comment to what she had to say and then, without mentioning this to Phoebe Astley, went off to take a statement from Stella Pinero.

John Coffin, meanwhile, drove back to his office, with a sleeping Augustus in the back of the car. He envied the dog his tranquil peace of mind. Then Augustus gave a tiny, muted growl from the depths of a dream. You too? thought Coffin.

In the office he checked with Paul Masters on all the matters that concerned them both in the day-to-day running of the Second City Force. No more riots, no more bombs and no armed robbery to take his mind off his own problems.

And then: 'There's a message from Chief Inspector Astley.'

175

The careful way of handing it over suggested to Coffin that it was not a message he was going to enjoy.

'How does she manage to get a fax out of Fish Alley?'

'Don't know, sir.'

Coffin grunted, reading what Phoebe had to say.

'The Todger is round here in Fish Alley,' Phoebe began without preamble, 'he has with him his young man, Pete Corner, the one we thought originally had been murdered, and who was the Todger's hidden man to check on the bombmakers. Not naming any names, but claims to have been following an interesting suspect from the theatre complex to Fish Alley over several days. Again naming no names, he says the evidence he has from the Anti Terrorist unit is that a group of six was responsible: four outsiders and two locally based. Pip Eton was one of the second lot. The feeling seems to be that he was killed by one of his colleagues. Apparently, this is not unknown in the business, so Pete says. Some connection with the old KGB, no doubt, trained there perhaps. Joke.'

But only half a joke, thought Coffin.

As an extra, Phoebe added: 'Found a lot of blonde hairs around, likewise fingerprints.'

Stella owns the bloody place, Coffin muttered, you know that. My fingerprints must be there, too. And it's pure chance that hair from my head is not all over the bedclothes, not to mention what are known as bodily fluids.

Phoebe could be very irritating.

'And we have what looks to be the murder weapon. I'm linking up with Archie Young, just in case.' A characteristic Phoebe Astley parting comment: 'Pete's a lovely lad, I can see we could work together well.'

Damn you, Phoebe, thought Coffin. For God's sake keep out of Pete's bed.

13

Chief Superintendent Young was sympathetic. 'What I have to ask you,' he began, then hesitated. He never knew how to address Stella in a formal way – when they met for drinks or dinner, that was easy but now . . . Should it be Miss Pinero or her married name? So he kept it professional, Miss Pinero. It did distance the Chief Commander a fraction. 'Just some questions about today.'

Stella looked at him, wide-eyed and apprehensive. 'But I've already answered –' she began. Her face was very pale.

'I have your earlier statement about Pip Eton and your involvement with him.'

He could see from Stella's face that she had begun to take in that this was a new and serious inquisition. She was an actress, of course, and knew how to milk a situation. He had to take that into account.

A picture came into his mind of all four of them at a police dance, and how lovely Stella had looked in a plain black dress with pearls at her throat. All real, too, by the look of them, his wife had said with envy. And how, when he had told Stella a few days later how beautiful both of them thought she looked in black silk and pearls, she had laughed and admitted the pearls were real but borrowed.

He hadn't wondered then if that was true, but he did now. And then he remembered how, on another occasion, she had comforted his wife when their eldest son was in a coma after a road accident. No silk and pearls then, just a little cotton dress. She had been more help than his own mother, who had sat there weeping; more help than he had given himself. And she had looked after the other child, then cooked an evening meal for the lot of them (well, micro-waved, but who said you had to be a cook?) and stayed the night so the two of them could go back to the hospital.

No acting there.

'Miss Pinero,' he said, 'we can take the statement here or we can go the station, as you prefer.'

He had brought with him the youngest and mildest of the detectives, Teresa Behr, known, as might be expected, to her colleagues as Teddy Bear. He had thought that Teresa might make Stella feel relaxed. Instead, he saw that Stella was casting uneasy glances at the pretty young woman with her air of quiet competence. Inspector Lodge had been busy in Fish Alley and unable to attend. Good.

The Chief Superintendent had passed Letty Bingham and Alice Yeoman on his way through the corridors, the first of whom he knew by sight and the second he could not fail to know by name since Letty was shouting at her angrily for not being around when wanted. 'But who is, in this place?' she had ended. 'Actors!'

Alice had broken away from Letty to ask the Chief Super-intendent what he wanted, then made a good guess and told him Stella could not see him.

He ignored this advice. An interesting woman though, with good deductive skills; they could do with one like her on the Force. He did not fail to notice that she threw off Letty, no mean feat in his opinion, and slid into the room behind them, stationing herself near Stella.

Guard or protector?

'I will talk here,' said Stella, her voice unsteady.

Alice spoke up. 'Can't you see she's crying?' she said fiercely.

'You've heard about Maisie?'

'Of course she has.'

'Let Miss Pinero speak for herself,' said Archie Young.

'Yes, I know,' said Stella quietly.

'Who told you?'

'Word gets round quickly here,' said Stella.

It was no answer so Archie sat there, waiting.

'I told her,' said Alice. 'It's all over the place, everyone knows. We're not dummies here, you know.'

Archie Young took action. He stood up. 'I think we will talk down at the station, Miss Pinero.'

Stella did not look at Alice. 'Hop it, Alice,' she said wearily. 'You mean well, but leave me to it.'

DC Behr held the door for Alice, thus tacitly passing her judgement. Archie nodded his thanks to her. She'll go far, that Behr, he thought. Mind you, the other one might, too; a fighter.

He turned back to Stella.

'She's a protégée of my husband, he got me to give her the job,' Stella said as Alice disappeared. 'I have wondered if she was his daughter, but he says not, says she is the child of a colleague, now dead, whom he owed . . . They don't look alike, so I believe him. She's not a theatre person at heart, but she makes herself useful.'

Archie was not sure if Stella was making a joke about Coffin's daughter or not. Probably not, he thought, so he allowed himself a smile, a soft-duty answer for everything, then took her through the story of Fish Alley.

She explained, with a good grace, that yes, the flat belonged to her, that she had suppressed this fact when she first told her story. Yes, she knew now that Pip Eton had been using it, but she had not realized it straightaway. Yes, she had been imprisoned there, or felt she was, even though in the end she had escaped with ease. She skirted round the nature of her relationship with Pip Eton, but managed to say she had heard a woman's voice, and Archie let her leave it there.

For the moment.

Then they talked about the bloodstained clothes, the jeans and so on. Stella seemed quite willing to discuss this matter. He moved on.

'You knew that the Chief Commander was going to visit Maisie about the clothes, your clothes, that were found under the bed in Linton House?'

179

'Of course, I knew. He told me. I wanted to go myself, I would have done, but I got caught up with things here.' She looked around her. 'It's always like that in the theatre, set one foot inside and the tasks descend on your head . . . I expect it's the same in your job.'

Archie agreed that it was.

'Did you make a telephone call to Maisie?'

Stella said: 'If you ask that, then you know that I did. I don't know how you know.' She considered. 'The answerphone, I suppose, she had it on, although she answered.' She shrugged. 'Oh, well, you know what it was about: the clothes.'

But we only know the tail end of the conversation, the bit that didn't get wiped. Erased, that's the word.

'What did you mean when you said to her: "You know what to say"?'

Stella studied her hands. 'Ah well, you see, I had told my husband that I passed on clothes that I no longer wore to Maisie for a charity shop. That was not quite true.'

'What was true?' He was aware of DC Behr quietly taking notes.

'I sold them. Some of my clothes were expensive and not much worn, and you know the theatre . . . we never have any money, a lot of us sell clothes, shoes and handbags even . . . Maisie did it for me. She took a rake-off, of course.'

Of course, she did, with knobs on, more than you knew, probably, hence her hidden money.

'And you didn't want the Chief Commander to know?'

'No, he has to know now . . . but I wanted Maisie to handle it tactfully. He's so generous himself, I didn't want to seem mean.' Stella shrugged. 'Oh, I don't know. I was all mixed up.'

'I see.' He wasn't sure that he did, nor if he believed her. 'And did she make a telephone call to you?'

Stella shook her head. 'No.' She shook her head again. 'No, I never spoke to Maisie again.'

She hesitated. 'How did Maisie die?'

'We think she let her killer in, and then was killed.'

'How was she killed?'

'She was stabbed,' he said reluctantly.

'So, is there a connection with the other deaths?'

'It seems likely, doesn't it? But we don't know yet.'

This time, the tears that sprang to her eyes were real.

The Chief Superintendent asked a few more routine questions about times and so on, more to keep the interview going while he watched Stella than anything else.

Finally he said, 'Well, thank you.' He looked at DC Behr, who stood up, smiled at Stella, and walked away. Archie followed. At the door, he paused and looked back.

'Sorry I had to make it so formal, but it seemed best.'

'Oh, sure. I understand. I'm glad it was you asking the questions and not someone else.'

Archie nodded. Like Phoebe Astley, for instance. She wasn't out of that wood yet, though she didn't know it. There was a going over from Inspector Lodge ahead of her, one of his specials, with his own particular brand of questioning. He would be there asking about Pip Eton and also about the first death of all, that of Francesco di Rimini.

He longed to light a cigarette and offer one to Stella, but he was a dedicated ex-smoker who still had hankerings when under pressure, as now: he was walking a tightrope here between loyalty to Coffin and loyalty to the job. And there was his own career to consider. He was beginning to see that they might sink or survive together. Tonight he would talk it over with his own wife and benefit from her advice; he trusted her judgement more than his own, which seemed to him the right way round in a marriage.

She admired John Coffin while being slightly envious of Stella's glamorous career. His wife had a career of her own, she did not mind being outshone by Stella, but she had once admitted rather wistfully that she would have liked those clothes!

He left Stella then, thanking her again for her help.

'Is that the end?' she asked nervously.

'Probably a few more questions, but don't worry.'

'That's what doctors say when there is everything to worry

181

about.' But she said it with spirit and did not attempt to detain him.

He admired her for that: she was a fighter. On the way out, he passed Alice, also a fighter, he judged. A hefty young woman, too; he couldn't see her playing Ophelia, but perhaps there was a place for everyone in the modern theatre.

As he took in the aggressive tilt of her square shoulders, he allowed himself a passing wonder about her sexual stance. If she preferred women, that explained her manner – half-protective, half-hostile – to Stella Pinero. Not likely to get any change out of Stella, who was enthusiastically hetero. He knew that performers could be any which way, but not Stella, not the Chief Commander's wife.

Archie Young nodded politely to Alice and moved on; he had a very straightforward attitude to sexual matters. Too straightforward, his wife had once hinted. A hint Archie did not take and, in fact, hardly recognized for what it was.

Archie's wife was herself a policewoman, currently chairing a committee on pornography and women, so she was a very knowledgeable lady. It might be a good idea to get her to take a look at Alice.

He turned back for a last word with Stella. 'Work on remembering the woman's voice,' he said. Wondering if there really had been a woman.

Stella gave him an opaque look.

John Coffin, with Augustus once again firmly attached to him, was working in his office, checking through reports with Paul Masters. If he himself was destined to be a life peer when he retired, as had once been sourly predicted, then he would see that Paul was promoted. Archie Young, so long his friend and ally, would have to be included in the pantheon somewhere, but he was a detective pure if not simple and without the administrative skills the top jobs demanded. And Inspector Lodge could be moved on.

But I am not going yet, Coffin told himself. Those who think so can wait and see.

Before he did anything else, he had to telephone Stella. She was in her office, so she answered promptly.

'You might have told me you were sending a great big dragon round breathing fire and asking questions.'

'I don't believe that Archie breathed any fire.'

'I admit he is a nice friendly dragon at heart, but he tried. He did a little bit of puffing and huffing. He sends out rather nice smoke for a dragon.'

'You're making me jealous.'

'No need, but you might be jealous of Alice, she's been eyeing me a bit.'

'Has she?'

'You don't sound surprised. But don't worry, I'm not really her style and she is certainly not mine.'

'Glad to hear it.'

'I think I know who is: Letty, judging by the way Letty was shouting at her. Angry.' Stella managed a laugh.

'Letty?'

'Yes, she picked it up and reacted. Energy was crackling through her.'

'You said anger.'

'Often the same thing with Letty.'

That was true enough.

'I've dropped you in it, haven't I?'

'We will talk later,' he said gently. 'In fact, I ought to apologize to you.'

'What do you mean?'

'I will explain, but later.' Not a superstitious man, he kept his fingers crossed.

They ended there and he returned to Paul Masters.

'I'm off to Fish Alley.'

Paul Masters nodded.

'The Chief Superintendent is talking Stella through various episodes.'

Masters gave another nod. He knew; he was the man who knew everything.

'I believe she will have to speak to Inspector Lodge . . . I shall see him myself.'

'He's at Fish Alley,' said Masters. Phoebe Astley would not like that.

'I know.' Phoebe had told him. Coffin asked: 'Anything further on the riot?'

'A white van was tracked to a house in Dedman Street, just beyond the Spinnergate tube station . . . the ring leaders were inside. They've been brought in to be questioned. Inspector Dover is well pleased.'

'Good. It was an arranged thing then, not spontaneous?'

'No, there was a bank robbery planned for the same time . . . didn't come off. The new CCTV cameras tracked three men in a stolen car on their way there . . . They have been brought in too.'

A busy day, but a commonplace in the Second City, and not without its successes.

This time he did not walk but drove himself to Fish Alley, where the kerb in front of Linton House was lined with police cars.

Inspector Lodge was standing on the stone steps to the front door, deep in thought. He looked up to see Coffin park his car. 'Thought I would find you,' said Coffin. 'Had a chance to look round yet?'

'A bit. I've been talking to Peter Corner.'

'Oh yes, he's the man you had planted with the building firm.'

'Yes, a building firm is always a good place to put a man, a sleeper, which is what Pete was more or less. Builders move around, get to know all the gossip.'

'So they do.'

'To tell you the truth, I had had my doubts about the firm I got him into. They had been doing some work on contract in Belfast, I thought they were worth watching.'

'And are they?'

'The Archers seem to be clean enough, although when Pete went missing I did wonder. And the dead man being found in a house they were working on . . .' Lodge shrugged. 'But nothing has turned up that incriminates them. Astley's got a nose for that sort of thing,' he said admiringly, 'and

184

she would have smelt anything there was. She says not. I could do with her on my team.'

Coffin said nothing. He knew well that the men and women who worked with Lodge were a group of individuals who followed their own line, investigated in their own way, and although loyal to their mates were not team workers. It was not always safe to think of yourself as a team in their questionable world. Phoebe might do well in it, he granted Lodge that much.

The flat was quiet, but not empty. You could feel the presence of the police all over it.

Phoebe Astley was in the sitting room with Peter Corner. She was pouring coffee from a tall carton into white plastic mugs.

'Like some coffee, sir?' she said as she handed a mug to Peter Corner, a tall, dark-haired young man with bright blue eyes. Coffin could see straightaway that she was giving Corner one of her more flirtatious treatments. It was a treatment, sometimes you felt the better for it and sometimes much the worse. Corner looked unmoved, which Coffin judged to his credit.

'Have a sandwich.' Phoebe held out a plate. 'We were so hungry that Pete kindly went along to Max's and brought grub back. Cheese and chutney, ham and salad, and smoked salmon. Try the salmon, Peter, it is said to be stimulating.'

She was deliberately baiting the Todger, who stayed expressionless but was probably chalking it up.

Coffin drank some coffee, black. Max made the best cup of coffee in the Second City. Even a plastic mug could not spoil it.

The whole feel of this room had changed since he had visited earlier that day with Stella. A forensic team, a clutch of photographers and several detectives had been through it, probing and looking, and changed the scent.

He stood in the middle of the room and demanded bluntly: 'What have you got?'

Phoebe took it upon herself to be the voice: 'In the first place, the clothes, the bloody bundle. From the nature of the

185

bloodstains down the front of the T-shirt, all down the leg of the jeans, and on the arms and front of the denim jacket, we feel sure that the killer was wearing them at the time of the killing. Forensics have taken them off to match with the blood of Pip Eton.'

'Right.' Coffin nodded. 'What else?'

Phoebe hesitated. 'No name tags, but they are good Italian jeans and denims . . . you say Stella thought they were hers.'

'Thought they could be,' he said tersely. 'She hasn't missed them. She keeps working clothes at the theatre.'

Phoebe spared a passing thought for a woman who could keep expensive clothes, which these were, as spare working clothes. 'Quite. Easily purloined.' She was rather pleased with her use of that word, put her in the Wilkie Collins or Edgar Allan Poe class as a commentator on crime.

'I want to look round.' He made a silent tour of the flat, followed by the others; he went into the bedroom where the clothes had been found, and looked under the bed. There was a fair amount of dust, which told him nothing he did not already know about Stella and housekeeping. He moved on to the bathroom, where he paused, studying the hand basin, the bath and the lavatory.

'Any traces of blood here?'

'Forensic took samples and will be coming back to us.'

Coffin nodded, and went on to the kitchen. He stared at the floor, which was carpeted. 'Looks a bit wet.'

'Forensics took a scraping.'

'And the sink?'

'From there too.'

He made no further comment, until they all came back into the sitting room.

He sat down and picked up his unfinished mug of coffee.

'That will be cold.' Phoebe seized the carton and shook it. 'Still some here, feels warm, let me give you a drop more.'

Coffin finished what was in his mug. 'I don't mind it being cold.' He turned to Peter, who was standing with his back to the window. 'Before we talk about anything else, what about those underpants of yours?'

There was silence. 'Is this important?' asked Phoebe.

'I think it is, I think it is very important. I wouldn't be surprised if Inspector Lodge did not agree with me. These were the ones found on the dead body in the bombed house in Percy Street.

'How do you think they got there?'

'I thought it was pure chance.'

'Did you? Why was that?'

'The reason I have my name inside is partly because the unit like us to be labelled in case we turn up dead – that's the hidden message for knowing eyes only – but I have my name written in marking ink because I use a laundry and they do get lost. I have lost several pairs. Other clothes too. If you have your name inside, the laundry is willing to refund you the loss.'

'And have they refunded you for these?'

'I haven't made a claim yet. I've had other things on my mind.' He had left them, of course, when he last visited di Rimini. They probably knew. Lodge must have guessed.

'You did not address your mind to how and why they turned up on a murdered man? I can see from Inspector Lodge's face that he has been wondering.'

Lodge moved his hands in front of his face, then drew them down as if he was wiping it.

'I had other things on my mind, you know, sir. I was following up a lead which led me here. I've been working as a temporary handyman in the local school, and doing the furnace here. It was my way to keep an eye on things here. But yes, I was out of touch, we don't always keep in touch in this game.' He was definitely defensive; ambition, rivalry with Lodge had driven him. Sex – unluckily he really liked di Rimini – had been a spur also. He wanted to avenge him.

'I think you knew where they could have been ... not who used them, because that would mean you knew the killer,' said Coffin carefully. 'But certainly where they might have been so the killer could use them.'

Peter looked at Lodge, then at Phoebe, who was giving him a careful scrutiny.

'Well, I never,' she said. 'I never would have put you down for one of di Rimini's pick-ups.'

'I was working a line, you often have to do things you don't like, act in a way that is alien, when you are on a job.'

'That's true,' said Inspector Lodge.

Peter shrugged. 'When the matter came up, when the question was asked, I would have said. But other clothes of mine have gone missing, including underwear.' To Phoebe's amusement, he spoke the words prissily, like a woman referring to her knickers. 'What do we call them now?' she asked herself, repressing her mirth. 'Briefs, bikinis?

'Oh, Pete,' she said, shaking her head. 'How you disappoint me. And I expect you are breaking Inspector Lodge's heart.'

'Cool it, Phoebe.' Coffin stood, drawing himself up to his full height. 'Did it never occur to you that you were compromised? That your work and status was known?' He turned round. 'I can see it occurred to Inspector Lodge.'

'Of course it did,' said Lodge irritably. 'I thought you were dead.'

'I came across Francesco – I called him Frank or Ed sometimes – at a pub down at Spinnergate. We chummed up, I thought he was worth working . . . And he was, it was something he said that put me on to Fish Alley and to watching this place here. I was already eyeing Miss Pinero. All right, I did keep mum and drop out, but we do in our business, and it was worth it. I got a strong lead on Pip Eton.'

'A strong lead,' said Coffin again. 'So what was it?'

Peter looked at Inspector Lodge, then made his own mind up. He was, so Coffin decided, fully the same rank as Lodge, and in the world in which both men moved, possibly his superior. How much of an act his mock repentance had been was not clear. God what a crew, Coffin thought. I wish I had never got mixed up with it all, but I couldn't keep out.

Briskly, speaking coolly and with command, Peter Corner said: 'We knew about Pip Eton, of course. He had been identified as a member of a small cell, associated with the bomb makers. He was a recruiting officer and the one with the money, but up to whatever he was asked to do, you can take

188

that for granted. He may have helped place the second bomb, he may not. Not sure.'

'Was his unit responsible for the bomb outside the shop in Spinnergate?'

'As I say, we can't be sure as yet. The main team came from outside. This lot were a reserve team, but they would have played their part. I've been watching them for some time, it's why I am in the Second City. Pip Eton hung around with some locals and was trying to make time with Miss Pinero. He was the paymaster, the money man, but also the professional soft man of the unit, the one that went out to make friends. He may also have been their M man, the one who got the transport, but his main use was to get a local contact. Well, he had one ready made, close to you.'

'So he did,' said Coffin. 'We know that.'

'But I didn't know about the house in Fish Alley, whereas Frankie did. He had a foot in the theatre world and these things get passed around. The woman Maisie knew, and she knew Frankie, they drank together.'

'She's dead,' said Coffin thoughtfully.

'Yes, now. And so is Pip.'

'So he is,' said Phoebe.

'Now, one school of thought says he was killed by a member of his cell for talking. Or for spending their money. I favour that view myself. I lived opposite for a week . . . sometimes I slept in my car, sometimes I didn't sleep at all. I watched Linton House. I was inside the place doing odd jobs, I watched Pip Eton go in the day his body was found. I didn't see him leave, but there is a back entrance where you could park a car. He may have left, dead.' This was the fullest statement the man had made so far.

'Any other comings or goings?'

With some reluctance, Peter admitted that a local bus ran past Fish Alley once an hour, that the stop was not far away from Linton House. No, he could not see who got on and off.

'So Pip could have got on it?'

'That is so. He wasn't a man who liked going on a bus.

189

Public transport was not his preferred way of getting about.'

Coffin ignored this.

'But he could have done?' Phoebe was not about to ignore anything.

'It's possible.'

'Anything else?'

'The second day I was watching, I saw Miss Pinero going into the house. Pip Eton had his arm round her, he might have been pushing her. Two days after that, I saw her leaving, on her own, she was walking fast. Running.'

'She herself has told me,' said Coffin.

'I confirm it, then.'

Score to you, Coffin thought, but did not like him any the better for it. 'You can confirm the days, can you?'

'If I'm not bullied. I get confused if I am bullied.'

'The Chief Commander will ignore that,' said Lodge quickly.

'All right, I didn't say it. Wipe it out, due to my absence of mind, when I forget where I am. But there is something else which might be of interest to you about the house.'

'What is it?'

'I went back to watch. There was another person there.'

'A woman?' Coffin asked quickly, remembering what Stella had said about hearing a woman's voice beyond the door.

'A woman, or a man? No, I can't answer. I only got a glimpse through the window, but it looked like a man.'

Coffin held out his beaker. 'Any more coffee, there? Thank you, and no, I won't have a sandwich.' There was a tension in his stomach that was not hunger.

He drained the coffee, lukewarm now, and put the mug on the table.

'I don't think Pip Eton was killed here. I can see no real evidence. The only blood was on the clothes, which could have been brought in.'

'The carpet in the kitchen –' began Phoebe.

'It was washed. If traces of blood appear, fine, let me know,

190

but otherwise, I think we have to look for another killing field.'

He walked to the door. 'Keep me in touch, Inspector.'

Lodge nodded assent, and got up to follow him out.

'Peter,' Coffin made his voice gentle, 'next time you have to leave anywhere in a hurry, take your underclothes with you.'

Phoebe closed the door quietly but firmly behind them. She and Coffin looked at one another.

'He's a clever fellow,' said Coffin thoughtfully. 'I could almost fancy him for the killing myself, but he's too sharp for that.' Oxford-trained, he thought, probably got a degree in philosophy. Or even theology, they were the really formidable outfit, weren't they? The real vultures, ready to pick the flesh off the bones.

'Shows you how they work, doesn't it?' said Phoebe. 'Turds.'

'Watch it, Phoebe.' She was letting her anger show.

'Oh, I get like that sometimes.'

She watched the Chief Commander go out to his car. The lovely Pete has made an enemy there, she thought. Good, and I'm another one.

'Sir,' she said, going up to the car. 'We found traces of a sedative in a bottle of wine, more in a teacup . . . Miss Pinero was probably doped. She may very well have lost track of time. In case you wondered.'

'Thank you.' He was grateful, he had wondered and never asked how it was that Stella had been imprisoned for several days without getting out. A sedative, she had mentioned that herself and I was sceptical even if I did not show it.

I know better now.

'Thanks, Phoebe,' he said again.

191

14

Once in the car, driving out of Fish Alley, he realized that Augustus had been with him, perhaps had been so all the time. No, that was not likely, Augustus was a dog who took his duties seriously, who would probably have snapped at Peter and snarled at Inspector Lodge.

No, not at Lodge, there was a man more deserving of sympathy than a snarl.

'Besides,' Coffin addressed Augustus, 'I snapped for both of us, didn't I?'

Off to the office, to tell Paul Masters that the Chief Commander was still around, and then off to find Stella.

The best place to look for Stella seemed to be the theatre.

Stella had decided that the theatre was a democracy in which every player, even those whose employment was temporary, should have a voice. Her own was loudest, of course, but the others were allowed a shout or two.

The local university supported the theatre with funds, so that some intellectual input was demanded. Out of every five plays, one might be an Ibsen or a lesser Albee even if the audiences were thin. She could rely on good reviews for these plays, however, in the university newspaper and in *The Stage*, even if their own dear *Spinnergate Herald* was hostile.

The democracy of the theatre was gathering in the bar to develop ideas for new productions. Stella was expected to look in later. She was admired for her skill as an actress and her ability to keep the whole show going. Letty Bingham was admired for her financial acumen, recognized to be vital, yet feared for the axe she could wield. But Letty, swift as ever, had sped away on a Concorde bound for New York. Checking her investments, one school of thought said, buying new clothes said another. No one disputed that while Stella was a lovely woman whose looks could survive slopping around in jeans and trainers, Letty had the best clothes, the sort you did not see and certainly could not buy in the Second City. This naturally did not increase her popularity.

Present that evening were Jane Gillam, Fanny Burt and Irene Bow. They had all three been in *Noises Off*, while Jane and Fanny had survived *An Ideal Husband*. They had started off with some scorn for the Wilde play but ended with an appreciation of Wilde's skill as well as his splendid jokes. As they worked they saw, contrary to what they had first thought, that most of his best jokes were at the expense of men. They had all enjoyed the Frayn, but agreed it used up a lot of energy because you were always on the move.

Jane went to the bar, returning with white Italian wine for them all. 'I would like to do a couple of the new, small Pinters, two together. One before the interval and one after.'

'I don't know. Thanks for the wine.' Fanny took a sip and considered. 'Would we get an audience round here?'

'From the university,' said Irene Bow. 'Not everyone round here wants light comedy.'

'Most of them do,' said Fanny. 'Or that's what Stella will say.'

'What about a Sam Shepherd? He's very strong.' Irene admired the American.

'Not for us,' said Fanny. 'Can't see it filling the seats, and you know what Letty can be like.'

Irene sipped her wine. She was happy to be in work, when so many of her friends were not. 'Just a suggestion.'

'You could put it up,' said Jane. 'Stella doesn't knock everything down.'

'Especially if there's a good part for her.' Fanny was a cynic.

'Oh well, you can't blame her, she invented this theatre.'

'So she could go on acting till she dropped.'

They were, all three, very young.

'She has turned down some good parts to stay here with us,' said Irene in support of Stella. 'Films, too.'

For a moment they sat in contemplation of a future in which they, too, might turn down a film offer. Except I never would, said Fanny inside her head. Not if the money was good.

'Do we actually count? I know it's a democracy and we have a voice,' said Fanny, 'but do they listen? Does Stella?'

Michael Guardian and Tom Jenks appeared through the door. 'I know who does listen, girls. We do, especially if you're buying us a drink.'

'Buy your own,' said Fanny. 'You earn as much as we do.'

'It is true', agreed Tom, 'that the money is equally meagre for us all, taking no account of the extra weight we men bring.'

'Which is considerable, in your case.'

'True.' Tom was complacent. He was a large young man, not handsome but pleasant to look at. He intended to be the sort of character actor, always in work, who ends up with an Oscar for playing himself.

'So what were you talking about?' Michael had brought some drinks over.

'Plays, productions, casting – what else do we talk about?' This was Jane, in one of her sharper modes. 'I wondered how much notice Stella takes of what we say.'

'A bit,' said Michael, who had been with the company longer than anyone else. 'I have known her do a modest late Pinter. You're jealous of her. But she did set this place up.'

'I've always wondered where the money came from,' said Tom.

'She had a series on TV and a film or two, and I daresay someone put money in. Anyway, it's run on a shoestring.'

'Yes, but it's her shoestring and we all dance to it.'

'Oh, Tom,' Fanny. 'You're jealous.'

'Aren't we all?' Jane asked.

'Yes,' said Tom. 'Fault admitted.' He drew his mouth down. He could look baleful when he chose. Or perhaps, Jane

194

thought, when he did not realize that he was giving himself away. He does suck up to Stella, she thought, but what's underneath eh? 'I'm jealous,' he went on, 'because you women have it easy, compared to men in the profession.'

Irene said, 'I'd like to try *The Women*, it has some wonderful parts . . . of course, it's period now, but that would be part of the fun, all thirties clothes.'

'Big cast,' pointed out Jane, who could see herself in it, possibly as the injured wife who wins out in the end. 'Some strong parts.'

'All for women,' said Michael, with emphasis. 'This isn't a girls' club, you know.'

Tom gave a groan. 'No, take pity on us and the audience.'

'Most of our audience are women,' said Jane. 'Especially at matinees.'

'They like to see a man, you know that, I know it, and you can bet Stella knows it.'

'True,' said Jane, the realist.

'Talking of which, our esteemed Stella has not been around much lately.'

There was a pause.

'She's in today,' said Irene quietly. 'She's looks white, though. Still, she's working as usual. Alice is doing props with her, the ones that were borrowed from the university. She said she would be along.'

There was another pause; they had all heard about Maisie.

'She must be upset about Maisie.' Jane looked sad. It was one of her best expressions, her features suited it, as she well knew. 'They've worked together for such a long time.'

'I can hardly bear to think about it.' Fanny shook her head.

'I'm frightened,' Irene admitted. A nervous look suited her also.

Tom said: 'I was nervous before, I don't mind admitting it. My digs got a blast in the Spinnergate bomb. I still haven't got glass in my window.'

'It's the third murder,' said Irene. 'Stella must feel safe, being married to top brass.'

195

'I suppose.' Jane was thoughtful. 'I think he's quite alarming himself.'

'Attractive, though.'

Michael said in a firm voice: 'I'm as sorry as you are about Maisie, she was a great old girl, part of the theatre, the old theatre. But the murders can't touch us.'

They were silent.

When Stella walked in, Alice by her side, they all started to talk at once.

'We're talking plays,' said Tom, blithely.

'Talk away. Now, I have consulted my six-month schedule – you know I try to work to it, although I sometimes fail –' her turn to smile. 'And I see we voted to do *Night Must Fall*.'

So much for our right to choose, thought Tom. His expressive face showed his thoughts which Stella read.

'Of course, none of you except Alice was with me then, but I assure you it was a democratic decision.'

There was silence.

'Yes, you're thinking what I'm thinking: not suitable at the moment.' She looked down at the list she carried in her hand. 'We had Bill Barton pencilled in for the killer, but, as it happens, he's involved in a TV series so he probably wouldn't have been free, although I believe he would have tried to honour his promise. So, no problem there.'

With a bit of make-up, I could have played the old lady in that play; there was one, wasn't there? thought Irene. Then she remembered Maisie and decided, maybe not such a good idea.

Stella went over to the bar to order a bottle of wine for them. She was talking as she went. 'I thought of Shakespeare, you always feel safe with Shakespeare, the play supports you, but I decided against; any Shakespeare needs more time, even though all of you will have done your stint in him. So I wondered what suggestions you have?'

Alice carried the wine over to the table, pouring it with a steady hand.

'Ayckbourn?' This from Fanny.

'Done him a lot here,' said Tom, who had been studying

196

past productions at St Luke's. 'In fact, there's a school production of one in the Experimental Theatre next month.'

'True,' admitted Stella, who had already made up her mind though she had no intention of showing her hand yet. 'But something light yet serious is a good idea.'

'*An Inspector Calls*?' Michael had played the inspector once, knew the part to perfection.

'Priestley is a good idea,' said Stella with conviction. 'I seem to remember we talked about it.'

'*When We Are Married*, then?'

'Now, that is bang on,' said Stella with even more conviction, grateful that she had not had to suggest the title herself. She had had the other play in mind if necessary, some tribute must be paid to democracy. But cheerful, rumbustious comedy was the thing.

She drank some wine before discussing parts. I really need a strong brandy, she thought. I should have left all this till later. But no, I wanted to get on with things, cling to normality, whatever and wherever that is.

'I think you are marvellous,' said Irene, 'when you must be so miserable.'

Stella did not answer. I am that, and more, said a voice in her head.

'I don't suppose I've taken it all in yet. First the bombs, then the murders.' I am well acquainted with unnatural death, she reminded herself, being married to a man whose work it is.

'Shall we be questioned about Maisie?' asked Jane.

'Yes, I expect you will.'

'I wonder what they will ask?' Jane sounded nervous.

What petty crime has she got on her conscience? Tom asked himself. Bet she's got a little stash of Ecstasy or such stowed away somewhere. Destroy it, dear, before they come.

'Oh, they will just poke around,' said Stella, vaguely.

'Answer up promptly and don't worry.' Alice, the child of a policeman, was firm. 'They aren't gods, you know, they can't see through you.'

Stella looked down at her hands. Sometimes I think my

husband can do exactly that. Not because he has some extra-sensory power, but because he is sharp, observant and clever.

'Don't be too cocky,' said Tom. 'I had an accident on my motorbike last year and they weren't nice at all.'

'I expect you were drunk.' Jane knew her friend Tom.

'Well, only a bit tipsy. All I did was to crack a shop window, but I broke my own nose.'

'Life's very unfair,' said Jane.

Suddenly, Michael said: 'I think Maisie was worried about something. She used to talk to me a bit – she liked men, liked a gossip with what she called her boys – and she let out to me that she was worried. She knew my father was a solicitor, so I suppose she thought I might be a good source of legal advice if she needed. "I could be in trouble," she said; she'd made me a cup of tea, she often did that. "Someone I knew years ago, an actor, as a young chap, I think he's got me into something I'd rather not be in. It could be big trouble."' Pip Eton, thought Stella at once.

'And he wasn't the only one. Maisie seemed more worried about what she called "the other one". I couldn't make out if she meant man or beast, then she laughed it off. "Take no notice of me." I didn't much at the time – she did go on sometimes – but now I wonder. Should I mention it to the police?'

'If they ask,' said Alice. 'Otherwise don't.'

'I think you should,' said Stella gently. Suddenly, she felt sick. The picture of Maisie, anxious and worried, melded with the picture of the dead Maisie, covered with blood. She put her hand to her head.

'Are you all right?' That was Alice. Even when she was being sympathetic she sounded steely.

'Yes, I'm fine, but I think I'll get off home. We'll have another work talk tomorrow.'

Stella met Coffin and Augustus in the corridor outside her office.

She embraced him eagerly. 'Take me home, I want out of

here. Just let me collect my things.' She gathered up her coat and briefcase.

Augustus gave a small, excited bark and leapt up towards her.

'Right, boy, right,' said Coffin, holding him back. 'She's coming with us.'

From the door, Alice said: 'Can I help?'

'I think she's all right,' said Coffin. 'We're on the way home.'

'She's not well, look after her.' Even a benediction from Alice could sound like a threat.

'I will be in tomorrow,' said Stella. Augustus was growling softly. 'Be quiet, boy. Quiet, all of you. I'm all right and I will be back at work tomorrow, Alice. We will go through those property boxes and cupboards.'

Alice gave a nod.

Stella and Coffin let themselves in through the door at the bottom of the tower in which they lived. Not a convenient way of living, with rooms on every floor and a winding staircase, but the rooms were large, full of light and had a curious charm. The belfry where the bells had hung was their attic. The bells themselves, damaged in the Blitz, had been repaired in Whitechapel, where they had been made, and now lived in another church, so they had not been silenced.

'Poor old Alice,' said Stella, over her shoulder as she ran up the stairs. A drink was foremost in her mind, then something simple but delicious to eat. She would probably ring Max's restaurant to get something sent over. He did a very good chicken dish. 'She'll never make her way in the theatre unless she learns how to move. She likes the life, I think, although I am never quite sure of that, but she's got to handle her appearance better.'

'She is a bit on the plain side, like her dad. He wasn't bad-looking as a man, but it won't quite do in a girl.' Coffin was carrying Augustus, who had decided that the stairs were too much for his short legs.

'There's a place for a woman who's not a beauty; probably a good place but you have to convince, not be hangdog about it.'

'Is she?' Coffin put the dog down as they reached the kitchen. 'Positive sort of character, I'd say.'

'Perhaps I see a different side of her.' Stella was reaching for the telephone. 'Pour me a drink, while I ring Max's.'

Coffin poured out some claret. 'I meant to be across to collect you earlier, but I got held up in the office.'

'You always do.'

'True.' Somehow he always did. Tonight, there was a report from London to skim through and yet another savage crime in the Second City about which he must be alerted: a double killing, the murder of a wife and child by the husband, who then tried to burn the bodies but only succeeded in giving himself third-degree burns. This terrible event might make the national press but would probably not figure on the television news, even locally. Coffin had noticed that the media liked an extra bizarre twist that they could get their teeth into, a domestic murder, even a vicious one, could be passed over.

'Let's not talk about what's going on until we've eaten,' said Stella. 'I know Maisie was up to something, I've caught that much today in the theatre. Stupid of me not to have noticed before. I thought when I threw myself into her house after being shut up in Linton House that she was . . . not exactly reluctant to take me in, but hesitant in a way I would never have expected of her. I didn't mean to stay, after all, just tidy up and settle my nerves.'

'We might as well get it over.' Coffin wondered whether brandy wouldn't be better than wine, or strong tea as good as anything. You could never tell with Stella: wine for celebrating, she had said once, and tea for support. 'Maisie was involved with Pip Eton, probably over a long period. He may have been blackmailing her. I suspect that her life was not unspotted.'

Stella nodded. 'Yes . . . plenty in her life, I daresay. Oh, how sad.'

'She must have taken money from him. She may have let him have the bag and the clothes that Francesco di Rimini wore, she may have been the voice you heard in the flat.' I say 'may', he thought. 'Or she might have sold your things elsewhere. The good clothes probably did not see a charity shop.'

Stella frowned. 'Could be.'

'She didn't kill Pip; not clear yet where he was killed.'

'And he couldn't have killed her; he was already dead,' Stella said quickly.

'No, nor did he kill Francesco di Rimini, although he might have wanted to.'

'He was violent.'

'I believe you there. You certainly had a struggle. Can you remember more now? Your arm, for instance, how did that happen?'

Stella looked down at her arm, and ran her hand down it. In a hesitant voice, she said: 'You know, I think the idea of biting was a fantasy . . . I was hurt or I hurt myself, I seem to remember something, but it is too much of a blur now, and getting more so with every day that passes, like a nightmare, so clear at first, then fading. I think I picked up a knife . . . I remember a serrated edge, like a bread knife.'

'That would explain something of the nature of the wound.'

'He got it off me . . .' She shook her head. 'I am sorry. It's gone again.'

'OK, so he didn't kill Maisie, he was dead himself then. I don't think he killed Franceso di Rimini either. Eton wasn't an irrational killer, he was a terrorist. These deaths bear another mark.' He was talking half to himself.

But Stella was listening. 'I bet there is a school of thought, and not so far away either, that thinks it must be me.'

'You can rule out Phoebe Astley. She told me that forensic had found traces of a sedative in a glass at the flat, and she thinks this was given to you. Which would explain why you didn't notice the passage of time.' He was not going to let her know how much this had troubled him. 'And also how confused you were.'

For a while there was silence. Stella got up, went to the window to look out. It was a fine, bright evening with a clear sky and a full moon. A cloud passed across the moon as she stared out. The cloud was long and angular, with what could be a tail. Sometimes I see a cloud that's dragonish, she thought . . . was that Shakespeare? Was it even true? That cloud looked more like a bird. Or Superman, she thought, with a hint of a giggle. She was coming to life again, she could tell.

'You said you would be apologizing to me,' she said, still looking at the moon.

Coffin said nothing for a while. 'That will come,' he said, at last.

I wonder if I could tell her, he was asking himself. Dare I do so? He poured her a strong brandy, and as he handed it to her, he said: 'Piece of advice, don't go into the theatre tomorrow.'

Can't she see that there is a strong personal element of hatred for her in this?

For once the telephone did not ring. Max's van delivered a hot meal of chicken and salad which they ate together, with Augustus receiving his share. They chatted idly of this and that: whether they should get another cat and what would Augustus make of it, whether Stella should get her hair cut. It was quiet and peaceful.

'I'll make some coffee,' she said.

'Don't bother.' He held out hand to stop her. Standing, she smiled down at him, then they walked up the staircase together.

Augustus hesitated at the kitchen door, then made a decision. He turned back to his basket.

Bed was indicated.

The delayed pleasures of the afternoon were performed, perfected even, in the night. They were almost silent, pleasured and friendly as only lovers who have been together for years can be.

'I expect those kids in the theatre think we are too old for this.' Stella rolled back upon her pillow.

'I'm quite sure Paul Masters does, I can see the look in his eyes.' Phoebe Astley did not, she knew better; a slight touch of guilt there, quickly repressed. After all, their relationship, if you could dignify it by that name, had been over before Stella came back into his life.

'I miss you terribly when you are away,' he said sleepily.

'So do I. Let's retire and live on a desert island.'

'Why not.' Sleep was deliciously close.

Except, thought Stella, I have had an absolutely marvellous offer of a thirteen-week contract from the BBC – these things have to be considered.

She raised herself on one elbow to look down at her sleeping husband with affection. He wouldn't come either, there would always be another crime, another crisis before he could leave, and he never would leave.

He was lying on his back, with his mouth slightly open.

Any minute now, you are going to snore, my darling, she thought. Now that is something that the crew down at Spinnergate Central HQ would never think of you.

Only I know that.

In the morning, they breakfasted quietly in the kitchen, drinking strong coffee and eating toast which Stella had burnt, then scraped clear. 'Still, it's crisp,' she said. 'And I expect the carbon is good for you.'

'True.' Coffin slid a bit down to Augustus, who liked charcoal.

'I'm going in to work,' said Stella. 'I heard what you said last night, but I want to go.'

Coffin nodded. 'Take the dog with you, will you? He may not have very big legs –' Augustus looked up and wagged his tail – 'but he's good little fighter.'

Stella did not believe in any threat to her, so she prepared for work without concern.

Coffin, anxious for Stella, was not worried about himself because he had not seen where the real threat was directed.

As they set off, Augustus was just happy to be going out with the two people he loved most.

At the door of the big theatre, a stone's throw from their own front door, they said goodbye with a kiss. Coffin patted Augustus and walked away.

Stella sailed into the foyer, followed by Augustus, tethered by a lead. She checked all was as it should be, she hated it when the theatre looked untidy, as if last night's audience had only just moved out.

But no, she was proud of it. Her office was tucked away in a corner of the building, strategically placed near the new young woman installed by Letty to manage money and accounts, but equally near the backstage citadels of costume and props.

There was a neat pile of letters on her desk prepared for her by her secretary-cum-assistant, a middle-aged, stage-struck local matron who worked for the minimum wage because she loved drama. Mrs Brighton was an ally and a friend, the more so because she never intruded. The spirit of Letty Bingham hung over them all.

Indeed, there was a fax from Letty on Stella's desk, with the message, threat even, that she would be back next week. Stella worked on, referring at intervals to her six-month schedule in which forthcoming productions were pencilled in, possibly more firmly than she allowed the democracy of the theatre to see.

In mid morning she needed to check the properties of the last production but one, some of which had been rented and should have been returned. She walked down the short corridor; Augustus, freed from his lead, came with her. He had the swaggering roll of a peke in good condition and fine humour. Together they entered the room where Mr Gibbs, he was always called this, was talking with Alice and an assistant. Working, too, Stella hoped, but she noticed long ago that work in the theatre involved much conversation. Coffin said it was the same with the police.

While she discussed the problem of the missing props with Mr Gibbs, the other two wandered off to the far end of the room and Augustus strolled around investigating. Had the missing items – one small chair and a pretty desk – gone back but not been recorded? If so, why not? Or were they still here, hidden behind other furniture?

Augustus was at the other end of the room, sniffing at a double door behind which was a large, walk-in cupboard. He was making a noise which attracted Stella's attention. Then he began to scratch at the door. Stella walked over to stop him. This made him go at it even harder, looking at her as he did so.

'Probably got a rat,' said Mr Gibb.

'I hope not.' Stella opened the door, switching on the light as she walked in. 'Bit stuffy in here.'

She took several paces into what was really a small room lined with shelves.

In the bright light hanging from the ceiling, she could see that the floor was stained.

For a moment, she hesitated, looking back at Mr Gibb, but Augustus pushed forward and snuffled at the floor, his body shaking with excitement.

An old brown stain of blood. A big old brown stain of blood. Perhaps someone had tried to wash it away, there were signs, but this blood was there to stay.

Augustus raised his head and began to howl.

15

Coffin sat at his desk staring at the assembled mass of letters and reports all demanding his attention. He did not find this side of his work boring or something to be deplored, he liked a tidy desk. He liked the feeling that he was in charge. If he could have run the whole Second City Force from one great computer, he might have been tempted to try.

Paul Masters came in with the internal mail which he had already read and initialled, making his usual sharp comments here and there.

'Sir Fred's been on the line.' He kept his voice neutral.

'Thought he might be. He's our action man.' He raised his head. 'And what did Sir Fred want?'

'He's coming down to see you.'

'Not today, keep him away from me today.'

Paul Masters considered the possibility of keeping out that commanding figure before deciding that it could not have been meant seriously. 'I'll try.'

Coffin laughed. 'We'll set Phoebe Astley on him, shall we? I think he is frightened of her.' And Inspector Lodge certainly is. But he did not say this aloud; one does not make too many jokes about a colleague. Or Coffin didn't. 'Take these reports with you, will you? Cast your eye over them and let me know what you think.'

Paul Masters took a brief look. 'About recruitment, is it?'

'That's right, we will have to talk it over.'

As Masters left the room, he looked around for that small figure he knew so well, and whose white hairs he had so often brushed off the edge of his trousers.

'Not got Augustus with you today?'

'No, he's with Stella.'

There was nothing in Coffin's tone to breed alarm, but for some reason, Masters felt uneasy. He closed the door behind him with extra care.

Once on his own, Coffin let his mind run over the picture he had formed of the three deaths.

Pictures were coming up, clear and sharp, in his mind.

The first one, the body in a bombed house in Percy Street. The dead body of a man who was dressed as a woman, and that woman, his wife, Stella Pinero.

No accident there, he told himself, Stella had been selected with deliberation, as had the victim, di Rimini – or Bates, to give him his proper name. They were both victims.

Stella was meant to be involved. Her jeans, her handbag with a few possessions in it. Coffin felt he could say now that all these had been appropriated, stolen, by Maisie, certainly with no idea what they were going to be used for, but either sold or given to some person who had a hold over her.

Pip Eton might have been that person. His figure was there in the story, but his own murder suggested to Coffin that there was a shadow behind him.

Coffin found himself pacing the room. You know who the killer is, he told himself, you have known for some time. Well, guessed, and you did not want to face it.

A colleague, investigating a terrible death, had once said: 'Don't you hate the human race?' At the time, Coffin had been able to say, no, there was always hope. But now, he felt a black depression. Guilt, you could say, because he had the idea that he could have prevented these deaths.

Hubris, perhaps, that dangerous pride to which we all, except the genuinely humble – and not many of them around in the police, he thought – succumb at times.

All my fault, you say, and quite enjoy the self-flagellation.

After Francesco, that shady character (though not without his attractions, if Dennis Garden was any judge), was the murder of Pip Eton himself. A lot still to uncover there.

207

Coffin paused in his perambulations: Why did I say 'himself' like that, as if he was the fulcrum on which all balanced? As far as my poor wife is concerned, he certainly was that central figure. She knew him, she had a relationship with him, and she gave him a key to the place in Fish Alley.

He gritted his teeth at the thought of the flat in Linton House. Stella could be a fool sometimes, in a way that only the theatre, and possibly politics, added a cynical undertone, seemed to bring out.

The first victim had been killed, without too much blood loss, by a deep stab wound. Then his face had been beaten to bits. The received opinion was that he had died where he was found, that he had walked there, prettily dressed, to meet his killer. You could see his walk on the video.

Right, that was murder one.

Murder two: Pip Eton. Stabbed.

He was not killed where he was found, obscenely dressed in a kilt and hat made of back issues of *The Stage*. He was dead when he was propped up there.

Coffin moved to the window. From where he stood he could make out the roof of St Luke's Theatre. If he turned his head he could study the roofs of Spinnergate near to Fish Alley, but he could not pick out one house from another. A bird might do, or possibly a wandering cat with a good knowledge of the rooftops, but he could not.

Anyway, Pip Eton had not been killed there, either. In Coffin's opinion, the bloodstained clothes were a plant. Where had he been killed?

It was probably crucial to finding his killer. Location was important here. Because a dead man is heavy, no easy object to transport into a public place.

You are telling yourself where he was killed, said Coffin, moving away from the window. Obvious. In or near the theatre.

Once again Stella Pinero walked the stage.

He moved away from the window while his assessment moved on to the next death.

Murder three: Maisie.

No doubt where she had been killed: at home. Murdered by someone she knew, whom she had let into the house, and to whom she had spoken on the telephone. You might say she had summoned her own killer.

Which suggested the motive: she was about to name that person to the police.

Coffin wished he had either Phoebe Astley or Archie with him to hold a dialogue, but he had his own reasons for talking to himself.

He was still a player in his secret game, as Sir Fred, no doubt carrying Inspector Thomas Lodge in his train, would be arriving to remind him.

He put his head round the door to ask Paul Masters if Sir Fred had said exactly when he would come.

'No, he left it open. He said he would ring when he was on the way.'

'And he hasn't rung?'

Paul shook his head. 'Not yet. I would have been straight on to you.'

'Good.' Coffin went back to his desk where he drew towards him the file on the death in Percy Street.

He took from it the shot from the video of the dressed-up figure of di Rimini walking down Jamaica Street towards his death. His killer, it was thought, was there before him.

But Coffin's eye was drawn to the blurred figure on the edge of the picture. He laid a magnifying glass over it to bring out what detail he could.

It seemed to be a man. A man dressed in dark trousers and a loose jacket.

He took it to the window to study it in the best possible light. Yes, swinging round the corner of Jamaica Street was the killer. He was following his victim, not waiting for him.

Those clothes, dark and neutral, reminded him of something.

Coffin put out his hand to the telephone, then withdrew it. No, he would take himself down to the Production Room where he would look for himself.

209

'I'm nipping out for a minute or two, Paul. You don't know where I've gone.'

'Just as you say.'

'If Sir Fred turns up, give him a drink and keep him happy.'

'I'll do what I can,' said Masters, watching the Chief Commander's retreating back.

On the staircase, Coffin met Phoebe Astley. 'Just coming to see you.'

'Good. Come with me on this call, then you can tell me what you think.'

'I don't know what to think about,' observed Phoebe mildly.

'You'll find out. Tell me, I suppose the usual teams went over the theatre after the body was found?'

'Still doing it, I think. It's a big job.'

'Not found anything?'

'Not yet, as far as I know.' Phoebe did know, but loyally said nothing about the fact that the forensic and SOCO teams had enjoyed the theatrical company so much that work had gone slowly. She herself had delivered a sharp kick to them only that morning.

'What's all this about?' She was moving fast to keep up with him.

'We're going to the Production Room.'

Phoebe raised an eyebrow, but followed without a word. When the Chief Commander was in this mood, it was best to do as asked, without fuss.

One lone figure, Sergeant Bailey, was in the Production Room. He looked up in surprise as the Chief Commander came in.

'Morning, sir.' He stood up.

'I want to see the register.'

Every artefact connected with any crime, great or small, was bundled up in a plastic bag, entered in the register, together with the name of the officer who brought it in, the date, and a few identifying details.

Silently, the sergeant handed the book over. 'It's all on the computer as well, sir. We've never lost anything yet.'

The joke was ignored as Coffin studied the register.

'I want to see Number 33741.'

He waited while Bailey checked the shelves, brought a step ladder, and climbed up to search the top shelf.

'Here you are, sir. Brought in by Sergeant Miller.' He pointed to the signature and the date. He was a man who liked everything authenticated, well suited to the job he did, which many considered dull. He found a certain romance in these objects once touched by a crime, so never to be let loose in the world again. Kind of sacred, in a way.

Coffin took the bundle to the long trestle table in the middle of the room where, under the centre light, witnessed by Phoebe and the sergeant, he opened the parcel.

A dark pair of trousers, and a very loose black jacket.

'These were found in the house in Percy Street. Thought to have been left there before the bomb fell.'

'So?' said Phoebe.

'I think they were worn by the killer over the killer's own clothes.'

'Is that just a guess, sir?' Phoebe was careful to be formal.

'No, if you study the video of the street scene you can see a figure dressed like this following di Rimini.' A wolf after his prey. Coffin was spreading the clothes out on the table. 'Did they ever come under forensic study?'

'No, they were not thought to be connected.'

'Sloppy thinking.' He stretched out the jacket and then the trousers, examining both inside and out. He was slow, taking his time. There was a stain at the crotch, to which he pointed. 'Now that is an interesting stain.'

'It's on the inside –' protested Phoebe.

'Yes, think about that. Get a proper forensic study done for me, and sooner than soon. I want to know about the blood.'

'I'll see to it, sir.' She looked at Sergeant Bailey, who moved towards the telephone, muttering about a messenger. 'But sir . . . no blood analysis is much good to us, without a suspect to match it to.'

211

'Use your mind, Phoebe,' said Coffin briskly. 'You are a woman.'

'So you've noticed,' Phoebe muttered under her breath.

He marched out of the room. 'Come on, the sergeant can get on with that, I want you with me.'

'Going where, sir?'

'To the theatre. You had better drive, I want to think.'

The entrance to St Luke's was blocked by two police cars. Phoebe double-parked her car beside them.

'Something's up,' she said. As she did so, her phone began ringing. She picked it up. 'Sir,' she called out, as she listened. 'Sir –'

But Coffin was out of the car before her, moving rapidly into the foyer. A uniformed constable greeted him with a surprised salute.

'What is going on?' demanded Coffin.

The constable was about to answer that he didn't know much but he knew that traces of a lot of blood had been found and that Miss Pinero –

He was interrupted by the appearance of a detective sergeant who seemed surprised at the arrival of such a high-level visitor, but also relieved.

'Sergeant Lomas, sir. We had a call about a lot of blood –'
He in his turn was interrupted by the sound of barking. 'That's the dog, sir,' he began.

Coffin was off, through the swing doors behind the box office, through the darkened theatre, following the sound of the dog. 'Thought you had a team going over the theatre,' he called over his shoulder.

'Must have got called elsewhere,' said Phoebe as she followed. Curse them, she thought, I'll have their lights and livers, or Archie Young will. 'There are about three cases on the go at the moment, sir.' Excuses, excuses, she was muttering, I will kill them regardless.

There was a WPC at the door of the property room. Inside, Stella, Alice, and Mr Gibb stood grouped together at one end of the room before the opened doors of a big cupboard.

Nearer the door, and huddled together, were a frightened group. Coffin recognized Jane Gillam and Irene Bow, and there were a couple of young men whom he did not know, except by sight.

Augustus was barking and whining, rushing between Stella and Alice. When he saw Coffin, his barking increased in fervour but he did not move away from the women.

Coffin walked up the room, nodded to Stella and Alice without speaking, then went through the double doors.

There were indeed traces of blood; stale, dried blood, and plenty of it, even though an effort to scrub it away had been made. A bucket with bloody water in stood at the end of the little room. There was more blood here. A trolley of the sort used to move props around stood, blood on it.

'Well, well,' said Coffin, coming out. 'So this was where Pip Eton was killed.' And how his body was moved. Cover it up with a sheet or blanket and you could move through the corridors with some impunity.

Stella began to say something.

'Be quiet,' ordered Coffin, his voice stern. 'And keep the dog quiet.'

Stella picked up Augustus, who kept up a low grumble.

In a low voice, he said: 'So this is where you killed your fellow conspirator.'

'No,' Stella cried out. She tried to take his arm.

'Not you.' He moved away. 'You, Alice, you.'

He was aware of Phoebe Astley, together with the detective sergeant, moving quietly up the room towards Alice. She was shaking her head from side to side.

'Keep away, you lot,' she called, without turning to look. 'Or I won't answer for who gets killed.'

'Oh, I daresay you have a knife up your sleeve,' said Coffin. 'But you won't use it.'

'I won't need to, everyone knows it's all her,' she nodded at Stella. 'Your lovely wife. All her doing.'

'No, that won't wash. Stella is in the clear. You are not. We can prove you were in the house with di Rimini.'

'The old transvestite? Oh, big deal.'

'The clothes you wore to kill him, you left them behind and went home in jeans and a sweater. We will probably track that down on the video.'

'You'll have a job proving they are my clothes,' she laughed. 'What rubbish!'

'We will track you at every street corner till you got back to the theatre: picture of a killer. And we will examine the clothes; there is blood inside the trousers . . .'

Alice shrugged. 'So what?'

'I'm making a guess it's menstrual blood, Alice. You were bleeding yourself when you stabbed him. Are you always worse at those times?'

'Stop it, stop it. I hate that talk. You're all doing it, shouting. The walls are shouting at me. I can hear them all the time.' She was still moving her head, then a steel blade had appeared in her hand. 'I may not be able to kill your wife, but a slash or two down her face won't improve her looks.'

Stella made a small noise.

'I don't want to harm her, it's self-defence. It was you we were after all the time. Orders, you know. Get close to you, compromise you, get you out. Pip was to do the job with help from Stella.'

'And he didn't get it right, so you killed him. Maisie knew it was you. She had sold you some of Stella's clothes, and was about to say so. Pip, first, then her.'

'It was me or him. I think he liked Stella, he was going to tell her everything.'

'Thank you for putting it into speech. There are witnesses.'

She did not bother to look round. 'Stop shouting at me. I won't be here. No one will touch me while I have this knife . . . And I have friends who will get me away. A pleasure to go . . . I hated you, you know. You would play the big bene-factor, the kind man, but you are selfish and cold. A proper careerist. Because of you, my father died. I knew that and I knew it would be a pleasure to drag you down. You think Pip Eton recruited me and Charles Mackie? No, I was looking for someone like him. I couldn't get in fast enough.'

She put out a big strong hand which gripped Stella by the

shoulder. The knife, long and bright, was in the other hand. 'I'll take her with me for safety. Touch me and I will drag this knife down her face.'

Coffin drew back.

Alice began to push Stella towards the door. 'Let me pass, you lot.'

But at the door, Augustus wrenched himself out of Stella's arms. As she staggered backward, free, the dog went for Alice. She kicked him away as she pushed into the group at the door and through them, Augustus following.

'Don't bother touching her,' called Coffin. 'A woman running through the streets with a peke pursuing her will be picked out on every camera in every street. Let her go. I'll warn them. She may lead us to the centre control she must have had, if not, a patrol will take them in whenever – Astley, take over.'

He walked towards Stella. 'Bloody you,' she said angrily, rubbing her elbow where she had fallen.

'I said I would have to apologize and I will . . . but later.'

Followed by the cameras, Alice was picked up some forty minutes later entering a house to the south of Spinnergate Tube station. Augustus was still with her, footsore and weary.

The house was later raided by a special police unit; three men were arrested in connection with the recent bomb. Bomb-making material was found in the garage.

'They aren't the whole unit,' said Coffin to Tom Lodge later, 'but a good part of it. Some others blew themselves up.'

'Good work,' said Sir Fred, even later. 'I congratulate you, Chief Commander.'

Later still, Coffin made his peace with Stella. Over a special dinner at Max's restaurant.

'You aren't really as angry as you act, are you?'

'Yes, I am. Furious.'

He looked her in the face and smiled.

'You can pour me some more champagne. We might need another bottle. I hope it costs.'

With a sigh, he said: 'I apologize, I repent, I confess – will that do?'

Stella considered. 'A bit more detail is required.'

Coffin buttered one of Max's special bread rolls. 'Even now, I can't tell you some things. I knew about you and Pip and the place in Fish Alley, I've told you that. I was to get you out of it all . . . I knew how dicey Alice was, her father had told me. I knew I was in the game, but I shouldn't have asked you to give her a job. For that I apologize.'

'Apology accepted.'

'I didn't know how much she hated me. I should have thought about it long before Edinburgh. But my game was to get Alice . . . unluckily, her game was to get me.'

Stella considered. 'Pip's death . . . She can't have done all that on her own. She must have had help.'

'Yes, I think Maisie helped. Not in the killing – I don't see Maisie as a killer – but afterwards – in the tidying up, in the transport of the body on that barrow, skip – whatever you call it. And keeping watch while the body was moved. Yes, she could have helped there, but I guess that was also the time when she took fright and thought about confessing. And so Alice killed her.'

Stella shook her head. 'And Maisie did all this for money?'

'Alice had her hooks well and truly in by then, but Maisie liked her, strongly.' Coffin studied his wife's face. 'Just guessing. You never noticed anything? I think one or two of the cast did.'

'I knew about Maisie, we all did, but she kept that side of her life from me, she knew I wasn't that way.'

'Money and sex,' said Coffin. 'They come in everywhere.'

Stella was considering what she had heard. 'And is that all? Was anyone else involved?'

Coffin decided that honesty was best. 'I expect so, my dear. You have to face it. This is not the end, there is more to be found out. But my guess is that the theatre will be in the clear. I wonder about those builders, though.'

216

Stella sipped her champagne. 'Let's take the rest of the bottle home. Max won't mind. We mustn't leave Augustus alone any longer. He is exhausted, poor boy.'

'He deserves a medal. I hope you aren't too tired?'

Stella looked at him under her eyelashes. 'Let's see, shall we?'

THE CASE OF ALICE YEOMAN

When the case came to court, a plea of abnormal menstrual tension was put forward by the defence. This plea was rejected by the court, which accepted the Crown's medical assessment of manic depression leading to a psychotic state.

The prisoner was committed to a secure mental hospital for the duration of the Queen's pleasure with the provision that if she responded to treatment she might be released into the community.

Coffin visited her in hospital, he being her last friend, or unfriend, in the world. She seemed normal, but probably was not.

She wanted to discuss the affair and her involvement with the bombers. 'Blew themselves up, didn't they, so I've heard.'

'Yes,' Coffin said. It had been in the papers. 'By mistake, as they were packing up to disband. They had rented an empty garage down by the river.'

'I know. I put them on to it.'

'I'm surprised they let you into their group.'

'I had a passport,' she said gleefully. 'You.' Then she added: 'And a lot of local knowledge – streets, houses, garages, that sort of thing.'

'I wonder that they trusted you.'

'Oh, they didn't, not a lot. Kept me on the edge, but I enjoyed it, because I meant to drag you in through Stella and see you go down, down, down.' She kept on repeating 'down, down'. Then she said: 'I expect they would have killed me, too, in the end.'

218

So they might, thought Coffin. You were hardly the ideal terrorist. A one-woman terror campaign.

'I was determined to soil you, degrade you.'

Thanks, he thought. 'Why did you leave di Rimini's finger in a handkerchief belonging to Stella?' Ask a silly question, get a silly answer; but no, what came out was rational enough.

'It implicated Stella in his death, like dressing him up in her clothes and using the other chap's underpants – well, I didn't think of that; Corner left them behind, I suppose,' she sounded shocked. 'Di Rimini must have put them on. As for me, I paid him, I knew his ways from that place we both drank in. He thought we were making a film, so he dressed himself up, he did a bit of porno posing for dirty pictures. I knew the chap who did them, that's how I got the picture of Stella faked, do anything with a camera, that man could. Give you his name, if you like.'

'We found it out,' said Coffin grimly.

'So?' She was disinterested. 'Di Rimini didn't have to do any acting, just lay there as asked, and then I stabbed him and hit him. Stabbed him first. He squeaked a bit; I reckon he owed a fingernail – and he didn't miss it, he was dead. Moribund, anyway,' she added thoughtfully. 'It does take time for some people to die. Then I went away. No one takes any notice of what you do in Spinnergate if you look as though you are working, as if you have a purpose.'

'You certainly had that. What about the other deaths?'

She shrugged. 'Oh, you know how it is. I had to kill Pip Eton, he knew it was me. I even went to the hospital with him to jolly him along. I thought he might kill Stella for me, but all he could do was to try to threaten her, and through her get at you. I went to Linton House and suggested he might kill Stella, but he wasn't up for it, and he was beginning to threaten me. So I did him. I fancied to by then. Maisie, of course, had to go, and she knew it. She knew I bought clothes off her and she soon knew why. Couldn't trust her to keep quiet.'

'A lot of killing in a short time.'

'I am nimble – you can do it if you are nimble.' She leaned forward. 'Don't tell them here, but I might be nimble enough again.'

Alice fell silent, no more to say.

All gone, Jerry, Andrew and Charles. And her victims.

And her father whose death she blamed on Coffin – had she really loved him so much that only a string of deaths could exorcize his memory?

At Christmas, Alice Yeoman sent a card from Bishoptown Hospital, Surrey, to John Coffin with the message:

SEE YOU WHEN I GET OUT.